Digitized

Ashton Moseman

ISBN 978-0-9976224-9-2

Dedication

Before you read this story, I'd like to thank
a few people for their help in completing
this book and supporting my efforts to
make this story a reality.
Thank you Mom,
thank you Grammy,
thank you Gerri,
thank you friends, and family,
for all of your support and
encouragement.

And to all of you who want to share a
story of your own…
just put it down on paper
before you forget.
It could wind up on shelves someday.

:)

Chapter 1

It's been eight hours since we had left home for our great uncle's place, and Adalyne and I were dying to stretch our legs. It has been nothing but highway for over 540 miles! Adalyne was next to me in the passenger seat, stretched out as far as she could go in a car packed with suitcases. I don't know why there's so many, we don't even own that much stuff. After a while I started to drive in a sort of autopilot, drifting in thought, counting the mile markers, or thinking about my relationship with Jackson. Oh… that reminds me, I need to call him and tell him I'm going to be in town early. I still can't get over how lucky I am to find someone in the same town I'm going to work in! I'm so excited to see him again. Though it's been nothing but a long-distance relationship for months, I'm really hoping that he will be there. I haven't told Adalyne yet, but she always finds out anyway. I reached down into my purse for my phone, pushing aside a bunch of junk. As I pulled it out and turned it on, I could see that I've received some new emails from my great uncle, but I swiped it aside, unlocked my phone, and called Jackson. I let the phone ring for a couple of moments… no answer. I called him again...no answer.

"Ok, one more time"

But before I could call a third time, Adalyne woke up and asked in a very big yawn, "How close are we?"

"We are about ten miles out of town"

"Well that's close enough for me."

Adalyne leaned up in her seat expecting to see trees and buildings but gave a disappointed look as all there was to see was grass, a few power lines, and a very flat horizon. I decided not to call again because my sister was awake, so we'll just meet him for lunch. We're all going to the Circuit Cafe for lunch anyway so there's no need for a phone call. On the other hand, I'm pretty sure that he would've answered a call from me unless he was doing something important. My thoughts were interrupted as Adalyne gasped very abruptly, causing me to swerve the car a little.

"Oh my God! What?!"

"Look at it, it's pretty."

I sat there squinting my eyes as the endless horizon was cut off by a steep hill that revealed the urban area of a large city below. The road then made a wide turn to the left and went down the side of a hill. Beyond the road was a ravine lush with trees and buildings. Near the edge of the ravine, on the far side of town, was a giant massive complex that was most likely the Tech Complex. Every building had trees of fall colors surrounding them, filling the ravine with beautiful red and yellow colors.

"Eight hours of driving, this better be worth it."

I looked at Adalyne with a sarcastic look.

"It'll be worth it."

Along the other side of the ravine was a river, a large river with fisherman at its rocky shores. As I drove off of the highway and down main street, I noticed a few signs outside of a store that read 'No More Machines, Stop Josh and Tom's Cybernetics!' And as we continued down main street there were a couple of other signs just like it. 'Boycott the Robots!' 'Destroy the Droids!' Adalyne looked at me and said in a concerned voice, "I hope this doesn't turn violent."

"I want to know why they are protesting Tom's company."

The protesters were most likely referring to what happened twenty years ago, when seven people were found dead inside the old company warehouse. Adalyne and I have indulged ourselves in as much history as we could before we came, and let's just say it isn't pretty. The original idea Tom and Josh had was to build this interactive workshop where adults and children could come build a robot of their own, and buy it if they wanted to at a reasonable price. Josh was the mastermind behind the androids. He had built many of the functioning robots that helped run the workshop, but then he started behaving weird. Tom noticed and became worried about his behavior. About a week later, four children and three adults were found dead inside one of the workshop rooms. The place closed, and an investigation followed. As soon as Tom thought the tragedy was over, Josh took his own life by hanging himself. Tom was heartbroken, but became the soul owner of the company. He began pushing ideas of his own by building two more locations, and adding a cafe along with each location, renaming the company 'Josh and Tom's Circuit Cafe'. The old location was left to rot, but most of the parts and androids were moved to a storage facility that Tom hasn't told us much about.

We finally pulled up to the workshop, and the first thing I saw was the big sign with Josh and Tom on the front holding a prototype robot, smiling with excitement. When we walked inside I saw a polished android walking around taking people's orders. The droid was dressed as a waitress and was about six feet tall, but the most pronounced thing about it was how smooth it moved. I guess you could say that there could be a woman wearing it as a costume. There was a room to my left filled with tools and parts for customers to come in and build. Standing on its own was an android built with heavy metal parts, and a boxy head with a single rotating camera for an eye. There were hoses attached from its center body spreading out to provide hydraulic power to its extremities. It was a simple design compared to the waitress, but it was still a very complex android. I continued looking around the restaurant checking out how it was laid out when Adalyne nudged me in the side and said, "Who is that waving at us?"

I turned and saw a man in a police uniform with a pistol on one hip, and a taser on the other. He had black hair that was cut very short, and a badge with B.P.D. printed on it. But something was familiar about him.

"Morgan! Over here!"

It was Jackson. As we walked over, Adalyne gave me a suspicious face like she realized who he was, and that we didn't just drive eight hours for a job at our great uncles business. As we approached Jackson, he stood up and looked like he couldn't decide which one of us was Morgan. Though we were identical twins, we had our subtle differences. My hair was longer than Adalyne's, she was a little taller than I was, not to mention the different clothes we were wearing. I knew Adalyne didn't know his name so I leaned in and gave him a hug.

"It's so nice to see you again."

Jackson's confused face went away and he hugged me back.

"It's nice to see you too, Morgan."

My sister broke in abruptly and said,

"Do you mind enlightening me on who this is."

"Uh... Yea. Adalyne, this is Jackson…"

"Your boyfriend?"

Jackson laughed and said,

"You didn't tell her?"

"No."

We all sat down in wooden chairs around a polished metal table that had a menu under a layer of glass. Adalyne then leaned over and whispered into my ear. "When were you going to tell me about this?"

"I was going to tell you as soon as we met him… like just now."

Before I could talk to Jackson, my phone buzzed as a new message popped up. 'Can't make it due to work delay at tech complex.'

"Well I guess Tom isn't going to make it."

Jackson leaned forward in his seat interested by what I said.

"Is Tom the one employing you?"

"Yea… is he employing you to?"

This would be the most amazing coincidence I've ever known. Me, my sister, and Jackson, working under the same roof, employed by a relative. It couldn't get any better than that. Jackson leaned back in his seat and thought about it for a couple of seconds, then leaned forward and spoke.

"Well sort of. I parole around town for eight hours, four before lunch and four after lunch. I then go patrol around the urban areas for a little while, but then I need to come back and sit in front of his building for another three hours before someone else takes over."

My sister cut in before he could say another word.

"How come you're watching the place?"

"Well…a group of people came by a few days ago and smashed in two of the giant windows at the front entrance. I arrested a woman with a nose ring, and she wasn't too compliant."

Jackson let out a heavy sigh and appeared to be a little frustrated about that incident. Then he shook his head as if he just forgot about it.

"Oh, have you noticed the taser I'm wearing?"

It just came to me that Jackson never had a taser before. The last time I talked to him, he was still learning from another officer on duty as part of his training.

"I just finished my training the day before yesterday, which included my taser training. Today I went to get a taser, so they took me into the back room of the police station. What they didn't tell me is that in order to get one, I had to be tased. I turned around to ask them why we were here, but two taser prongs stuck me in the side. It hurt so bad, I became stiff and fell flat on the floor."

He turned his left side to us and lifted his shirt cautiously revealing two tiny marks where the taser prongs were, and then gently let his shirt back down.

"It was the most painful experience I've ever had, but I got the day off because of it."

"How far do the taser prongs go?"

Jackson gave a short smile.

"They can go up to 10 feet…"

"No I meant into your side."

I seemed to be more interested than I should have been in this whole taser thing, but if I was going to get a taser for the job as a night guard, I'm going to be well prepared for it.

"Oh, less than half a centimeter. They have little barbs that will stick into your skin, but I can assure you that there is enough juice in these things to knock you out if it hit you just right, and you are not going to get up from it anytime soon."

Our conversation was cut short by a machine-like female voice that was ear shattering and directed straight at us.

"What would you like to order today!?"

It was that android waitress I saw when I walked in. She had fake, plastic hair that was pulled up in a bun, and her skin was transparent, showing all of the mechanical parts underneath.

"What would you like to order today!?"

Jackson looked at us and appeared to be waiting for us to order. Adalyne spoke up and asked for a chef salad, then Jackson and I ordered two sandwich wraps. The plastic waitress spoke up again, and said in a very loud mechanical voice,

"I'll be right back with your order."

She turned around and walked straight into the kitchen, and soon after walked right back out towards another table. I looked at the clock on the wall that read 11:47, and turned towards Adalyne who was watching the other androids on the workshop side of the building.

"We need to go to the complex as soon as we are done here, alright?"

"Ok, I'll keep track of the time."

It was 12:25 by the time Morgan and I were full enough to get a small travel box for our leftovers. We needed to go to the complex as soon as we could, but I needed to make a quick bathroom break. On my way out of the bathroom, I bumped into a man in his early 30s. He was blinded by the boxes he was carrying and we ran into each other, spilling the boxes of paper everywhere.

"Oh…. I'm so sorry ma'am."

"No, it was my fault, I wasn't paying attention."

I started stacking papers on the ground and I couldn't help but notice

5

one of the files titled 'Repurposed Androids'. I pointed it out to him and he responded in an uneven tone.

"Oh... um, that? My boss brings these androids, at least two dozen by now, from wherever he finds them, but a couple don't function.... correctly."

He reached over, took the file from my hand, and put it in one of the boxes.

"What do you mean they don't function correctly?"

"Most of them have some missing pieces, a bad program, or just need a little tune-up. But these two have a tendency to turn themselves on without anyone being there to flip the switch. Oh! You saw that android out in the kitchen that is made of plastic?"

"Yes."

"Well... they have the same design, but they are pretty damaged compared to the other repurposed androids Tom has brought over the past four-five months."

Gee, this guy might know what happened to the older models. I wonder if I can see these androids in person? Maybe he knows the location of the original workshop. There are too many questions I wanted to ask him.

"What's your name?"

"My name is Adalyne."

"Well I'm Josh, after my father."

"Your father, as in the Josh who..."

"Yes, as in the man who started this company. I wish he was here to see what it has become."

"That would be nice. Are you the only one running the place?"

"There's my boss, the design team that works at a different building... and there's me. My boss isn't really here often because he's over watching that new tech complex come up."

"And your boss's name is...?"

"Um... Tom."

"Yea, He's my great uncle."

"Really? Wow what a small world."

"Do you happen to know what he's doing at the new complex?"

"I think he's got a plan for the new rows of rooms that he will rent out to people who want to build an android there. He's going to have a testing room for the androids that is about three stories tall, and has an obstacle course and a rock wall to test on. Besides the point, have you seen the two new models the design team put together?"

"No, I just got in town a little bit ago."

"It's a humanandroid, and a lion."

"And why did they design a lion?"

"I have… no idea. I think it has something to do with proving that J.T. Cybernetics can build or replicate anything with their technology."

"Neat. My sister and I are going to work night shifts at the complex only because we have training. Tom asked me to come work on some android because I'm a mechanical engineer. And he asked Morgan to come because she was trained in security for the marines. After I'm done there I could help with these projects."

"It would be really nice to have someone to work with me, but I prefer…"

There was a sudden loud hollow bang followed by a long screech that sounded like metal scraping metal. Everyone in the building fell silent. There was absolutely no sound until I heard a bit of laughter that broke the silence, and the chatting resumed between people. I turned to look at Josh, but he had slipped something into my hand, and left through the 'Employees Only' door before I could say anything. I figured that something fell over in his office like a shelf or an unsteady ladder. In my hand was a small metallic remote looking device. The words on the front were scratched off, but I could make out a T, Y, and an O. Why did he give me this? He does look a little cute, maybe he already has a crush on me. I put the remote into my purse and started walking back to the table. I couldn't help but wonder how Josh could run the entire cafe by himself. The thought went away as I saw that there were chefs in the kitchen preparing meals for everyone, so he wasn't completely alone. I walked back over to where Jackson and Morgan were standing, both of them trying to stack a sandwich in a box that clearly wasn't big enough. As I walked up to Morgan, I poked her on the shoulder, harder than I should've, to get her attention causing her to jump and spin around.

"You've got to stop scaring me like that Adalyne!"

"I'm sorry, but how else am I supposed to get your attention?"

"I have a name."

"Ok, I'll remember that."

Morgan has always been jumpy, even as a little kid, and you don't really need to try that hard to scare her. I bet when that sound hit the wall she must have jumped out of her seat. I leaned over and asked Jackson what Morgan did when she heard that sound. Jackson started snickering, but pretty soon started laughing. Morgan turned and said, "Are you still laughing about that?"

"Yup."

"Well stop, you're going to make me laugh again."

Jackson turned around and told me that when that sound occurred, Morgan had barely taken a bite out of her sandwich when she jumped, and smeared that sandwich up the center of her face. I looked at Morgan and couldn't help but laugh. Pretty soon we were all laughing at Morgan, our faces red and hot. A little while after we left the building, Jackson drove off in his police cruiser, and Morgan and I got into our car. She then turned to me and said,

"You know that Jackson's parents died in a car accident."

"Oh God, that's horrible. When did that happen?"

"About a month ago. He's taking care of his 9-year-old brother James and his grandpa who lived with his parents. He's kind of stressed with it all going on."

"Did you already know about this?"

"Yes, he told me soon after it happened, and he doesn't like talking about it too much."

Morgan put the car in drive, and we left for the complex not discussing anymore of today's events. But something bothered me. If an object did fall over in Josh's office, wouldn't you have heard the screech first and then the bang?

Chapter 2

I kind of like Adalyne, she's different. Will you get your head out of the clouds! You have a job to do. After walking through the employees only door holding a stack of boxes, I figured out what that sound really came from. I just wanted to pretend that it didn't come from them. I looked around like I knew what I was doing, trying not to appear distracted. As I entered my office, with the stack of boxes in my arms, I could see the giant six foot by eight foot window that peered into the generally large storage room. I sat down in my office chair, turned on my computer after placing the boxes in the corner, and as I waited for the computer to power up, I did a quick spin in my chair to see if anything had been moved. Nothing was, so I looked back at my computer. I pulled up a picture of my father, and then a few more. There were pictures of him putting androids together, walking alongside them, and interacting with finished models. He always seemed to have a smile on his face. I then pulled up a video of him and Tom talking with one of their finished models.

"So, what should we name the model Josh?"

"How about… Bill, or Trinity…"

"Trinity." Said the android.

"Alright Trinity, what do you want to do?" asked Josh.

"I don't know. What is there to do?"

Tom spoke up while looking at the computer monitor.

"The program seems to be holding up, but let's shut it down before the process line overheats."

Josh reached behind the android's head, but hesitated before he shut it down. I started to watch some more footage of my father and Trinity…

BANG!

"What the hell!"

I immediately turned to grab my flashlight and shined it through the window and into the large storage room. My heart was beating slow and heavy as I looked into the dark room. I didn't notice it at first, but there was a shadow at the end of a shelving unit seeming to be staring at me. It moved slowly out of view and when I saw it, I yelled,

"Ha… that's right, I caught you. Go back to where you were!"

I sat there for a moment letting my adrenaline calm down. There should only be two. I've been dealing with this for a little while, so why haven't I gotten used to it? It has been getting more and more active over the three months that I've been here, so that could be why. I collected myself together and kept on doing my tasks, organizing files, typing in documents on repurposed androids, and ordering parts from local vendors. I was partly expecting an interruption or something to drag my attention away from the monitor, but all I could hear were the people in the workshop having conversations, laughing, and enjoying themselves. About ten hours passed by before I finished up the last task. I happily hit the log off button, and stood up from my chair to leave. As I started closing my office door, I saw something that I missed. It was a note from Tom. I looked at my watch and it read 11:24. Ok I guess I have time to read the note, anywhere other than here though. I won't stand being interrupted again. I took the note and left my office for the main dining room. There were a couple of patrons left so I told them that we were about to close. I walked over to the kitchen, relieved the last kitchen aid from cleaning, and opened the breaker box door to begin flipping switches. First the overhead lights, then the kitchen appliances. Then I activated the charging cord for the deactivated android. I also left a light on over the patrons, and opened the note that I had. It read,

> Josh,
> I found another prototype just outside the back door. There were a couple of people that dropped it off. I talked to them a little and they told me that it appeared on their lawn a month ago. They just gave it to me! Awesome isn't it? Well I'm not going to write a massive letter but I left the android in the spare office behind yours. You don't need to assess it tonight, but I do prefer you get it done right away tomorrow.
> Tom

"Yea… totally awesome."

How many of these is he going to find. I don't get it! I am a little suspicious of what he found and I do need to wait for the patrons to leave… I guess I could assess the prototype tonight. Walking past the patrons, clearly seeing they were done eating and were just enjoying the conversation they were having, I entered the hallway through the employees only door and walked down towards the spare office. I walked into the office and at first, I thought it was a new model, but then I noticed that the plastic shades were wrong and its right thumb was gone. It was just sitting there on a wooden chair with no supports. There was a file on the table labeled repurpose and reuse. I walked around the table towards the deactivated droid and studied it carefully. There were wear and tear marks across its hard plastic covered body, as if it was out in the open for a while.

"What have you been up to?"

I continued to study the droid until I noticed that there was an all too familiar company stamp on the back of the skull. 'J.T. Cybernetics.'

"Oh, yea. This is my father's."

I pressed the back of the skull's plastic plate and removed it. Each android had a time stamp on each limb indicating when each part of the prototype was built. Most of the androids I've scrapped have been the same design, except one. The first android Tom brought had a very old metal covering that could only been removed by unscrewing some bolts. Its frame was extremely tough and sturdy, its movement system was hydraulic, and its weight was tremendous. I pulled myself back to the now, and continued my assessment of the android in the wooden chair. I removed the plastic plates from the limbs, and found the time stamp for each piece. I walked over to a shelf in the back of the room with the plastic covers in hand, and set them down next to a roll of heavy duty straps. I turned around to leave for my office, but I noticed that the android's eyes were looking straight at me.

"Uh… Uh uh… No-no. I'm not doing this again!"

I walked across the hall into my office and grabbed an empty file from a desk drawer along with a number stamp for the android. Number 126-F. I walked back into the spare office and saw its head turned towards the door with its eyes glaring into my own.

"Ok… That's it!"

I angrily walked over towards the shelf, grasped the heavy duty straps, and began tying the android to the chair. Once I finished, I stamped the number tag on, walked back into my office, pulled the taser from my desk, and walked back into the spare office happy to see that the android hadn't moved from its previous position. I sat down across the table from the android, and began filling out the repurpose form in front of me. I was careful to keep an eye on the droid, hoping to spot if it moved any further.

The form required me to describe the droid's condition, its represented gender (male), what kind of internal 'organs' it has, if it has hydraulics or synthetic electric muscles, and if it functions correctly. Most of the androids my father made were with hydraulics. The electric tendon wasn't really used until Tom found a way around the voltage and amperage issue by using a Xenon Difluoride battery. It's a very powerful battery, but I don't remember too much about it. I stood up and walked over to see what kind of battery the droid had, but as soon as I could view inside, I noticed that the entire internal system was covered in mold and some old brown rust. The battery connectors were corroded and most of the computer chips and processor line were broken or torn. And then I noticed something peculiar. There were what looked like six bullet holes in the chest of the android that I didn't see before. I leaned away from the android and spotted another bullet hole in the shoulder.

"What the hell happened to you?"

This type of android had its brain in its chest simply because the computer couldn't fit in the head. I then realized that the android's memory compartment was still intact. So I walked over to the shelves on the other side of the room, grabbed a monitor and cable, plugged the monitor into the memory unit, and began playing some video footage. There was a terrible screeching sound from the monitor, and the android started shaking violently in its chair, unable to move its arms due to the straps. I jumped, falling backwards out of my chair and landed flat on the ground, drilling my head into the floor. There was a burning, stinging pain in the back of my head from landing on the cold tile. With the sound added on top of it and my eyes watering, I could kind of see the droid struggling in his bonds. His seat was leaving the floor and for a wooden chair, fiber straps, and a 450-pound android, it was holding up quite well. I thought I was deaf from the impact because I couldn't hear the servos or any droid's 'screams', but I could still hear the chair slamming around on the floor. I stood up and reached for the taser, but before I could, the android had broken free from the straps, smashed his fist into the monitor, and through the table splitting it in two. The taser went tumbling under the shelves. I leaped for it and almost reached it when a hand grabbed my leg and pulled me backwards. I turned over and saw 126-F's hand reaching for my face. I brought my foot up and started kicking him in the head hoping to stop his approach. Once, twice, three times, pushing off with both feet and finally grasping the taser in my hand. I stood up to shoot the taser but the android was there in my face and slammed both of my hands against the shelves. I was face to face with him, close enough to pick out all of the individual scratches in his plastic face. He leaned in and started pressing my hands harder and harder into the shelf. He was going to break my wrists, then what could I do? I would be defenseless. The droid continued to press harder into my wrists and the wood shelves started to creak and moan. Wait a minute, the shelves are made of wood! I brought my foot up and slammed it as hard as I could down on the bottom shelf. With a loud crack I felt it give way, and it began to lean forward slowly. The droid released a little pressure allowing me to get my hands free and I ducked down as the shelf fell over onto him. When the dust settled, I got up slowly through the shelf, pulled my taser from the mess, and walked over to where the droid was struggling to get up. Pinned belly down on the floor, he looked at me with his head twisted in a one-eighty, expressionless in a non-threatening way. I stood there for a moment and said to him, "Why do you want me dead? I know what happened to my father and I think that's why you want me dead. I don't know why you're still here, but if you want to leave, I can't help you with that. All I want is to talk to my father, but he doesn't recognize me yet… And I'm not going to leave until he does."

I pulled the trigger on the taser and shoved it into the droid's neck, holding it there until he quit shaking. I stood up and looked around the room eyeing the disastrous mess that was made. Imagine explaining this to Tom. I've never had this happen to me before. I started to pull on the android to get him out from under the shelf, but it was useless. He was too heavy and the shelf was pinning him underneath. I'll save it for tomorrow. I walked down the hallway and entered the main dining room, which was completely empty. I noticed that one of the big vent slats was knocked out. I wonder if an android was on its way to the spare office? I hope not. I knelt down and shined my flashlight into the vent and saw nothing, so I slid the cover back on. Thank goodness no one was around to hear all of that. Or was that why they left? Oh, forget about it. I'm tired and ready to sleep in a comfortable bed at my own home. I grabbed the keys from the front desk and went through the front doors to lock them. I turned the lock quickly and quietly, then shoved the keys into my pocket. I started my car and left the workshop parking lot thinking about why this android attacked me. He could've easily punched me in the face to knock me out, but he didn't. His voice box was damaged and that may have been a reason. Maybe it was the monitor. It did make the worst sound I've ever heard when I plugged it into the memory compartment. That was most likely the reason why, but it smashed the monitor and kept on attacking me. Why… Just forget about it! My head was hurting and I needed to rest my shaky body.

"Grandpa, James, I'm home!"

I closed the front door, headed to the kitchen with a bag full of groceries, and looked around to see if anyone was home. No one that I could hear.

"Grandpa! James! Hello, anyone!"

"I'm in the basement!"

I went downstairs to discover Grandpa had completely rearranged the furniture, drinking a can of beer, and was sitting in his favorite chair watching the news on TV, cursing it out at the same time.

"Grandpa, what are you doing down here?"

"I'm drinking!"

"I know that. I mean why are you down stairs?"

"Cause I wanted to watch from the big tv. I can't see like I used to."

"Well you can't be going up and down those stairs, you'll fall and hurt yourself."

"Watch me."

I know that Grandpa has been stubborn ever since he… well forever, but I wasn't about to tolerate this behavior.

"How'd you move around this furniture?"

"I didn't do it. James did. He wanted to set it up exactly like his old home."

My brother, who is only nine, was in the car with my Mom and Dad when they crashed into an on-coming truck. Investigators told me that they swerved to miss a deer and then hit the truck. They then sat there for a while because the truck driver was knocked out as well as my parents. The only reason they were found was because my little brother James walked most of the way back to town before being picked up. The strangest thing they told me is that my brother was seen along the road with another person close to town, but they never did find this person. My brother won't give a description to anyone, and they left him alone because he was just in an accident. The driver of the car who found James said it looked like a very pale man, but when the driver went to confront this pale man, he took off. I shrugged it off and sat down on the couch next to grandpa and told him how my day went.

"Hey grandpa? You notice something that I'm carrying?"

"What?"

"A taser."

"Oh, I knew that. One of your buddies sent me a video of you being tased."

"Really, that was definitely Thomas then wasn't it?"

"Yea. You screamed like a girl. Oh! Speaking of girls. Did you meet up with your girlfriend today?"

"Yea I did."

"Is she hot?"

"Grandpa come on."

He turned and looked at me with one eyebrow raised up and a suspicious look on his face.

"Ok fine... She's hot."

"Ha! Knew it."

"Well what else did you want me to say."

"I don't know. You could've lied."

"I'm not going to lie about my girlfriend."

"You used to."

"Alright, goodnight Grandpa. I'm going to go see what James is up to. Enjoy your beer."

"Oh, I will."

I went upstairs, down the hallway to my brother's room, and knocked on his door. He was inside his room making shooting noises and flopping around on the floor, doing whatever came to his imagination.

"Hey James?"

"WHAT!"

"Can I come in?"

"Ok!"

I opened the door to his room scattered with Legos, toy trucks, cars, Nerf guns, paper and pencils. The papers on the floor had realistic figures drawn on them, better than what I could do but most of them were of the androids from the Circuit Grill. He loved art, and was very good at it, so I sat down next to him on the floor to talk to him about doing an art class. I picked up a picture that he drew of the androids making a conversation with a customer and he was next to me coloring in a sketch he must have just made.

"Hey James? What are you drawing there?"

"Nothing."

"Come on let me see it."

I leaned over and got a look at the drawing he was shading in with a pencil. It looked like an android from the Grill, but it had no right thumb and it seemed to be weathered. I stood up and said that it was time for bed, but he wanted a little more time to finish what he was doing.

"Alright but only five minutes, ok James?"

"Fine."

I started leaving his room when he asked what the yellow gun on my holster was.

"This? This is my new taser."

"Can I see it?"

I pulled it out of my holster, removed the end cartridge so it couldn't fire, and let James hold it. James' eyes lit up in excitement as he held the taser in front of him.

"It's heavy."

"Yes, they are heavy. Do you want to know how I got it?"

"Yea."

"I had to get tased by one."

"That sounds painful."

"It is… Well you need to get some sleep, so goodnight James."

"Goodnight."

James handed me the taser and I closed the door as he continued drawing on his paper. I reattached the end cartridge on my taser and put it back in my holster. I really hope that he's able to cope well with this. He was really bad the first week after the accident, but it's been getting better as time went on. I walked into my bedroom, removed my holster and bullet vest, and put them on my nightstand. Then I looked at the time and it read 11:24. Wow, time flies when you're tired. I flopped onto my bed and turned on my tiny 10-inch TV I bought at a garage sale. Two more days to sit and watch the complex. After that, I can come home much earlier. I leaned over and turned off the lamp while watching TV, and slowly fell asleep.

My joints ached from following my uncle around the construction site after lunch today. The size of the place is just mind boggling. It's three stories tall and is the biggest workshop I've ever seen. He showed us what was going to become the oversized testing area, and later showed us the forty unfinished workshops, including where some technology retail stores were going to go. The entrance is going to have a giant Iron replica of an android he called Trinity. He described the android as Josh's perfection, but, so far they only have the pedestal half finished. There is the courtyard in the middle of the complex that is about a couple of acres. Tom hasn't quite decided on how to design the third floor area, but he said that he's planning to turn it into a young kids engineering and entertaining area. After all of that, he showed us the warehouse, boiler room, and the workshop in the basement, each room packed to the brim with parts and supplies. We were walking around that complex for at least seven hours, and for a 77-year-old man, he out-walked us both. I guess I could use exercise… a lot. After that, Adalyne and I went to the gun range to practice with the new guns Tom gave us for our job. After arriving at Tom's house for the night, I was walking down the hall to my bedroom and passed a few pictures of him, his wife, and his daughter Martha. I've never met Martha and I'd never heard a lot about her. Tom said that some drunk man ran her over with a car right outside of the workshop when she was only ten. The story is so sad, but I feel like he wasn't telling me the whole truth. His wife, since passed, had blond hair that was curled in a large blob over her head, the same late 70s hairstyle was in the rest of her pictures as well. She was a little taller than Tom, and was also wearing a silver chain link necklace. I continued into the bedroom Adalyne and I were sharing, and I could see that all of our suitcases were brought in… except one.

"Adalyne, where did you put my large suitcase!?"

"It's still in the car. I'm getting it right now!"

I opened my smaller suitcase and put all of my hygiene supplies in the bathroom across the hall. I then opened my bag of clothes and put them on the hangers in the closet next to Adalyne's clothes. My security uniform my uncle gave me was already hung up on a hanger. No bullet vest and thankfully no taser. I am in no mood to get tased. When Adalyne and I practiced with our new 9mm pistols at the gun range, I noticed that the pistols kicked back more than they should've. We would always come and practice shooting pistols with our great uncle since we were 13. I still have my 9mm at home, but I figured I didn't need it. What was I thinking? I'm a security guard, of course I needed my own pistol. I looked at my watch and it read 11:24. Wow, no wonder I'm so tired. It's almost midnight. I walked back down the hallway, to the balcony, and down the stairs where Adalyne was carrying four suitcases.

"You know I can help right?"

"Yea I know. I just feel like I could run a mile."

"It's almost midnight, how could you run a mile?"

"Oh my God Morgan, I'm being sarcastic."

"We walked around the entire complex with uncle Tom out walking us the entire time. That's almost six to seven hours."

"Ok fine, I'm tired."

I took a closer look at Adalyne. Her posture was higher, her mood was lighter, and she was carrying at least one hundred pounds of suitcases. I know this behavior because I acted the same way when I met Jackson here fifteen months ago, and now Adalyne met someone? I wonder where, or how. Adalyne had never been interested in anyone that I know of. I looked at her and asked in a suspicious tone.

"Who did you meet?"

"What?"

"You heard me. Who did you meet?"

"No one."

Adalyne had that look in her eyes that just proved that she had met someone, most likely at lunch.

"You're in love aren't you?"

"What? No I'm not."

"Yes you are. You're hyper, you're acting very strange, and…"

Tom suddenly yelled out our names in a loud voice making me jump around towards the basement door.

"Morgan! Adalyne! Come over here please!"

"Great, what did we do?"

"I don't know, but you jumped like you were under attack by a dog or something."

We walked down stairs to where Tom was, each wall piled with boxes upon boxes of files and blueprints. Tom turned to us and held out a key and a small maroon book the size of my phone. He gave me the key, Adalyne the book, and told us that he needed us to do something before the place opens. Tom described everything he and Josh did, 1970s and up. He talked about the old location, but it was demolished almost 15 years ago. Tom also mentioned a small complex his company built called the J.T. Robotics Workshop. I've never heard about it before, but he said it was the first location they built. The complex was built over an underground bunker that he said was to serve as a fallout shelter just in case a nuclear war broke out. By the time he finished the bunker in 1980, the cold war was beginning to de-escalate, but what shut it down was the bad structure of the bunker itself. He and Josh only had this place open for a week before they had to close it to the public. Tom said that Josh had been using this bunker as testing area for a very long time. After Josh committed suicide, Tom had turned the place into a storage room to hold blueprints and unused circuits. I knew that Tom was the owner of the company, but I didn't know that he built an underground bunker. Tom and Josh were close to being self-made millionaires, but they put almost every dollar back into their company. Tom then specifically said that he needed blueprints that were located in his partner's old office next to the east side of the bunker.

"You understand what you need to do?"

"We understand Tom."

"Get some rest then. You have a big day tomorrow."

For a while we thought about why he never told us about the bunker, but we could never find a solid reason why. It would explain how he was able to come up with all of the supplies out of thin air, but it didn't explain why he kept it a secret. We walked back up into our bedroom and I started making my bed. Adalyne didn't bother making hers, she was too tired from the day's activities. But I on the other hand, prefer to be in a neat bed so I don't wake up with aches and pains. Come to admit it, I need to get some exercise before we go see that underground bunker tomorrow. I wonder what's down there? Maybe an old prototype or some parts for one... I need some sleep. My thoughts are all over the place.

Chapter 3

"Morgan…Morgan…MORGAN!"

I tossed a pillow at Morgan to get her out of bed. She tumbled over the side and stood up in a sloppy fighter pose still half asleep.

"Morgan, it's time to go to the bunker."

I looked in the closet for some clothes and noticed that Morgan had brought her Marine uniform zipped inside a dust jacket. She was in the marines for four years, and she has a black belt in martial arts. She helped run security where she was stationed at, but it didn't help with how jumpy she is.

"Why did you bring your uniform?"

"For the complex's grand opening. You know, to look nice."

"Uh-huh, You just want to impress Jackson don't you."

"Maybe both."

I looked at her with a joking face and tossed her some of her clothes off of the closet rack. I put on some fresh clothes to wear for the fall season. Then we put on our matching Conkling Bay jackets we got from Coeur D'Alene Lake. We walked down stairs to the kitchen and found Tom sitting at the dining table irritably watching the news, and drinking his coffee.

"Hey Tom, what are you watching?"

I sat down next to him and saw, on the TV, a man standing in front of the new building that was under construction. There was a reporter next to him, with short blond hair and a nose ring, that was asking what this new place will be like when it is finished.

"What can you tell us about this place?"

"All I can say now is that it is a one of a kind building, but the projected completion time of the tech complex is about another year and a half."

"Can you tell us what is unique about this tech complex that makes it different from other facilities?"

"Well we are the only complex in the world that will give customers the ability to customize and build their own android at a reasonable price. And if you want to hear any more, you're going to have to wait and find out."

Tom turned to us and pointed to the man that was being interviewed.

"Do you girls know who that is?"

Morgan and I both shook our heads, and Tom continued.

"His name is Ben, and he's programming the new androids that I've been designing. I have only been working on one brand new prototype just to see how they will function. So far it's been a smooth process, but we ran into some difficulties and we need some help with the programming."

"So... you didn't just hire us to be a night guard and a mechanic?"

"Yes, and no. You will still be there during your shift," he said pointing to Morgan, "but you Adalyne, can work on the function and program of the prototype."

"When do we need to be there?"

"You don't need to be there till seven tonight, but I do prefer you go a little earlier and get in some extra time on the droid's programming. After your shift, you girls can do whatever you want. You'll most likely be sleeping."

Tom stood up, opened the fridge, and threw some frozen waffles into the toaster. He then put on his coat and slid his car keys into his pocket.

"There are more waffles in the fridge if you're still hungry. And take my truck, the road you'll take is in bad shape."

And with a fast pace, he walked out the door to the garage, and slammed it shut behind him. We just looked at each other and shrugged it off.

"Well, now we know what he looks like when he's grumpy."

We giggled a little and started eating our toasted waffles. I wonder why he was in such a grumpy mood, and in a hurry. It was 7:43 by the time we were in Tom's pickup, driving to where he said the J.T.C. shop would be. It didn't take too long before we left town on Molt road, heading towards the old bunker. Eventually we approached a turn up ahead that had no sign, and there was an old decrepit asphalt road that was being overgrown with weeds. I turned down the road and began weaving my way in and around the coulee next to a small creek. Eventually we came across an old brick and concrete building that had a somewhat desolate vibe to the place. There were no trees, except on the tops of the hills, and there were no signs up anywhere.

"This looks right."

I looked at Morgan and I could swear that she was about to burst with energy. Almost too excited for a little treasure hunt.

"Morgan, we can't spend too long here. Tom needs these blueprints right away."

"Tom said we didn't need to show up till seven. We've got plenty of time."

Morgan walked up to the front door and looked at the padlock on the door holding the entire entryway shut. She took out the key Tom gave her and unlocked the padlock. I was looking at the front of the building that had wood planks over where the windows used to be and there was stripped grey paint on the side from being exposed to the weather for too long. We made our way inside and I thought that it looked almost identical to the J.T. Circuit Cafe where we had lunch.

"Hey Adalyne, look at this."

Morgan had found a poster that was hidden behind some old wood planks. She picked it up and studied it with a very disgusted face. I walked over to her and looked at the poster with excitement. On the tattered poster, there was a line of androids dressed in human outfits from the early eighties. They were all standing in a line as a worker in front of them was giving instructions to follow. As I studied the face of one of the androids, I realized that the design of it was almost exactly the same as the waitress android at the J.T. Circuit Grill in town. Morgan looked at me and said with an uneasy tone, "Don't you find it strange that the droid on this poster, and the one that took our order at the cafe look the same?"

"Yea, you'd think that they would move onto a newer design."

Each droid had a creepy human appearance to it that seemed to be way ahead of its time. The facial expression of the droids then were permanent compared to today's models that could change their facial expressions to whatever they wanted. It gave me goosebumps. We left the poster where it was and found a hall that ended with two massive doors with large windows. In front of the doors was a number panel. I took out the maroon book that Tom had given us, and started flipping the pages. I then realized that there was no power in the building to run the panel.

"Hey Morgan, go try and find the breaker box. It should be by the old checkout counter somewhere."

"Ok Adalyne sir!"

Morgan stood in a salute to make fun of my instructive tone, and then walked off towards the kitchen. As I was figuring out how to get down into the bunker, I noticed a sign above the door that said "Fallout Shelter". I stepped closer to the window and saw that the elevator cables were the only thing visible. Morgan broke the silence with a quick and sharp voice.

"Adalyne, there's no breaker box by the checkout counter."

"Ok, check the back office. I'll check and see if there's any closets around."

I left the elevator door and walked over to an old, withered, door. I slowly opened the door to what looked like a small storage room. There were shelves up against the walls on either side of the room. The shelves were completely empty except for some lonely bolts and wires. I thought that I saw everything there was to see, until I noticed something peculiar. I noticed that there was a cupboard shaped wood plank up against the back wall. I walked up to it and tried to pull it open, but it wouldn't give. I ran my hand around the edge of board hoping to find a latch or something, but found nothing.

"Come on you stupid thing, open up."

With a little irritation, I lightly hit the wood panel. To my surprise, it popped right open. I closed it and pushed it in, again causing it to pop open. It must have been one of those push-open cupboards. I pulled the door open and sighed a heavy sigh as I saw at least eighty breaker switches.

"Morgan, I found the breaker box!"

...

"Morgan?"

I turned around looking for Morgan, but I couldn't see her anywhere. I walked over to the checkout counter and she wasn't there. Oh that's right, she was in the back office. Walking down the opposite hallway I noticed multiple doors on either side. Close to the end of the hallway to the left, was a door wide open where Morgan's flashlight shone out of it.

"Morgan?"

"Yea?"

"I found the breaker box and I need you to see which one turns the elevator on."

"All right"

Morgan was holding a blueprint that looked like an android ball and socket joint design.

"You found a blueprint already?"

"Yes, it's a joint design and I wanted to familiarize myself with it."

"But it has to be twenty years old."

"It's still cool though."

We left the office and headed back to the storage room and the breaker box. Morgan went over to the elevator door and I started flipping switches. Click.

"Working!?"

"No."

We continued this pattern for at least ten minutes, but none of the switches activated the elevator.

"You know what, I'm just going to turn them all on."

I took my arm and started turning them on ten at a time. Lights, the back office, and all eleven of the workshop rooms. Main hall, back hallway, and then the outside light turned on. I finally finished switching all of the switches as the indoor lights came flickering on.

"Adalyne! It's working now."

I ran over to Morgan and the number panel, opened the maroon book and found the password for the elevator. I reached down and typed in 9-1-8-2-3-6-6.

The elevator started whirring, electricity humming, and the lights in the elevator shaft lit up. I peered down the shaft through the window.

"Wow, that is a long drop."

Morgan was behind me trying to look down the elevator shaft as well, but wouldn't get close to the door. I pulled her closer to get a better look, but she pulled away.

"You aren't that scared of heights are you?"

"I don't like how far down that goes."

We sat there waiting for the elevator to come up for some time. Finally the elevator cast a shadow over the door's windows, and opened revealing a very large space inside.

"Well, at least there is plenty of room," Replied Morgan.

She slowly walked inside of the elevator stretching her arm up to touch the top of the elevator door, but there was two feet of space between her hands and the top. I looked at Morgan as I pressed the down button on the elevator control pad.

"What do you think will be down there?"

"I think there will be the blueprints we need, and I hope that there will be something special like an abandoned droid limb..."

Morgan turned to me with her eyes full of hope.

"Maybe there will be an entire android down there."

"I highly doubt it. Tom was pretty thorough about getting things that he needed out of the bunker."

Morgan turned away as the elevator doors closed and the elevator started moving back down towards the bunker.

"Yes, but it is good to hope for it."

By the time the elevator door opened, we had our flashlights on and looking around expecting to see a grand open room. There was, however, a door on the far side of the room with a breaker box off to the side of the room. I walked over to the breaker box and opened it. It was exactly like the one in the wall in the closet, but this time the switches ran sideways and there were twice as many.

"Alright, let me do it."

Morgan pushed her way forward and started flipping switches.

"Morgan, what are you doing?"

"I'm not going to sit and wait to find the right switches. That will take too long."

A soft flickering light came on behind the door, shining through a tiny inch and a half thick window.

"Wow. They sure weren't messing around when they put up this door." Stated Morgan.

I walked over and turned the lever on the door to release the lock holding it shut. We both pulled it open and stared into this large, stadium sized room that had these huge eight foot thick pillars of concrete holding the structure up.

"Did Tom say that his office was on the west side or the east side?"

"He said east, but... which way is east?"

We decided to split up and look around for a while. I began walking around the perimeter of the entire shelter, passing a couple of other, smaller rooms. A kitchen, a boiler room, a couple of large bathrooms, but then I found a large hallway with doors lining either side. As I walked down towards the end of the hallway, I read each sign over each door. Every single necessity was thought of and prepared for, each door appropriately labeled, and each door hiding another massive room behind it. I did become a little curious of what was behind one of these doors, but when I tried to open one, it was locked. I looked through the window into the room and spotted rows upon rows of bunkbeds, each one covered in boxes of supplies. I continued my way down to what looked like a row of offices, and finally spotted a sign with the name Joshua on it. I turned around and yelled,

"Morgan, I found the office!"

I walked over to the door under the sign and was happy to find it unlocked. I walked inside and saw a desk, a chair, and a shelving unit in the back of the small room. I looked along the side of the door frame and spotted a light switch. I flipped it on expecting a quiet little buzz, but jumped as a loud clank echoed through the room when the lights turned on. I shrugged it off and continued into the room. The desk and chair were covered in a dust sheet, but there were boxes of materials and supplies stacked on the shelves and on top of the desk seeming to be free of dust anyway. There was a monitor sitting under the dust cover, so I walked over and pulled the sheet off. The monitor was plugged in, but it didn't appear to work. Never the less, I pressed the power button and to my surprise, it turned right on. There was static for only a moment before the image began to clear up. It was a camera system for the bunker!

"Now that's cool."

I continued to observe the monitor and wondered how to change the camera angle. The camera's angle had a view of the hallway pointing towards the room I was in. There were no buttons other than the on-off, and volume. There was probably a circuit board sitting in one of these boxes, but I was not about to look for... I spotted a note card on the side of the monitor. I took a look at it; '1-2-2-2-3-6-6'. Beneath that was another set of numbers '1-2-4-2-3-6-6'.

"This looks important."

The door to the room opened and I turned around to see Morgan, who was covered in rolls of blueprints, reaching for another roll in the corner of the office behind the door.

"Morgan? Why do you have so many blueprints?"

"They looked important."

I started to laugh but suppressed it so I could speak normally again.

"Everything looks important to you. You're carrying about fifty rolls of blueprints. Tom only needed the blueprints for the suit design, and his early prototype design."

"Ok, but I'm bringing these up for me to keep... if Tom will let me."

"I don't think Tom will let you take any blueprints you find, unless they are irrelevant to what he's doing, or simply out of date."

"Well it's worth a try."

We found quite a few designs of these androids, and some plain endoskeletal design for a prototype android, but that was pretty much it. Morgan had a bunch of designs that were about the processor line, the processor system itself, and many other small things for an android. We messed around for a little while looking at old blueprints trying to find more stuff. We walked back into the massive stadium room and over to a stack of boxes that appeared to stand out from the other boxes. There was a box made of metal, the only one in the entire bunker, sitting under a bunch of other boxes. The box was screwed shut and there was no way to figure out what was inside. There was only a small word in red printed on the very front of it. Trinity. Above it was a blinking green word that said CHARGING.

"What do you think Trinity is? An android?"

"No clue. But it is getting a little close to lunch. We should get going."

We were walking back to the elevator when I glanced at the note card that I found behind the monitor.

"1-2-2-2-3-6-6."

"What?"

"Oh, I found a note card behind the monitor in the office."

"Seven digits?"

I then realized that there was a seven digit code for the elevator as well.

"I think this could be for the elevator, but the elevator doesn't need another code to ascend. Right?"

I walked through the door leading to the elevator shaft and walked over to the control pad inside the elevator. Morgan went over to the breaker box and started switching them off. She then walked into the elevator and reached for the ascend button.

"Wait!" I yelled.

"What?"

"I'm going to try this combination really quick just to see what it does."

I pressed in the numbers one at a time, each appearing on the number pad. 1-2-2-2-3-6-6.

"I really hope you don't get us stuck down here." Morgan replied in a concerned voice.

I pressed the enter button and stood back in anticipation. In a moment's time, the elevator doors closed and we started to ascend. It wasn't ten seconds before the elevator stopped, and opened its doors revealing another small room.

"Tom never mentioned a second level above the main bunker, did he?"

"No, I don't know what this is," Morgan replied while walking over to the edge of the room.

"There is no breaker box here, but there is a number pad next to the door. Bring over that note card."

I walked over to the number pad and started typing in the numbers. This time there was no sound effect to tell whether or not the numbers were entered. 1-2-2-2-3-6-6... nothing happened; no sound, no change in anything.

"Ok, wrong one."

1-2-4-2-3-6-6... There was a faint click followed by the door creaking open slightly.

I followed Adalyne into this dark room with a flashlight at my side, looking for any switch to turn the light on. There was a computer on one side and file cabinets on the other in this tiny cubicle of a room, but it was in a better condition than the office in the lower bunker. I looked to my right and saw a dark hallway through an open door with railing on the right side of the hall.

"Adalyne, I'm going down this hallway really quick. I'll be right back."

"Don't get lost. We don't know this part of the bunker."

I started walking down the hall, hand on the rail, and flashlight at my feet. I walked for a little ways until I came upon a wall with a small breaker box. I opened it revealing only eight switches inside. I took my hand and flipped them on all at the same time. I turned left to the sound of a buzz and then the lights of a stage came on in a blueish hue. I walked towards the stage in curiosity as the rest of the lights turned on. The wall on my right suddenly lit up and there was something there. I turned to my right and my heart stopped dead in my chest as I screamed at the sight of a black face with bright blue eyes staring down at me only inches away, its mouth opened just enough to reveal its bright white teeth. If I had been a couple of inches closer, I'd be touching its nose with mine. I flung myself away and backwards onto the floor in desperation. Adalyne came running in but stopped short upon entering the room. Her face surprised and mouth wide open. Against the wall, there were two canine like figures hanging from the ceiling by four giant steel arms, attached to the back of their shoulders. The one that I had almost ran into, now that I could get a better look at it… or her, had black fur on her face and body. Her face was a near perfect resemblance of a dog, but with a human look added on top with blue eyes complete with eyelashes. She had canine ears, with white earrings that were more realistic than any I've seen on an android. She had black hair that ran over her head and covered her left eye. On the back of her head was a bright white bow pinned behind her ears, and beneath the bow her hair ran down the back of her body to the top of her hips. The top she had on was a perfect white color with a V neck spanning to her shoulders. Over each shoulder were pointed shoulder pads that came out four to five inches. Her top ended just above her abdomen revealing that it was mostly the same color as the rest of her body, but the front of her belly was a dark grey color, lighter than the rest of her black fur. She was wearing white bell bottoms with triangle folds over her belt going all the way around her waist, about seven on each side. Her body structure was feminine with rounded hips and torso, but it was still unnatural. Adalyne walked over and picked me up by my shoulders allowing me get a better look at the one to my left. It was the same design, but this one appeared male. His body structure was more square than the other android. He had no hair over the existing fur on his head, and there was nothing covering his chest exposing his muscular shape. He was wearing the same bell bottoms as the other android, but there were no white triangles folded over the belt of his pants. Adalyne broke the silence with a quiet voice.

"I think they're off."

They haven't moved at all since I first saw them, and now that I've gathered myself back together, the androids actually looked kind of pretty. They were about six and a half feet tall to the top of the head and about seven feet to the tip of their ears. The biggest thing I noticed is that there were no gaps at the joints of the androids' skin. I turned to Adalyne and said, "Yea. I think they're off."

"You screamed so loud, I think you could have woken them."

Adalyne nudged me in the side jokingly. I looked around for a desk or shelves or something to explain these androids, and that was exactly what we found. On the opposite side of the room was a single shelf with two very large boxes underneath, and five smaller boxes on top of the shelf. Behind the two large boxes were what looked like two very long gun cases, about ten feet long each. I walked over with Adalyne towards the boxes, while keeping an eye on the two animal androids. We pulled out one of the larger boxes from the bottom shelf and opened it. There were layers of nicely folded fur packed to the top of the box. I reached down and touched the fur... but ripped my hand back revoltingly.

"What?... It feels just like skin!"

Adalyne reached in, touched them, and reacted in the same way.

"It does feel like skin."

I pulled out a very heavy chunk that took up half the box. and laid it out on the floor. It was an extra skin for the androids. Adalyne turned to me and said,

"You know what that looks like?"

We both had the same thought.

"Yea, it looks like one of those barbie dolls with no clothing."

"So that must mean that the androids can be dressed however we want?"

Adalyne and I looked at each other with faces full of ideas. We pulled the other skin out and laid it right next to the other one. They were almost perfect imitations of the barbie and ken dolls, but these skins had nothing to support them, and they were flat on the ground. They also had wires with small connectors sticking out where the skin split. The skin split perfectly down the back of the legs, arms, torso, and up to the top of the head.

"Hey. Maybe I could wear the skin."

Adalyne caught me by surprise.

"You think you can get that thing on? It must weigh more than eighty pounds."

Adalyne walked over and picked up the replacement skin for the female android.

"It's like a coat, but it's too heavy to wear."

Adalyne changed her mind and put the skin back down on the floor. She walked back to the shelves and took another small box from the shelf and I took a smaller box from the top shelf. Inside my box was a tiny booklet and a few blueprints. I took out the booklet and the front of it read, 'Function and Programming' and handed it to Adalyne. There was another one beneath it and it read, 'Design and Construction'. Adalyne leaned over and showed me a blueprint on the ears of the androids. The ears were capable of pinning themselves up to a point or folding all the way back against the head, just like a dog. I pulled out a small blueprint that looked like the head of one of the androids. Unlike the androids at the restaurant, these used a small version of pneumatic actuators to move the lips, ears, and some sort of magnet to move the eyes and eyelids. They could even move their eyebrows. Looking at the blueprint closer, I picked out the framed details of a small speaker in the back of their throat...and a tongue? How far are they going to go on the details? I pulled out a larger blueprint of just the metal skeleton. The entire frame was made of a steel alloy that held the android upright. It looked very similar to the human skeleton, including the joints. The shoulder, ankle, wrist, and hips were ball and socket joints, and the elbow and knee joints were simple hinge joints. On the ball and socket joints were something similar to hydraulics, and were connected crossways around the joint making an X appearance. It was repeated over the joint so it could twist, but I noticed that the hydraulics on some of the joints were larger in the front and back, seeming to imitate human muscles. I pulled out a third blueprint that seemed to be on just the hydraulic-like pneumatic actuators, but this design ran on fluid, not air pressure. Connected to the end of the hydraulic arm was a steel fiber cable simulating a human tendon. Adalyne looked at my blueprint and I looked at hers. We continued passing blueprints until I found the one I was looking for. Inside each android were xenon difluoride batteries capable of running for a seemingly endless amount of time, and were no bigger than a car battery. I've read about these batteries somewhere before, but I'm not too sure when they were invented. There was an electric pump inside the android used to power the hydraulics. It was silent and ran on the little amount of power that it was given. There was a manual switch on the back of the pump that when pulled up, the android would lock up its hydraulics, ceasing its movement.

"Hey Morgan, look at this."

Adalyne handed a blueprint to me that was a cut out of the skin. Inside the skin were hundreds of tubes filled with an adhesive to reattach the skin if it tears. Just below the skin above the tubes were thousands upon thousands of sensors attached to a network of wires that would connect to their main processor. I turned to Adalyne and pointed out the sensors.

"Look at how well this is designed. The skin is just like a touch screen."

"That's nothing compared to the programming. I don't understand it but it's very thorough."

Adalyne handed me a small blueprint that had the design of the computer in the android along with the 'Function and Programming' booklet. The booklet had everything from joint movement to programming the behavior of the robot. I turned to Adalyne quickly, "You know what I haven't seen yet?"

"What?"

"There aren't any names for the androids. That's usually the first thing we know."

We sat there digging through the rest of the boxes, but there was nothing in the box that had the skins. We tried to open the long gun cases, but they were locked with some type of magnet twist lock. I tried to pick one up but, with both of us at either end, we could only get one case off of the ground for a moment.

"Maybe we missed something in the office."

I walked into the office shuffling through drawers and shelves. I then turned to the wall behind the desk where a mirror was hanging. I bet that there's something behind this. I reached up and pulled the mirror off of the wall and to my disappointment, there was just more wall. Darn, I was hoping for a safe or a hidden key. I held up the mirror, and as I put it back on the wall, something fell onto the floor. I pulled out my flashlight, pointed it at the floor, and lo and behold, there was a small TV-ish looking remote that appeared to mirror its buttons on either side. With excitement I picked up the remote and ran out to Adalyne.

"Adalyne! I think this controls the droids!"

"You sure?"

"Yes I'm sure."

I turned the remote over and flipped a switch on the back. The buttons on the remote lit up and there were names above the buttons that weren't there before. On the left side was the name Jackson, and on the right side was the name Lexis.

"Well Adalyne, I found their names."

"Ha! That's the name of your boyfriend!"

I wonder what Jackson would have to say about an android with his name? I examined the buttons that were initialed VA, AB, and RPB. Most of the other buttons had numbers on them, but there was one button that was missing. Where's the on button?

"There doesn't seem to be any power button."

I looked at the remote closer making sure that I had seen every button. I handed it to her and she started pressing buttons one at a time. Each time she pressed a button, we'd look at the androids to see if they had changed.

"Maybe it's broken."

I looked back at the androids wondering how someone can turn these on. Perhaps the button wasn't on the remote, or maybe the hydraulic lock was on. I walked over to Lexis and started looking on her back for any switches. I looked up to her head and noticed that the skin of the ear and the skin of the head were separated in one small spot. I reached around the big steel arms holding up the android, and stuck my ring finger into the hole behind the ear. There was cold metal and plastic. I then poked around with my other finger to reach in further, and there was a plastic switch on the metal plating under the skin.

"Gotcha."

I pulled the switch towards me and immediately pulled my hand out. There was a small buzzing sound followed by a low hum. Adalyne jumped at the sound and threw the remote backwards into the box behind her.

"Morgan, What did you do?!"

The giant metal arms began lowering the android down to the floor. As the arms disconnected from the android, she lifted her head up and suddenly became sprite with life. I was backing up from Lexis as she started walking towards Adalyne with her bushy tail swinging behind her. Was there a tail there before? I didn't see any in the blueprints, but I haven't seen all of the blueprints yet. She then stopped three feet in front of us with her hand extended towards me. She then opened her mouth and asked in a static female voice, "Hi, nice to meet you. What's your name?"

I hesitated for a while, but then extended my hand into Lexis' fuzzy hand not knowing what to expect. She then shook my hand in a formal greeting and repeated,

"Come on, you can tell me your name."

I stood there staring into the androids bright blue eyes wondering what kind of programming was in this thing's head. Lexis' hand was almost twice my size, same with her feet, but her feet looked like a normal human foot instead of paws.

"My uh…my name is Morgan."

The way this android moved was very accurate, or organic you might say. The mouth was even conforming to fit the words coming from the speaker in the back of her throat. She then turned to Adalyne and asked the same thing, but Adalyne just stood there and stared at Lexis, frozen in her thoughts. Lexis was holding her hand out to greet her for at least a minute before she said.

"Come on. I know I look like a dog, but I'm a friend."

Adalyne slowly brought up her hand, but stopped midway. Lexis then reached down, took her hand, and shook it. Adalyne tried to pull her hand out of Lexis', but Lexis let go and Adalyne fell backwards into a box behind her. Lexis backed up and put both her hands on her hips and laughed quietly.

"What are you doing?" asked Lexis.

I helped Adalyne out of the box, brushing the dust bunnies off of her back. Adalyne just stood there and stared at the android with a flicker of wonder in her eyes, slightly fogged with fear.

"Adalyne, tell her your name."

Adalyne turned and looked at me with a face screaming 'please don't'.

Lexis spoke up again and said,

"Your name is Adalyne? I like it."

Lexis turned to the stage, and then to Jackson who was still hanging on the other two giant arms. She walked over behind Jackson, reached behind his right ear, and flipped the switch. There was a short buzz, a low hum, and Jackson was disconnected from the two giant arms.

"Morgan why did you say that?"

I looked at Adalyne surprised.

"These androids seem friendly enough, so why not interact with them. And for once, you're the jumpy one."

"I'm not jumpy, I'm being cautious."

"Sure."

I turned and looked at where Jackson and Lexis were. They were just staring at each other almost like they were having a silent conversation. Jackson turned to look at us, then back at Lexis, and back at us again. He walked over and stood in front of us the same way Lexis did and held out his hand, but this time he said.

"Morgan, right?"

We shook hands in a formal greeting.

"Yes… I'm Morgan."

Jackson turned towards Adalyne, but didn't bring up his hand to greet her.

"And your name must be Adalyne."

"Yes."

"Do you mind if we shake hands?"

Adalyne turned to me, then back towards Jackson. She stood there for a moment before she brought her hand up towards Jackson to shake his hand.

"See Adalyne, they aren't so bad."

"Yea, but why didn't Tom tell us about this? Something doesn't seem right here."

"Doesn't mean it can only be bad though."

I turned to the stage and saw something I hadn't noticed before. There was a small metal handle sticking sideways out of the stage. I went to pull it out, but before I could, Jackson, who was right behind me said,

"I'll get that."

He walked around me and knelt down near the handle. He pulled on it, twisted it clockwise, and with a loud crack the door opened and pieces of the door handle fell onto the floor.

"Wow. We weren't made to break stuff Jackson."

Lexis was right behind me talking jokingly to Jackson.

"Sorry."

Jackson reached in and pulled out two guitar cases and handed one to Lexis. I was puzzled about what they were doing. Perhaps they were just gathering their belongings. Why would androids be gathering their belongings? Or have a conversation to themselves? Jackson then pulled out two microphones on stands. I looked at Lexis and she had opened a guitar case revealing a bright white guitar with black lightning bolts running parallel with the strings, and she was pulling the strap around her neck.

"Lexis, what are you guys doing?"

"Well, our duty is to perform for people. There's you and Adalyne so why not. Do you happen to have any song requests?"

I looked at my watch and it read 11:45.

"No, I just thought that we'd be out of here by now because we have somewhere we need to be, but we can stay for just one song."

Adalyne grasped my arm and spun me around.

"Morgan, what are you doing?"

"We discovered a couple of androids that I've never seen before, there is technology in them that shouldn't have been invented in the time period they were built, and they behave like they're alive!"

"I know, that's what scares me. They were made to simulate humans, but still somethings off."

In the time span that we were arguing, Lexis and Jackson had set up the stage with one speaker and two microphones. They had matching guitars in their hands waiting for us to pay attention. Lexis leaned into the microphone and said,

"You guys ready!?"

Adalyne and I jumped at the loud voice coming from the speaker. She was looking at us with her bright blue eyes, guitar at the ready.

"Well? What do you guys want to hear?"

I looked at Adalyne with an idea to test these things, so I turned back to Lexis.

"Surprise us!"

Lexis turned to Jackson and they both nodded their head in synchronization. There was a quick drum intro, followed by Lexis and Jackson playing their guitars in an eighty's rock style tune. Pretty soon Lexis' guitar became more pronounced and she stepped up to the microphone and sang. They were both swinging their tails in synchronization with the song, almost like they were enjoying their own performance. Lexis was singing into the microphone barely touching it with her top lip. When she wasn't singing, she was dancing… dancing as if she were human. Then Lexis did something I've never seen before. She turned the guitar around and played an electric keytar on the back. The dance style was very unique because it seemed to be a subtle combination of programming and fluid movements. It was too… perfect. The moves she was doing were exact. Deliberate and on the spot every time. When she struck the guitar, it didn't seem like the sound was coming from a recording, it was coming from her guitar. Unlike many older performing androids, she was actually playing the guitar. It also seemed the same way with their voices too, like they were the recording. Lexis and Jackson were up on stage singing this song for about four minutes before they decided to stop. They walked over to us, and that's when I noticed something that scared me. They were breathing, but not just any breathing, they were panting like dogs trying to catch their breath. The breathing didn't sound real, but mechanical.

I was watching Lexis and Jackson as they stepped off the stage, and noticed that they were breathing, heaving their chests like they were exhausted. Lexis walked over, stood next to me and asked,

"Would you hang on to this for a moment?"

Lexis held out her guitar and that's when it hit me. Her breath was hot, and it smelled like metal. I took her guitar and backed up from the wretched smell, waving my hand to disperse it. She then walked over to the stack of boxes and picked up the two long gun cases as if they only weighed twenty pounds. I turned to Jackson who was standing next to Morgan and breathing just as hard as Lexis was.

"Jackson, why are you and Lexis breathing so hard?"

Jackson turned to Lexis who nodded her head, and let Jackson speak.

"We have a type of battery in our design that when under use, tends to heat up. To keep it cool, our designer built us something similar to lungs to push and pull air through our bodies. There are coils of coolant tubes wrapped inside my snout, so when I breathe cool air in through my nostrils and breath hot air out of my mouth just below my speaker, I cool my battery."

I pulled Morgan off to the entry of the hallway that led to the tiny office and I told her,

"Morgan, these androids should be left down here! They cannot go anywhere but here!"

"But Adalyne, think about the people that would show up to see these androids perform! They can do everything a human can do and they can do it better."

"They are too perfect. What will the protestors say? What will anyone say when they see them?!"

"I don't know, and I don't care. We discovered these things and I am willing to do anything to get them out of here."

Morgan was leaning into me, her voice sharp and her attitude meaningful. She turned and walked away from me towards Lexis and Jackson, then spoke to them quietly. Jackson then turned and put his and Lexis' guitars into their cases, picked them up in one hand, and walked to the stage. He put the speaker and two microphones back under the stage, closing the door as best he could since the latch was broken. When he didn't put the two guitars back, I knew at that moment, Morgan had told them to come with us. As we walked back to the elevator, Morgan and I didn't share a word with each other. Instead, we closed up everything the way we found it. I switched the breakers off, closed the lid, and as I turned around with my flashlight, Lexis, who was at the end of the hall, was completely invisible except for her top and the bell bottoms that she was wearing, along with her blue eyes, white earrings, and teeth. Jackson was also invisible against the dark abyss, with the exception of his blue eyes, teeth, and bell bottoms. The elevator was lit up just enough to see into the office a little, and as Lexis, Jackson, and Morgan were putting their stuff in the elevator, I stepped on some paper on the floor. I knelt down and studied it. There, in the picture, was Tom's coworker holding his arms around what looked like a woman with a late eighty's curly hair style. In what little light I could see, she appeared to be slightly taller than him, and she wore jeans with a red V neck T-shirt with a silver chain link necklace. The bottom of the picture read Josh and Sarah Korice. Morgan then spoke up from the elevator and asked,

"Adalyne! You coming!?"

I looked up to see Morgan standing there with her arms crossed, Lexis standing next to the two long gun cases leaned up against the elevator wall, and Jackson standing next to the guitar cases looking at me with those blank blue eyes.

"I'll be right there."

I took the picture, stuffed it into my pocket, and ran for the elevator. I hopped inside and pressed the up button mildly anxious to leave the dark bunker. Not a second later, the elevator doors close, and begin ascending. I turned to Morgan and said,

"Sorry for yelling at you earlier. I just don't think it's right to do this."

"I'm sorry too, but we can't leave this kind of technology abandoned."

We stared at each other for a little before Lexis asked.

"Are you two sisters?"

I was puzzled at the question because we were such obvious twins.

"Yes. We're sisters."

"You look very similar."

"Well, we're twins. We were born at the same time by the same mother."

Lexis looked at Jackson and then looked at us and responded,

"I guess you could say we are twins because we were built at the same time."

I guess that makes sense. Wait... How can an androids' programming be capable of such human-like behavior? Capable of comparisons and logic? It doesn't make any sense! The four of us stood there for a while until the elevator broke the surface and we could see the workshop through the glass windows of the elevator doors. The workshop's lights were still on and the closet door was still open, it was all the same when we left.

I pulled out my phone and it read 12:04.

"Um, Morgan. We need to get going."

Morgan ran over to the breakers in the closet and started pulling switches. One by one the lights overhead shut off and the whole abandoned building became silent again. Jackson pointed at my phone and asked,

"What is that? It looks just like the screen of a computer."

"It's a touch screen."

I held it out for him to touch, the screen lighting up his face. He poked it with his finger and swiped sideways, sending the phone to the lock screen. He then pulled his hand away and looked at his finger.

"Why is it so hot?"

"What?"

"The phone. Why is it hot?"

I put my finger on the screen and it felt cold to the touch. Though it's been in my pants pocket all day, it shouldn't be that hot.

"What do you mean? It's cold."

Jackson stood there for a moment, appearing to be frozen in thought.

"I bet that phone screen works the same as the sensors under our skin. Like some kind of feedback."

These androids are clearly knowledgeable about their own anatomy, but they weren't around to see the technological advancements of twenty to thirty years. I wonder how long they have been abandoned. They also seem very willing to learn about this new technology too, but it scared me that they could. The four of us hopped into Tom's truck, and we were almost ready to take off when Lexis said,

"I don't think these E.W. cases are going to fit."

"E.W. cases?"

Morgan was turned around in the driver's seat looking at Lexis and Jackson who were placing the long 'E.W' cases and guitar cases into the back of the truck. I looked at Morgan, silently asking her why they brought these cases. Morgan knew what I was asking, and she just shrugged her shoulders. We were finally all situated, so Morgan started the truck, and we headed down the road for the complex.

Chapter 4

It was 11:46 by the time I parked my car in front of the Circuit Cafe, ready for the 'Model Showcase' tomorrow that Tom keeps telling me about. I unlocked the front door, flipped the closed sign around, and started turning on the workshop from in the kitchen. First the lights, then the workshop rooms, and finally the androids that helped run the place. Every corner was flooded with a soft glow from the nine giant overhead lights, giving a cozy cabin vibe in the atmosphere. The waitress android was standing deactivated in the corner to the right of the kitchen, plugged in all night to ensure that the battery was well charged. I pulled the cord out of her wrist, put the plastic cover over it, and turned a switch inside of her neck. There was a short buzz followed by a low hum, and she stood straight up gazing around to find the place empty. I walked into the back hallway, through the Employees Only door, and down into my office ignoring the fact that the android was wandering around trying to find someone to take an order from. I had my fingers crossed hoping that nothing would be out of order in my office. I opened the door and I couldn't help but yell, "Damn it!"

The office was completely trashed, but aside from that was the writing of two words 'I remember'. The writing was on almost every conceivable area that could be covered including the computer screen, and the drawings children had made that were hung on the wall. I touched the smear on the computer screen and pulled a little off to smell. It was hydraulic fluid, or grease I hope. It was sticky and had a wretched smell like it was dead and rust-mold ridden metal. I took some paper towels from the kitchen and cleaned the screen of my computer. I threw away all of the messed up papers into a garbage can with the same 'I remember' sentence written on them. The children's drawings that I had hung were smeared with the same bad smelling grease. I took the drawings and, with a little regret, threw them away. My office had to be spotless with no paper on the floor, everything had to be the way I left it. It's like a pet peeve of mine. I turned on my computer, taking me to the same boring blue screen it had since I began working here. I left the office and headed down the hallway, and just as I was opening the door to the kitchen, the bell on the front door rang. I turned to see two cooks walk in to begin their work day.

"Ready for the showcase today?"

"That was today? I thought Tom said it was tomorrow."

"Josh, Tom has been saying 'Model Showcase on Friday' ever since we got here… and today's Friday."

My thoughts were twisted around each other giving me a mild headache. I rubbed the back of my head suddenly aware that it was swollen from landing on the ground last night.

"You alright Josh?"

I turned to the two cooks who were just standing there looking at me. Behind them was the waitress who was also looking at me with as much as a confused face an android could express.

"Yea I'm fine."

I walked off into the bathroom and threw some warm water onto my face. I wonder which android made those smears. There was only one that I could think of, but there shouldn't be any grease left in him. The other two I'm sure don't use grease on their joints because the connectors are magnetic. Unless… how could I be so stupid. Of course it's 126-F, the rust would explain the red color in the grease. 'I remember'…'I remember', what are you saying? What are you telling me? I stood there thinking what is it trying to communicate to me, but nothing came to mind. I walked out of the bathroom and into my office ready to start my tasks. I pulled out files upon files of blueprints on the designs of the androids, looking for any hint on their behavior. I finally found a blueprint on their processors. Reading through it, I found a page that had something interesting on it. 1-2-9-2-3-6-6. Is that a password? I reached over and typed it into the computer home screen. The computer responded, incorrect password. Ok, maybe it goes to something else. I clicked through the screens on the computer, trying to find somewhere to type in this password, but turned to a sound similar to keys scraping a car coming from the storage room through the window.

"Oh come on! I have barely started my work day yet!"

I flashed my light through the window to scare off whatever was in there, and was relieved to find nothing. I stood up and walked into the spare office to check and see if the android I assessed yesterday was still under the shelf, but all I could find was a messy floor and no android. The vent slats on the nearby wall however, were knocked in, bent in every which way. Something definitely came through here, and isn't coming back this way soon because of how I treated it yesterday. I shrugged it off and continued working on my tasks. Printing flyers for today's Android Showcase, ordering supplies, and organizing papers and files; which was all I did for an hour. I left my office to meet the first customer that came in. It was a party of three children, all under eight, and six adults. The children came in and were immediately everywhere, but thankfully one of them was in the children's workshop area. The other two went running all over the place playing a game of tag. Running under tables, around counters in the workshop area almost knocking over the cyclops android standing in the far corner.

"Oh no you don't. Excuse me! Whose child is that?"

One of the parents went down the hallway to find the children, and I went to the kitchen to make sure that everything was ready to go. There were only two kitchen staff members, but they get the job done. I peered over the counter and watched as the two children ran out of the workshop and into the employee's door.

"Oh crap!"

I took off towards the door as one of the cooks replied,

"They're just kids, what are they going to do?"

Forget it, you wouldn't know. I ripped through the door just in time to see the parent of the children open a door to a room looking for the kids. I ran up to her and asked where they went, but she just stared into the room ignoring my question.

"Ma'am..?"

I turned the light on in the room and I could clearly see the two children… playing around android 126-F! He was sitting on the floor following a child with his eyes, moving his head slowly around as well. They were tripping over him and were hopelessly trying to lift up his hand, and it was just sitting there, watching them.

"You guys can't be in here."

The two kids turned their heads in surprise and the android seemed to do the same. Their mother walked in, took their hands, and walked them back out, scolding them as she took them to be with the others. I looked at the android, and he looked at me. We stared at each other for a little while, but then I slammed the door and made sure that it was locked. I walked down the hallway and locked my office door. I entered the main workshop room and locked the employees only door ensuring that no child would stumble across one of the worst monstrosities. I didn't want to find out what would happen if a child was killed by one of these things. But the more I thought about it, the more I realized that 126-F had all the chance in the world to harm those children. In fact, he seemed to be enjoying their company.

"Excuse me sir?"

My thoughts were interrupted as two children were standing behind me, and behind them their mother.

"Sorry for going where we weren't allowed to go."

I knelt down to their eye level.

"It's ok, everyone makes mistakes."

I stood back up as the mother told the children to go play, but then turned to me with a vulture's glare.

"What was that in the back room?"

"That was a decommissioned android."

"Why was it on?"

"Maybe the children turned it on."

"I doubt that. I've read everything about your androids and their designs. Never once did anything mention that android."

This woman who was 'interrogating' me had short blond hair with a nose ring shining in the workshop lights. She had obviously done her homework on these androids. She's probably one of those reporters. Ever since this location opened, reporters disguised as parents would come in with groups of children, hopefully distracting me, so they could sneak off and find important information on anything they could get their hands on.

"Why would it? It's official business that you don't need to be nosing around in."

"I'm going to find out about it, and when I do, I'm going to shut you down."

She then walked over to the other adults, most likely to tell them what happened. I walked in the opposite direction and through the employees only door. I locked it behind me and entered my office, making sure that nothing was following me. I pulled out a drawer filled with files and searched for an androids blueprints. I took it out and made a quick copy onto the computer. I edited the shape a little and removed the right thumb making him appear the same as the 126-F android. I printed the new blueprint onto a smaller blueprint piece and studied it to make sure it looked perfect. Though it looked like a real blueprint, I had removed most of the info that would surely drive this woman nuts. I walked back out into the main workshop looking for the woman. She was standing alone in a corner writing in a little booklet, trying to ignore the noise coming from the workshop.

"Was this what you wanted?"

I held out the fake blueprint for her to take, but she just glared at me with a confused look in her eyes.

"Didn't I just say I'd shut you down?"

"You can't shut me down, nothing that I'm giving you will ruin my reputation. I thought that since you wanted the scrapped android blueprints, I thought I'd give you a copy."

She took it from my hand and studied it carefully.

"It's fake."

"I said it was a copy. You think I'd actually give you an original blueprint?"

She looked at it again, and then her whole demeanor changed.

"Why are you giving me this?"

"Cause, what else could I do? The thing is motioned activated, that's how it turned on. And you threatened to close me down, so I wanted to prove to you that there is no wrong in what is going on here."

She smiled a little, but then she frowned again.

"That isn't going to change anything."

She walked off towards the front door, swung it open wildly, and walked off to her car. Sheesh, she's rude.

I looked at Tom like he was crazy.

"I'm sorry Tom, you want us to do what?"

"I want you to try on these suits."

I was looking at this weird suit that appeared to be an android endoskeleton, but had just enough room to fit a human inside. The joints and hydraulics were covered by sliding metal plates, the hydraulics were running up and down every limb, mimicking human muscles. On its back was a giant flat metal box that contained the power source of the suit.

"I want you, and Adalyne, to see if you can operate this new security pilot suit."

"How?"

Tom walked to the left side of the suit and pressed a small grey button. The front folded open and Tom, with excitement, slid his hands and feet inside the gloves and boots, immediately triggering the rest of the suit to collapse around him. He then started to move around with the suit mimicking his movements.

"See, it functions just like power steering on a car. No harm in trying."

He took off sprinting around to the loading ramp and jumped high into the air, almost touching the ceiling. It appeared as if the suit was part of him, moving with his thoughts, and simulating everything a human could do. He landed next to us with a loud thud, shaking the floor of the building. He reached over and took the handle of a four hundred-ish pound crate, and held it in the air with minimal effort. He dropped the box, and reached around his side to release himself from the suit with the press of a button.

"See, it won't hurt you unless you land wrong, or land in a way that an object gets through the gaps in the metal plating."

I looked at Adalyne and she looked at me. We had the same crazy idea like all twins do. I stepped inside placing my feet in the boots and sliding my hands into the metal gloves. The suit immediately closed around me, like a loosely wrapped rubber blanket over the whole body. I lifted up my hand, quite easier than I thought, and made a waving gesture to Adalyne.

"This is nice. I could get used to this."

"Well, once the battery dies… you're kind of stuck in there until someone charges or replaces the battery." said Tom.

I started to walk around a little, but there was too much space inside and I was being knocked back and forth inside the suit. I needed to get out!

"How do I get out of the suit?"

"Press the button on your left side."

I pressed the button and was released from the suit. I turned to Tom and said, "It's a little too spacious in that suit."

"You calling me fat?"

Tom had a joking look on his face, clearly showing that he was messing with us.

"I'm kidding, I've got one more suit I'm finishing that is specific to your… body shape. And the reason for that is because if there's too much space, like what you just experienced, you'll get knocked around inside."

Tom walked off towards the workshop adjacent to the room where we hid the two androids we found yesterday at the bunker. We looked at each other with worried expressions. Is he going to go into the other room? I hope not. He turned the lights on in his workshop, and pulled a sheet off of the other suit. Immediately I could see what he meant when he said, 'body shape'. The size of this security pilot suit was slimmer and had a more polished design.

"I started working on this model as soon as I was done with that one out there. It is stronger and lighter, it even has a helmet to go with it!"

I studied the suit closely. It seemed to be a little shorter and less bulky than the other one, but it was still towering over us, about eight feet in all.

"Tom, you try it on first."

He turned to me surprised.

"I can't fit in this suit, according to you I'm too fat. Besides, it isn't finished yet."

Adalyne laughed and nudged me in the side as Tom turned to get something off of the workbench.

"Morgan, try this one on."

"Fine."

I stuck my hands into the metal gloves, my feet into the boots, and the suit closed around me just like the other one. This time though, there wasn't much wiggle room available. I tried to adjust myself, but the suit just moved with me, not allowing me to move into a more comfortable position.

"You comfortable Morgan?"

Adalyne had her phone out videoing me in the suit.

"Come on Adalyne, put that away."

I reached down to press the button, but it wasn't there.

"Where's the button?"

Tom stood there with a hand over his mouth, not saying a word. Adalyne, catching Tom's reaction, asked,

"What, she's fine isn't she?"

"No."

I tilted my head sideways and asked worriedly.

"What do you mean no?"

"I said it wasn't finished yet!"

I looked down to where the button should be, and instead there were wires sticking out of its place. I slowly lifted my head and looked at Tom. His face was beat red, and very soon he started laughing. Adalyne stood there, with her phone still out, and started to laugh with him.

"Come on, this isn't funny. Tom, why didn't you say anything?"

"I-I assumed you wouldn't put it on because I clearly said it wasn't done yet!"

Tom and Adalyne kept on laughing at me; stuck in a suit for God knows how long.

"Get me out of here!!"

Tom turned to the table and started to work on something, still laughing at the current situation, and began messing with a button that had complex inner parts to it.

Adalyne asked, "How do these buttons work?"

"There's a magnet under the plastic connected to a spring, and as long as the magnet is held back by the spring, nothing can press in the button. Your metal gloves, however, connect to the magnet through the plastic, allowing you to press the button."

"Are you going to attach it any time soon?"

Tom tilted his head sideways. "Eh… I'd say you're stuck for a while."

My thoughts scurried in my head as I pondered what to do. What could I do, there wasn't anything for me to do while I was stuck in the suit. I started to move my arms around to see what the limitations were, but so far I couldn't find any. I started to walk around, but I felt heavy, almost like a newborn baby learning how to walk. Pretty soon I started to get the hang of it. I turned to Adalyne and said, "Let's try our secret handshake while I'm stuck in this thing."

I reached out for Adalyne, dwarfing her hand with mine, and we started doing our handshake we had since junior high. First a fist bump, then two high fives and two backhands, and finally finished with a rock paper scissors game. I spun around in a three-sixty turn to get a feel for the suit, almost losing my balance. I then started to do some of those Fortnite dance moves, but again almost lost my balance.

"If you guys are going to do that, go do it somewhere else." said Tom with a stern, but humorous voice.

"How long did you say it would take?"

"I don't know, it takes as long as it takes. Oh, actually you can go learn how to use that suit, you know… show off your martial arts in that suit, see what you can do."

I looked at Adalyne and we had the same crazy idea in our heads , the same one from before I got stuck. We walked down the loading ramp, and out into the parking lot. I couldn't help but make very loud footsteps as the boots scratched into the parking lot pavement. I followed Adalyne over to a tree at the edge of the parking lot and she said, "See if you can pull this tree out of the ground."

"You want me to pull out a tree?"

"Yes, see if you can do it."

"I don't want to pull out a tree at the edge of a parking lot. Besides, someone could see that."

Adalyne shrugged her shoulders and we started walking out further into the forest. Eventually we reached the point where we could no longer see the tech complex, or the parking lot.

"Ok, punch that tree."

I looked at a smaller, yet taller tree. I stood back a little ways and began to think of what to do. Should I try to snap it? Should I kick it?

"Are you going to hit the tree, or are you just going to look at it?"

"Fine."

I brought up my left foot and kicked the tree causing it to whip backwards, snapping it at the base, and leaving a gouge where it hit the ground.

"Wow, I didn't mean kill it!" Adalyne yelled.

"Well you try fighting a tree in a big metal suit then."

We continued on joking with each other, and as we crossed the top of the hill, I could see, on the road to the complex, a police car.

"Hey Morgan guess what?"

Adalyne looked at me and then looked at the police car and I responded, "Don't you even think about it!"

As I walked up closer to the police car I hid behind some lilacs along the road. Inside I could see a man in his early twenties sitting and enjoying some coffee. I got closer to the car and was able to sneak up around the car without him seeing me. I looked up to see if it was Jackson, and it was him alright. 3...2...1... I jumped up and slammed on the window causing Jackson to jump up out of his seat. His face was serious and he looked like he was reaching for his gun, but he stopped himself when he realized who he saw. He rolled down his window and spoke, trying to conceal his anger.

"My God Morgan, what the hell?!"

"Oh, I'm not Morgan."

Jackson looked out the window, turned his head both ways down the road, and asked,

"Where's Morgan?"

"She's up there on top of the hill and is in a little bit of a situation."

"Is she stuck?"

"No... Well actually yes, but she's still able to move around."

Jackson opened the door of his car and stepped out to look up on top of the hill. We soon started walking up the hill towards the last place Morgan was. Eventually we got to the same spot where I saw the car, but Morgan was nowhere to be seen. Jackson cupped his hands around his mouth and yelled, "Morgan, where are you!"

Jackson's voice was filled with concern as he looked around for any sign of Morgan.

"I'm over here."

Jackson and I walked over to the sound of her voice, and finally I could see where she was. A little piece of metal was sticking out from the side of a bush that she was hiding behind. Jackson walked up to the bush and started pulling it back slowly.

"Morgan?"

Morgan stood up from the bush and towered over Jackson from the suit she was wearing. She was also covering her head with a big metal hand, trying not to show her face to Jackson.

"Oh my God! What did you get into!?"

"Take a guess."

I butted in and told the entire story of what happened to her. Jackson smiled, then started to laugh.

"Oh, come on. Not you, too."

We couldn't help but laugh at Morgan's ordeal, but pretty soon Jackson reached up to pull Morgan's hand down, but as he tried to, he only pulled himself off of the ground.

"Morgan, come on. Please show your face."

Morgan slowly let her hand down, revealing a very red face. She was either red from blushing, or from being frustrated. Probably both. Morgan looked at me and said, "I wish you didn't do that."

"Do what?" asked Jackson.

He was standing to the side of Morgan examining the suit that she was wearing.

"Oh, nothing Jackson. Sibling stuff."

Jackson glanced at his watch and then spoke up again.

"Morgan, there's this really cool place at the ridge of the ravine back here a ways, but it's quite a walk over there. Want to see it?"

"We could check it out. We've got time cause Tom isn't going to have the button ready for a little while."

We followed Jackson over to where he said the cliff was. Morgan was next to Jackson talking to him in a quiet voice, and I couldn't tell what they were saying. Morgan seemed to become more adjusted to the suit, and even though she was making the loudest crunching sounds anyone could make under fall leaves, she still seemed to be light footed. Her mood changed too, no longer quite as frustrated as before, and no longer red faced. I looked down at my watch, it read 7:33 pm. The sky was turning a dark blue color, and the clouds were reflecting orange and pink hues. We broke the tree line and there was a flat boulder jutting out from the cliff. We faced west along the cliff, and it was the most beautiful sight I've ever seen. The copper colored clouds, blurred with pink and blue, were broken amongst the dark blue sky, giving an other-worldly appearance on earth. Jackson broke the silence between us.

"The sunrises around here are more beautiful than this. Nowhere else can you see something like it."

Jackson was trying to hold Morgan's metal hand, but she was staring blankly into the sky, unaware of anyone around her.

My phone buzzed in my pocket notifying me that Tom was trying to call me.

"Hello?"

"Hey, I just finished the button and you need to get back before the suit's battery runs out. I'm not going to be there to attach the button cause I have some business at the workshop, but I'm pretty sure you can do it."

"Ok, we'll be there soon. Bye."

I hung up the phone and stuck it back into my pocket. I turned to Morgan and Jackson who were now holding hands, and said,

"Not to be a party bum or anything, but Tom has the button ready."

Morgan turned around quickly with an excited face.

"Finally, I can't wait to get out of this thing."

By the time we walked back to Jackson's car, it was pitch black outside. We stood there and talked to Jackson a little bit more before we walked back to the complex, exhausted from today's events. It took me three frustrating hours to attach the button, but Morgan was finally released from the suit. She was sweaty, tired, and her hands were covered in suit marks from the gloves. It turned 11:00 by the time we arrived at Tom's house. He wasn't home so I immediately went to take a shower, but before I could, the entire house rumbled as if something massive had crashed into the neighbor's lawn.

"Morgan! Did you feel that!?"

"Yea, what was that?"

"I don't know. Earthquake!?"

We argued over what it was for at least a couple of minutes before I went to shower. I couldn't help but rethink what happened today. Why is Tom building these suits? And how? Morgan said that she couldn't find any joint or movement limitations, and she also said that it was almost like being a part of the suit. Tomorrow. I'm going to try it on, and I'm going to work on the other two androids to see how they function. I wonder if they are the same?

I walked out to the main room of the workshop to see these two brand new androids that were being displayed by the company. One was made to replicate a human, and when I say replicate... it is an understatement. The android was a male that had a bald head and a beard. He wore jeans and a red T-shirt with a pair of grey-black tennis shoes. He stood deactivated, silent and motionless which was very wrong for how human he appeared to be. His eyes were squinted, but not shut. They were lifeless and dark grey as if he were dead. If I didn't know any better, I would've thought that he was just a man in deep thought. Tom walked behind the android, lifted the red shirt to activate it, and let the shirt fall back down. The android almost seemed to wake up and take in his surroundings almost as if it was a newborn child. It walked over into a group of people to introduce itself as if it had done it every day. I looked over at the lion the company had put together. This one did not have realistic skin or fur, it was instead synthetic. Mostly to show off the internal workings, but was also to allow a scanner to watch the internal parts as it ran so it could pick out any imperfections. The lion was activated, and seemed to move in a more mechanical way than the humanoid android... Humanoandroid... Humanandroid. Hey, I actually like that description... humanandroid. It has a ring to it. There were people in the building that came from out of town, and some were from much further away, as if they were foreign investors.

"Excuse me, is your name Josh?"

"Yes. Are you just going to ask me questions about my father?"

"No, I'm Ben. I'm not an interviewer. Tom hired me."

"Oh, nice to meet you Ben. Are you the one working on the new androids for the tech complex... tech factory... tech center... whatever it's called?"

"Tech Complex... and yea, I am. It's getting really tough though. I can't figure out how to create the program for an interactive behavior with this specific android. I've done it once before and that's why Tom hired me. I kept the template for it, but for some reason I can't get the android's computer to process it correctly. And it spits out weird functions and responses when I ask it questions. I did come close once, but I almost fried the processor line."

"Now that's a problem my dad had when he was working with his androids. The more human they seemed to behave, the more often that processor line would overheat."

I have some experience with this kind of stuff, programming from scratch. But I learned only how to use pre-created programs when constructing the behavior of the android.

"Alright Josh, I need to go. I'll see you later."

"Ok, maybe when I learn how to program better than you."

We both smiled, and I watched as he went to examine the android lion walking around the room. I walked over to an android that had a single rotating camera for an eye, with a plaque describing what it can do. 'Constructed by Jeffery and Bailey, this android is capable of using martial arts to defend or attack people. It's main purpose is to serve as a body guard or servant for the military.' My thoughts were interrupted as Tom began speaking to the current audience in the room.

"I'd like to thank everyone for coming tonight. It's been quite a long day, but now I'd like everyone to go over to the field so we can show these things off."

Everyone in the workshop began moving with the android models outside, leaving me and Tom alone in the room.

"Hey, you don't mind staying here and shutting everything down do you?" asked Tom.

"No, I don't mind."

"Great. Tell you what. Since you're staying behind to shut the place down, I'll make sure that you get a paid vacation to… let's say one of the coasts. East or west, it doesn't matter. No longer than a week though."

"Oh, really? Thanks. I think it would be good to take a break for a while."

"Good. Alright Josh, I'll see you tomorrow."

I just remembered a question I had in my mind for a long time. It was about my father. I've never had the time to actually talk to Tom about him. I was eight when he died, and I was never comfortable to learn more about him. But now, I think, is better than never.

"Hey Tom?"

He turned around and looked at me, patiently waiting for my question.

"Do you know anything about the android my father made, the one named Trinity? And why did he spend so much time working on that specific prototype?"

Tom opened his mouth, but hesitated before he spoke.

"Why don't we wait till tomorrow. I'm a little too tired to tell you the entire story right now."

"Yea, ok."

"All right, get this place closed down, then go home and get some rest."

"See you tomorrow."

Tom walked through the front doors and waved his hand goodbye as he left the workshop. I was the only one in the room… or I thought I was until the waitress android asked a question right behind my ear.

"What would you like to eat today sir!"

I jumped around, scared half to death, and almost punched the android square in the face.

"It's me damn it! Don't do that."

After deactivating the waitress, I walked down the hall into my office, sat down in front of my computer, and began closing everything down. I felt this… this weird feeling of something looking down my spine. I turned slowly around my office, and stopped facing towards the window and storage room. The room was pitch dark except for the faintest glow near the back. There was this very faint outline of a figure standing right outside the window. I slowly pulled my phone out, and then reached for my taser on my desk. I activated the flashlight on my phone and saw a horrific figure standing there, glaring into my eyes. It was a repurposed android that Tom had brought to scrap a while ago. What scared me about this model was that it had absolutely no damage to it, and its movements were as if it was brand new. We continued to stare at each other until a second model walked up from behind, and stood only a few feet from the glass barrier. There were numbers that I had put on their chests to identify them, 124-F and 125-F. I have gained a total of at least thirty models over the past year, but for some reason only these three have expressed this behavior including the one I acquired yesterday, model 126-F. The two androids continued to stare as I backed out of my office. I opened the door to the hallway, but stopped as I spotted 126-F standing near the end of the hall facing the opposite direction. I slowly closed the door, but before I could close it all the way, 126-F ripped his head around in a one-eighty, spotting me with his dead eyes. I quickly closed the door and locked it. These things have never done anything like this before! What is going on!? I looked over into the storage room and watched as one of the androids backed up a little ways, and ran straight for the window. It leapt into the air, and with a loud thunk, bounced off of the window and onto the floor, leaving only a scratch on the glass. Then a loud bang echoed from the wooden door, crackling under the weight. These things were trying to break into my office! I crouched and slid under my desk, and pulled my chair up to hide myself, but I was sure it wasn't going to work. The giant glass window shattered into a million pieces as an android landed on the floor in front of me. As it slowly stood up, it looked straight at me. I raised my taser to fire, but then the door to my office came blasting open, and the 126-F android came running in. He didn't stop until he ran right into the other android, sending it back into the storage room. 126-F sent the android flying into the other robot standing in the storage room, and they both fell to the floor. The door to my office was wide open, and I needed to leave now! With both of my feet, I pushed the office chair into 126-F, and bolted for the open door with my taser still in hand. I made it almost half way when I heard the vent behind me rumble. The vent cover at the end of the hall flew out of its place, and an android desperately came crawling out of it. I ran up to the employees only door and tried to open it, but was locked.

"Oh, come on!"

I fumbled the keys out of my pocket and began unlocking the door. Right before I turned the key, the entire structure shook. The end of the hall lit up like a bonfire, and a blast wave slammed me up against the door, and onto the floor. I was dazed from the blast, and I could feel the heat of an approaching fire raging at the end of the hall. I slowly leaned up and spotted what looked like the android 124-F, and it was crawling towards me through the inferno. I stood back up and attempted to unlock the door, but that's when I realized that the blast had knocked the keys and taser out of my hand. There was a loud thud along with the bangs and clangs of steal hitting against each other from behind me. I looked back down the hall, and saw 126-F wrestling the android on the floor. They both threw punches at each other until 126-F took a hold on the other android, and they both fell into the approaching fire. I knelt down and began searching for the keys and taser, which I quickly found. I unlocked the door, threw myself onto the cold tile floor, and rested for just a little bit. I then realized that most of the place was on fire, and I needed to get out! I began to wobble my way over towards the exit, and that's when I noticed something near the kitchen. An android with the numbers on its chest burned and unrecognizable, was standing near a blown out vent. It stared at me with its black and deactivated eyes. It closed its fist in a threatening gesture, and began to walk towards me. With one large swing of its arms, it sent a table tumbling out of its way in pieces. I raised my taser to fire, but it ducked under another table and flipped it sideways to block my shot. The fire was beginning to inch its way around the rest of the building, melting or burning mechanical parts that it touched. The flipped table began sliding towards me, and it was then I realized that I had nowhere to go. The only exit was blocked by this android, and the fire was pinning me against it. I backed up into the waitress android, and an idea came to me. The waitress android had a program for splitting up fights that break out between kids. It may distract this android long enough for me to escape. I unplugged her wrist from the wall, flipped the switch on, and ran off towards the side of the sliding table. The android behind the table sprung out sideways and stopped in front of me only inches away. But then it caught me off guard… because it spoke.

"You aren't going anywhere Josh."

I quickly raised my taser to fire, but the android took it right out of my hand. It shoved me onto the floor and aimed the taser at me. But when it pulled the trigger, the waitress android stepped in front of the shot and took the full charge of the taser saying,

"No…n-no fighting is allowed… in…"

The waitress android fell to the floor with a loud thud. 125-F dropped the taser, then stomped it into pieces with its metal foot. I tried to stand back up, but I was knocked down by a heavy shove as the android came closer and closer. The android stepped on my foot causing me to yelp in pain, and kept me from scooting away any further. It knelt down with its foot still on mine, and spoke to me again.

"You have nowhere to go Josh, just like I had nowhere to go… just like my friends had nowhere to go. And now it's your turn… to be… one… of… us."

It raised it fists into the air, and at that moment, I spotted 126-F standing in the employees only doorway. 126-F came running out and tackled the android, causing its descending fist to clip my right ear, and hit the floor instead. The two tumbled towards the flames until 126-F managed to throw the other android into the fire, and stand up. He walked over and pulled me up off the ground by my left hand, and seemed to brush me off a little bit.

"You."

It said, pointing to the front door.

"Run."

It then shoved me towards the door hard enough for me to get moving. As I looked back I saw the other android sprint out of the flames in a fury of rage. It tackled 126-F to the floor, and threw a few punches into its chest seeming to be going for its brain. I ran through the front doors and out into the parking lot where I continued to watch the two androids fight it out. 126-F managed to tear away the chest plate of the other android, but his left hand became pinned against the wall, and 125-F managed to break that hand. 125-F began hammering 126-F, and with each blow, it became more and more clear that 126-F was losing. In a desperate move, 126-F brought up its legs, and put the android into a leg lock. The two stumbled into the flames as the structure began to fail. Pieces of debris were falling from the ceiling, feeding the fire below. Something in my mind nagged at me. Why would 126-F be protecting me? Every other android in there was trying to kill me except for 126-F. Why? I thought about everything I had experienced leading up to this moment. The mess in the office, assessing 126-F, fighting 126-F. What was the reason? The thoughts bounced around in my head, trying to fit together like puzzle pieces, until I realized… that the search for my father was the reason I got a job here, not because of his legacy. 126-F was protecting me from the other androids, he had to be the spirit of my father! I began to frantically run around the front of the building to find him. Through each window, I only caught a glimpse of him before he disappeared back into the flames.

"Dad!"

I ran around the corner of the building to get closer and yelled again.

"Dad!"

I ran back and forth in front of the building trying to find him, and I finally did. He was pulling on something in the other android, and it seemed to be giving way. With his wrist pushing the face of the android away, and his free hand on something inside, he slowly pulled out a xenon difluoride battery. It was right then that I knew what he was doing.

"Dad!"

126-F glanced up, his face mostly scorched from the fire. But this time he managed to say something through the roar of the blaze.

"I won't be gone. Run away, Josh."

He pinned the other android to the floor and pressed the battery down onto the floor. The ceiling above began to give way, and as a large beam fell upon him, the xenon battery blew. A massive fireball erupted through the front of the building, and I was sent flying backwards into the parking lot. I laid on the ground as if I were dead. Unable to move from the pain that stung every inch of my body. I saw someone run by, but stop short as they spotted me lying on the ground.

"Josh? Josh, it's going to be ok."

It was Tom. Pretty soon there were many people over me as the party returned to see what was going on. I remembered that I gave Adalyne the only thing that could stop these machines. When I can, I need to make another one. I never should have given Adalyne that remote. I began to fade away into sleep, and I couldn't help but think, I'm sorry Adalyne. I hope you and Morgan are smart enough to leave this place, and never come back.

Chapter 5

I was half asleep when my phone started to buzz, sounding like a strained bee in a plastic bag. I picked up the phone and noticed that Tom was calling. The time was 6:43 in the morning.

"Hello?"

"Adalyne?"

I sat up in my bed, still partly asleep.

"Yea, what's up?"

"You and Morgan need to get over to the Circuit Cafe right away! There's been an explosion, and I need some help to get things cleared out, ok?"

"Who all was there?"

"Just one person. He's in the hospital, but he's ok."

My heart fell, seeming to stop for a moment.

"Ok. Uh… We'll be right there."

I hung up the phone and immediately started to get dressed. An explosion at the workshop? I hope Josh wasn't there when it blew. I threw Morgan's clothes on top of her.

"Morgan!"

To my surprise, she didn't jump thirty feet into the air. Instead she got up and asked, "What's going on? Did someone get hurt?"

"I hope not."

We dressed ourselves rather quickly, and we were out driving to the workshop in moments.

"Adalyne, what's going on?"

"The place we ate at just a couple of days ago exploded last night for some reason."

"That doesn't sound right. What if it wasn't an accident?"

"You mean the protesters? I doubt they would go that far."

We sat in silence until we arrived at what used to be the Circuit Cafe. There were a few corners of the building still standing, and some firefighters were putting out remaining piles of smoking rubble. To the far left of the parking lot, there was a partly burned car that was damaged from the fire. Other than that, the building was completely demolished. We spotted Tom talking to the sheriff, and Morgan spotted Jackson in a different direction.

"I'm going over to see Jackson, I'll be right back."

Morgan took off to see Jackson, but I went straight to Tom.

"Tom, what happened here?"

"I don't know for sure. The fire chief is going to do an investigation and I'm going to salvage what I can. Whatever you find, you need to bring it up to me first. As soon as the firefighters are done, I'm going to go make sure that the media doesn't do anything stupid."

I looked around for a moment, but didn't see an ambulance anywhere. I turned back around to Tom and asked,

"How come you never told us about Josh?"

Tom turned away from the sheriff, forgot what he was telling him, and looked at me with an expression I've never seen him use before.

"I was going to mention him, but I never got around to it."

"Why? Why had you never gotten around to it?"

My anger was starting to show, and Tom noticed.

"I was busy. And how come you... You like him, don't you?"

I could feel my face blush. I was not prepared to tell anyone yet. I wasn't even prepared to tell Josh himself.

"Well... we met Thursday, for the first time. He was busy moving some stuff around, and that's when I bumped into him."

Tom seemed to relax a little and motioned to the sheriff to hang on a little longer.

"Why didn't you just tell me? He's in the hospital, but excuse me Adalyne, I need to finish my conversation."

He gestured to me to go as he turned around to continue his conversation with the sheriff. I got in the car and drove over to Morgan and Jackson. They were standing there talking to each other, and again, Morgan was happy to be around him. She always was, and always will be, an open book. I told Morgan where I was going, and I sped off towards the hospital. As soon as I turned down North 27th Street, I could see the three story hospital through the tall trees. It, too, was under construction expanding into a previous parking lot, and adding another three stories to the place. I parked the car, walked inside, and the first thing I did was ask where

Josh's room was. They asked who I was and I told them I was a friend. They gave me the directions to his room and I found it in no time. Inside was Josh, dressed in a hospital scrub that only doctors wore, looking out of the hospital window. He turned around and looked at me surprised.

"Adalyne... How'd you know where I was?"

"Tom told me."

Josh had some small bandages on his face and arm with a brace over his right ankle. He was also carrying a bag in his other hand filled with medical supplies from the hospital.

"Oh my God Josh, what happened?"

He stood there and pondered over the question, not knowing what to say, but I cut in before he said anything.

"It's fine. You don't need to say. Do you have a ride here for you?"

"No, but I just need to go get my car. It was next to the building when it blew, but it should be ok to drive."

I wanted to tell Josh about the destroyed car at the site, but I couldn't bring myself to tell him. He started to walk to the front door of the hospital, and I helped him all the way out to my car.

"What happened to your leg?"

"It's sprained. The doctors told me that I have second degree burns on my right leg and arm. I also have a sprained ankle so I'm going to have this brace on for a while."

We drove back over to the destroyed restaurant only to find Josh's half burned car next to the scene.

"Well... so much for my car. I just bought that thing."

"I can give you a ride to wherever you need to go."

"Thanks, but I need to talk to Tom first."

Josh got out of my car and began to waddle his way over to Tom. Tom spotted Josh and looked at him with a sorry expression. I stayed in the car and wandered my eyes from place to place around the scene. It didn't take long before I noticed that Morgan and Jackson weren't anywhere to be seen. I stood up out of the car and looked for them more carefully, but I still couldn't spot them. My attention was drawn away towards the sound of a crane pulling something out of the rubble. I walked over to the workers running the machine.

"What are you guys doing!?"

"We're pulling out one of those robots that survived the fire. It looks like something from a horror film!"

Wrapped in chains, there was a very dark android covered in ash. Its once shiny, plastic skin was now burned and molten, even some joints were melted together. It didn't take long to recognize the android waitress who took my order, but now she was molten and… Oh God, that smell! The worker and I covered our faces with our sleeves.

"Holy crap that smells awful!"

The worker retreated behind the crane to breath in fresh air. I walked as fast as I could back to where Josh and Tom were talking. Free from the wretched smell of the torn machine; I took in a long breath of air.

"You all right?"

Josh was looking at me worriedly, concerned about me. Maybe he likes me, too. It reminded me of what he gave me the day we met.

"No, the rubble over there just smells terrible, right after they pulled out the waitress android."

Tom told Josh to wait as he walked over to the rotten android that was now hoisted up in the air, pausing for a moment as the smell hit him. A crowd of people started to form on the other side of the street. Some with posters, and some only yelling words happily. 'No more droids! No more droids! No more droids!' They were chanting these words again and again until a police car with four officers stepped out to move them along.

"Do you mind giving me a ride to my apartment?"

I turned to Josh who was glaring at his burned car as if there was a part of him that was lost.

"Sure."

We hopped back into my car and drove over to his apartment. He directed me to an apartment called Grand Slam Patio Apartments downtown. The building was only one story tall, but it was about the length of a football field, like a motel.

"My apartment is the one right at the end, by the tall oak tree."

I parked the car next to the oak tree, helped Josh out of the car, and opened the door to his apartment. The first thing I saw was the kitchen and the living/dining room. To the right of the kitchen was a short hallway with only two doors. That was all there was. That was literally the entire apartment.

"This looks cozy." I said to Josh.

He looked at me like I was crazy, but then he smiled.

"I know, but it's the only thing I could afford right now. I'm saving up to buy this two bed home on the hills far west of the city."

Josh hobbled off into his bedroom as I waited out by the door. His apartment was very simple. There was a small TV in front of his couch, and the kitchen was not big enough for more than two people. There were cupboards hanging from the ceiling, jutting out from the wall above the counter that also came out from the wall. The kitchen sink was full of dishes, and his couch had some clothes on it, hanging over the pillows. On the wall over the couch was a large, old, lever action, 12 gauge shotgun. Most likely from his Grandparents or someone like that. He doesn't appear to be that proactive with chores, but he does seem to handle money ok by the way he speaks of it.

"Sorry about the mess. I wasn't expecting any visitors."

"Oh, it's fine. My sister and I don't keep our place clean either."

Josh was now dressed in different clothes, including a long sleeve shirt and sweats to cover the brace on his ankle, probably more comfortable than the hospital scrub he had on a moment ago. He walked over to the fridge, opened it and asked, "Want something to eat?"

It came to me that neither Morgan or I had breakfast this morning. That might be what Jackson and Morgan went to go do, go on a breakfast date.

"Sure. What do you have?"

Josh dug around in his fridge with his left arm for a couple of seconds.

"I have some frozen waffles…but no syrup. I have some breakfast burritos, and that's pretty much it. Darn, I thought I still had some German pancakes left."

"We could go out to eat. I'll buy."

Josh shut the fridge door and turned to me with a smile on his face.

"Sure, that sounds good. What place do you have in mind?"

"Well, not the Circuit Cafe."

I smiled at him, hoping he would smile back at my joke, but he just froze and stared into empty space. I stood there for a moment before I waved my hand in front of his eyes, but he didn't blink. His eyes stared straight through my hand as if it were nothing.

"Josh? Are you ok?"

He broke his stare and looked at me with a blank face. He appeared to be offended by my joke of the now destroyed restaurant.

"Yea…I'm fine."

"Sorry if I offended you."

"No, it's fine, but it is too early to make a joke about it. I was in there when it blew after all."

We got into my car and drove to a Perkins only a mile into town. Silence filled the cab of my car, not discussing anything about the restaurant. Josh was fiddling with his arm bandage trying to get it in a more comfortable position. I reached over to help but he said let it be.

"The doctors told me to change it twice a day, and because they removed all of the dead skin and tissue, the bandage will get dirty and gross really quick for a couple of days."

"Gross."

My mind flickered with thoughts of what a 2nd degree burn looked like, but I could never clearly picture it in my head. We arrived at Perkins at around 8:00-ish, and we seemed to be one of only a handful of cars in the parking lot. We sat down in a booth close to the door, and right away, a waitress was there to ask us if we wanted anything to drink.

"I'll have coffee please."

Josh studied the menu for a little, but soon gave up on it.

"I'll have coffee too please."

I turned to ask him a question, but the phone in my purse buzzed. I reached down to answer it, but I realized it wasn't my phone. It was the little remote that was just buzzing continuously. Josh looked at me and asked,

"Is that the remote buzzing?"

"Yea, how'd you know?"

Josh pulled out his phone that was also continuously buzzing.

"Why is it buzzing?"

"Well... it only buzzes when you're close to someone else with one of these on. I managed to turn my phone into one to see if it would work. The harder they buzz, the closer you are to another one. But they both need to be on"

"Is that all they do?"

"No, but I turned those functions off. You can turn them on, but I would need to teach you how to do it."

"I'm an engineer, I can figure it out."

I turned the remote over and saw a little screw-driver looking hole, it turned freely. There were small letters printed around it as well. I had no Idea what they meant, but I turned it with my pinky nail until it stopped buzzing.

"Well, I guess you don't need help."

Josh smiled at me and I smiled back. Maybe now is the right time to tell him, but I've barely known him for a couple of days! Morgan and Jackson, I guess, have been dating each other since they met over a year ago. That's what Morgan told me right? Over a year ago? I think that's right. I need to spend more time with Josh, I need to know him better.

"Your coffee ma'am."

The waitress handed us our coffee, then she asked.

"What would you like to eat today?"

I hadn't looked at my menu yet, and I don't think Josh did either.

"We'll need another minute."

"Ok, I'll be right back when you're ready."

The waitress walked off again, and I turned back to Josh to finish my conversation.

"Why did you give me this...this remote anyway?"

Josh rubbed the back of his neck and sat there thinking for a couple of moments.

"Well...uh, I gave it to you..."

"Because."

"I don't know, you're different. When I bumped into you in the hallway, I thought you were one of those reporters that were always snooping around in the restaurant. Always trying to find some secret that would end Tom's business. But then you talked to me like a friend. You helped me with that mess of papers, and that's when I realized that you weren't a reporter."

"So you gave me this?"

I held up the remote, and Josh seemed to have a harder time explaining why he gave it to me. He seemed nervous, on the edge of saying something, but yet still hesitant.

"Josh, you can tell me. It's not like I'm going to stop being your friend."

He leaned forward slowly and said hesitantly, "So we can find each other."

He had his head down looking at the phone in his hands. I was staring at him with bright eyes, trying not to blush. So he does have a crush on me, but should I tell him I do too?

Josh looked up at me and I could tell that he wasn't quite telling the truth, but I wasn't too sure.

"Josh, listen..."

His facial expression changed to worried. Afraid of what I would say next.

"...I'm sure that we uh...we have the same...feelings for each other. But we only met a couple of days ago."

"I know that, I just didn't expect to meet you again so soon, and it was you that found me in the hospital... right?"

Josh looked at me with one eyebrow raised, and I couldn't help but smile and break eye contact with him.

"It's fine Adalyne, Let's talk about this later, ok? I'm going to order something for breakfast cause I'm starving."

We eventually ordered some French toast and crepes, basically dessert for breakfast. It was a nice break from my great uncle's frozen waffles or omelets. I peered back into my purse and looked at the remote. It still had a little light on, didn't I just turn it off?

Jackson and I drove up to the complex with his younger brother James. We couldn't find Adalyne anywhere at the destroyed workshop, so we thought she came here. There were three androids that were found in the rubble, along with the weird plastic waitress. They were all being unloaded at the basement loading ramp near the storage and boiler room. I had to get to the room where Adalyne and I hid the Lexis and Jackson androids two nights ago, and keep anyone from going in there. This was going to be a surprise to Tom. Trying to get those things deactivated was a challenge, or at least I thought. Since we lost the remote, there was no way to turn them off of whatever mode that was running when they were turned on. Eventually I just asked them to deactivate, and they did so themselves, falling limp into the chairs they were sitting in. Tomorrow is also our first day on the job, up till six in the morning, asleep till two the next day. Jackson parked his police car next to the loading ramp, and we made our way inside. Most of the walls had drywall already up, but there were a lot of places near the center of the complex that didn't have any drywall up at all. There were forklifts running, taking the three wretched androids to Tom's workshop. The one currently being carried by the forklift was a rather simple android that had been built by a customer. It had only a single rotating camera in the center of its face for an eye. The next forklift was carrying what used to be the waitress, her face half burned, her plastic skin molten and torn. Some of her rubber teeth were missing, and in their place were the screws that held them. The entire android looked like it would be from a paranormal show. A third forklift came in with an even worse looking android. This one was missing its left hand, and in its place were long wires that were nearly dragging on the floor. They were all things of nightmares, and that smell… holy crap that smells awful. I stepped back far enough to get some fresh air. I looked back at Jackson who was holding onto James' hand as they were also backing away. James stared at these partly destroyed androids without fear. He knew they were just pieces of metal. The forklifts drove all of them into Tom's workshop and hung them on steal arms jutting out from the wall. They were surprisingly similar to the ones in the bunker, but these arms had regular hooks on them, not magnetic couplers. I was surprised to see a man with a beard walk into the shop with no shirt on. I was about to say something when he turned into the storage room, and exposed his skinless back showing that he was an android. Following behind him was a lion. It had clear synthetic skin and fur on its body, and it walked as if it were a real cat. Shoulders moving like a cat, tail swinging like a cat…

"Morgan!"

I jumped a little ways up into the air, spinning around to see Adalyne standing at the door adjacent to the loading ramp. She had her purse with her and she was light footed…again. I bet she was with whoever she liked this morning.

"Where were you? I looked for you at the burn sight but you weren't there."

"No, I went back to Tom's house."

"Oh… I thought you came here."

"No I was eating breakfast because I couldn't find you… Wow that smells awful."

Uh huh, I thought. We are going to have a long conversation about keeping secrets. But we're sisters, why would we need to keep secrets from each other? My thoughts were interrupted as a man to my left spoke to us.

"Have any of you seen Tom?"

I turned around and noticed that bandages covered his right arm and a bit of his face. I said to him, "He went up to the main lobby, someone said that this morning's rain leaked through the ceiling, so he went to check it out."

I wonder what happened to that guy, must have been in a bad car accident or something. I turned around to ask Adalyne if she was ready for the night shift tomorrow.

"That's tomorrow? I forgot."

"What happened to that guy with the bandages? He's so… broken."

"He was the guy running the restaurant last night. He's lucky to be alive."

I turned to look at him one more time before he disappeared into the only functioning elevator in the building. There are going to be more, but they haven't even started on them yet.

The rest of the day went on without a hitch. We pulled usable pieces from the androids, and we even managed to turn one on to see if it would work. Surprisingly, the waitress was the only android that was still able to function, the other two needed some new parts. Jackson took his brother James home after he had a tantrum, he seemed tired anyway. That boy isn't scared of anything. He was crawling into the androids to get parts from them only because we couldn't fit ourselves. He also wanted to try on the pilot suits that Tom made for us and himself. I still don't understand why Tom made those suits as strong as he did, and I don't believe that he made them to catch anyone breaking into the building trying to steal anything. You could hear them stomping around a mile away. Tom came down a little after Jackson and James had left, carrying a box of sub sandwiches in his arms.

"You guys deserve a break. You got up at around six this morning, and you aren't going to get home till about…"

He looked down at his watch for a moment and said in surprise, "It's already 8:50!? Sheesh, time flies."

"I guess these sandwiches are our dinner then huh?" I said jokingly.

"Ah, but I'm too fat to eat any."

We all started to laugh again. I put down the small screwdriver after finishing taking apart a tendon group from an android's arm to respond to Tom's statement.

"You're still hanging onto that?"

"And I'm not going to let it go till I'm not fat."

Tom paused for a little letting the laughter silence itself.

"Do you remember Ben from the news a couple of days ago?"

"Yea."

"He's going to be here tomorrow to help with the programming for a while, but he's leaving for France the following morning. He's going to represent me and my company, and the programming that's going into the new androids at this year's convention of technology. If he succeeds, we'll get sponsoring from multiple companies, and hopefully from a German tycoon as well."

"Wow, that sounds expensive."

"Well my company already has sponsoring from Microsoft, Tesla, Apple, and a few smaller companies. That's one reason my company can afford to build this massive place."

We talked about finances until we had the electric tendon group completely apart. I looked around the room to see everything that we had. There were the two suits, the three androids, and the brand new android that we were still working on. Since the other location had burned down, the lion and body-builder androids were being kept in the storage room. The lion was my favorite because it looked the most realistic, even though its pelt was synthetic. There were parts and pieces of androids scattered across the workbench, and tools were placed away sloppily into tool boxes. We swept up the dirt that fell from the wretched androids into a garbage can. As we left for the night, Tom walked over to a hole in the drywall next to the elevator, then he pulled out something strange.

"I've ordered some brand new, top-of-the line fire prevention equipment, but I have no Idea why this was left here."

Tom held out a fireman's axe that was hidden in the hole of the drywall.

This axe had a red signature handle, but unlike a fireman's axe, the blade was on both sides instead of just one side. Tom put it in the room we were just in, and locked the doors behind him.

"Someone had to have left it there on accident, but you'd be an idiot to use an axe to cut a hole in a wall. It's a nice axe too."

We all hopped into my car and drove to Tom's house exhausted from today's work. We all arrived and fell asleep by around 9:30, we didn't even bother to shower. We did however make sure that we were going to sleep in until noon tomorrow. I have a feeling that it's going to be harder than it sounds.

I was sitting in a truck with a couple of Tom's employees, heading to the burned workshop. There was one thing I needed to find, then I could finish building the processor for the brand new android. It was going to showcase everything J.T. Cybernetics could do, and much more. Once we arrived at the workshop, we pointed the headlights into the rubble of the destroyed building. I needed to find something electronic, but my next concern was the cabinet in the back room. It had the blueprints for the processors that ran the androids, including the waitress android. The cabinet was like a safe; it needed a password and it was fire resistant. It was most likely still buried under the rubble where we haven't excavated yet, but I need those blueprints tonight. We unloaded the skid steer from the back of the trailer and began moving rubble into the dump truck next to us. I slowly walked over to where the front of the building used to be and began walking through where the main room had been. It was hopeless to find any paper outside of the safe. I'm surprised that the androids we did find weren't as destroyed as they should've been. I walked around the pile of rubble when I noticed a joint sticking out of the ground. I pulled at it, brushed some dirt away, and pulled at it again. I took out my flashlight and shed light on something I missed.

"Hey! Over here!"

One of the employees came running over to me and shone his flashlight down on top of it as well.

"You found another android?"

"Yes. Now go get the skid steer, and we'll get this thing out of here."

I began digging more rubble out from around the head of the android. Most of the face was destroyed, but the android's head frame was remarkably intact. We dug around it until it was no longer covered in rubble. We brought the skid steer over and lifted it off of the ground. There were no arms and no legs left on this android, nor was there any plastic covering the body except for the front of the face around the eyes, and on the bottom left part of the jaw. We hooked up some chains, and moved it to the back of the truck. The last light of dusk was starting to fade away. My watch read 8:50, and I could tell that we were all tired from today's work. I was sad that the workshop burned down the day of the big show-off. I was kind of excited to see the company's androids do their thing. We finally located the cabinet and stuck it on the trailer with the skid steer. The limbless android, which surprisingly didn't smell as bad as the other wretched androids, was tied down to ensure that it didn't roll around. By the time we arrived at the loading ramp at the back end of the building, there was no light left from the sunset in the night sky. We put the cabinet-safe and android inside the room with the rest of the other androids, and the remaining employees left for the night. I walked around the room making sure that everything was in order… something began talking to me. It came from nowhere, but everywhere at the same time. I didn't freak out, nor did I try to ignore it. I knew who it was.

"No. No one knows… No… They wouldn't… I'll find a way."

I looked around and spotted Tom's Security pilot suit.

"It'll be a little while. Maybe a day… Yes… Relax, I'll get it done."

I pulled out a toolbox from the corner of the room, another that was near the shelves, and hid this thing behind the two tool boxes in the back corner adjacent to the new android. Hopefully Tom won't find it here. He'd toss it out faster than a rotten banana peel. I stood back from the two toolboxes that were covering the corner the thing was sitting in. You couldn't tell if there was anything back there from this angle. I was stepping side to side trying to see if I could spot it through the toolboxes. So far though, it's pretty well hidden. I turned the lights off in the room and locked the doors again, leaving for the night. It was all mysterious to me as to why now? He's been so quiet until now. But what matters is that I get what he wants done, no questions asked.

Chapter 6

It was around noon when I decided to go to the Kay Jewelry store on the edge of town. I parked my police car in the parking lot and walked inside with my police uniform still on. Inside there were pictures of jewels, rings, earrings, necklaces, and a glass display case that held jewelry of every type in them. I walked over to the front counter and a man dressed in a work suit asked me, "What law has been broken officer?"

"No law was broken. I'm just here to get a ring."

The man disappeared behind the counter and came up with a bunch of rings of different sizes.

"What kind of ring are you looking for?"

"Silver, with a small white diamond."

This time, the man brought up a case of just gems of different sizes, the metal rings absent. He pointed at the third to the smallest gem and asked,

"Is this the size you're looking for?"

It was about half the size of a pea, but was just as expensive as the rest of the gems. After about a half an hour of picking and choosing, I finally chose a one quarter karat, princess round-cut diamond with a white gold ring at the price of about three thousand dollars. I've been saving for a ring for a couple of months, and if my parents hadn't left me their estate, I wouldn't be making this purchase right now. I wish my parents were still alive. They would've enjoyed having Morgan around. She's fun to be with, sympathetic, and silly, but she's too easy to scare… even when it's not on purpose. We get along really well. Though we have had a couple of fights in the past months, we still enjoy each other's company. It has been nice to see her face to face after so much time in a long distance relationship, and I feel we need to move forward. I sat down in the driver side of my police car and began to drive down main street towards the freeway. Today is Sunday so, Wednesday morning at the cliff edge, the best time for a beautiful fall sunrise, I'll ask her. How am I going to get her out there though? Her shift ends at six, long before the sun comes up. She'll be asleep at her house by then. I'll need to catch her early in the morning and tell her about the sunrise, get her out there without Adalyne following, and propose. It's all planned out, and I'm ready for it. I drove past the coffee shop and picked up Thomas for patrolling the freeway. We left town as if it were just another day on the job.

I walked into the room with the three wretched androids hanging off the steel arms. It's quite early in the morning, but I need to get this done. I pulled the two toolboxes out from the corner, relieved to find that the limbless android was right where I left it, and dragged it over to the counter. I took some chains and hoisted it up into the air on a spare set of hanging arms from the ceiling. The android hung with no limbs attached to its body. Instead, there were wires hanging in their place. I didn't need to remove anything to dig around inside of its body, and there wasn't really anything in there to retrieve. I opened the chest that contained the processor inside, which didn't seem to be that damaged. I walked over to Tom's automated pilot suit and started to take off the metal coverings, then I removed the plastic coverings as well. The only place I left untouched was the feet and the hands. The entire suit was in its raw frame supports and hydraulics including the constricting bars collapsed around the individual. I stepped inside the suit and the bars collapsed around me like they were supposed to, and since there were no metal coverings on the suit, it was much lighter, and agile. The only thing I needed to figure out was how to allow this machine to operate the suit without any limbs. It does work like power steering on a truck, but it will take a lot of time and programming. With the suit still on, I picked the android up off of the chains that were hanging, walked out of the workshop to go find a better spot to hide this thing and the suit without anyone noticing, but I better hurry. I picked up all of the steel plating from the suit and took them with me.

My alarm on my phone went off at noon today. Ensuring that I had enough sleep for my shift tonight. I rolled over to face Morgan's bed, but she wasn't there. I got up and put on a fuzzy robe that was hanging in the closet, then walked into the kitchen to find Morgan eating some leftovers in the fridge. She was watching a news reporter talk about the burned down Circuit Cafe. Behind the reporter was the building, bulldozers flattening the rubble to make way for a new building. You could hear the chant of protesters on the side of the street celebrating the destruction of the place. The reporter was standing in front of the camera, talking negatively about the company's history. Morgan heard me walking downstairs and said in a tired voice, "You have a good night's rest?"

"Yea. When did you get up."

"Not too long ago. I had a dream that Ben, the programmer, was messing with the androids that we're scrapping. They came to life and started to out-function the androids we found in the bunker, but then they started to take people and simulate them into one of their own... It was...weird"

"Well, considering how ugly they are, I would've expected a bad dream like that."

"Yea. It woke me up a couple of times last night."

Morgan continued to eat her leftover dinner for lunch, watching the TV and occasionally cursing at the reporter. I took my crepe out of the fridge from yesterday's breakfast, and began to eat the rest of it. We sat there at the dining table for a while until we both finished our... brunch. Then I went back up to our room and put on the clothes to wear under my uniform for the day. I looked outside my window, and for a brief moment, I thought I saw a snowflake. I walked over to the window and spotted a large storm cloud approaching.

"Hey Morgan!"

"What!"

"Was it supposed to snow today?"

"What?"

I walked out to the balcony overlooking the living room.

"Was it supposed to snow today?"

Morgan took the remote and flipped between news channels until she came across one with the weather forecast. The meteorologist on the channel said, "There's a seventy percent chance of precipitation over most of the state today with a possible on average accumulation of one half to two inches of snow. The storm will soon give way to a high pressure system with warmer temperatures, possibly melting off the snowfall. Today's highs are expected to get around the high thirties, and the low tonight will stay in the low twenties."

Hmmm. Better take a coat with me when we go. There wasn't much for me and Morgan to do besides watch television and eat brunch. We had seven hours to do whatever we wanted to do.

I wonder why no one had shown up to work today? The area was completely empty of construction workers, or any employee for that matter. Now might be the perfect chance for this. I ran back to the elevator and went to the second floor of the building. The android and suit were hidden next to some finished walls tucked behind the soon to be testing room. Oh… It's Sunday. Of course no one is going to show up on a Sunday. Maybe there was a daytime guard, but I think I would've ran into them by now. I had some assorted tools and a laptop with me to work on the programming of the suit. Since the suit was hollow, I could just put the android inside. The complicated part is connecting the processor from the head to the rest of the suit, and deactivating the power assist function... This will probably take all day.

It was about six when I turned back towards town and officer Thomas and I noticed a car with an expired tag. I activated the lights and siren, and followed that car close behind getting a detailed view of the license plate. The silver Toyota pulled off to the side of the road and into the gravel. I hopped out and walked, through a layer of snow, up to the driver side window. I could only see the driver and no passengers. Before I could knock on the window, the driver started to roll it down.

"Is this why you pulled me over?"

He held out two pieces of paper stapled to a smaller piece with the renewed tag on it. I responded to him with a small amount of laughter.

"Yes, the reason I pulled you over was for an expired tag."

I took the papers and read them carefully. He had a receipt for the registration and another copy to keep in the car with him. Stapled on the back of these papers was the tag, clear as day.

"Well, you better get the tag on soon because officer Thomas over there isn't hesitant to make new friends."

He laughed at my joke as I walked back to my patrol car. I sat back down into the driver seat and entered the license plate of the car into the computer. There were no warrants for the owner of the car, his license checked out, and the registration for the car was valid. I turned to Thomas and said, "Nothing wrong with his registration or license. He's not on parole and hasn't had any recorded incidents with police before. I say he's good to go."

Thomas nodded his head in agreement. I walked back over to the Toyota and gave Mr. Barta his registration and license back to him.

"You have a good rest of your day officer."

"And you as well. Get that tag on ASAP."

I walked back to my car as Mr. Barta took off in his. Sitting down in my seat, I couldn't help but think that there was something familiar about him, but I couldn't remember what. I looked at Thomas who was now holding the ring I bought this morning.

"Let me guess… For Morgan."

I took the ring back from him and put it back into the black box.

"Yes, and you aren't going to tell anyone else. This is a surprise."

"Don't worry. When are you planning to ask?"

"Wednesday."

"Are you sure about this? Most first relationships don't last."

"Oh shut up. I've been with her for more than a year. I'm sure we're meant for each other."

Thomas held up his phone with Morgan's contact number on it. Attached to it was a video, about twenty some seconds long.

"Does she know about the scream you made when you were tased?"

"She knows I was tased, but please don't send her the video."

Thomas started laughing hysterically. Knowing that he would do such a thing just to mess with me, so I decided to just let him send the video, and he did. I immediately regretted my decision.

It was around 6:30 when I received a text from an unknown number. I clicked on it and the message read 'Jackson getting tased' followed by two laughing emojis. I wonder who this is from? I sat up on the couch and tapped the link that brought up this video with Jackson in it.

"Follow me Jackson, We're going to get you all set up for the taser."

I know that voice, that's Thomas. The video showed jackson walking into a room with no windows. Soon after, the camera left Jackson and pointed at a taser in the other officer's hand.

"You ready?"

Jackson turned and looked at Thomas.

"Ready for…"

There was a loud pop and you could see two wires sticking into Jackson's side. The taser started clicking from the power inside, and you would not believe me when I told you that I could not scream any higher than Jackson. I turned the volume down on my phone as Jackson fell flat on the floor, ridged like a mannequin, causing me to burst out laughing uncontrollably. Adalyne looked at me like I was having a medical crisis and was quick to ask, "What's so funny?"

I kept laughing at the video, handed Adalyne my phone, and she played the video right away. Right on cue there was that scream again and Adalyne burst out laughing with me. We replayed the video a couple of times, each time laughing at his unnatural scream. I was laughing so hard that it was causing my lungs to hurt.

"I… I never knew that Jackson could scream… "

I couldn't finish my sentence for all of the laughter I had in me was almost choking me. I tried to finish my sentence, but all I could utter was, "Like… He screamed like…"

Eventually, we both calmed down to the point where we could speak full sentences.

"I never knew Jackson could squeal like a little pig."

"It sounded more like a voice crack to me."

We kept on giggling for at least a couple of minutes with the video replaying over and over in my head. I haven't had a laugh like that in a long time. Adalyne stood up from the recliner next to me and asked,

"Did Jackson send you that video?"

"No, his friend Thomas did."

Jackson's pretty cautious about any embarrassing film or photos of him getting to anyone, especially me. My thoughts drifted to the time, only fifteen minutes left until our shift starts. We might as well leave now just so we are well prepared.

"Hey Adalyne. We better get dressed in our uniforms cause it's almost call time."

Adalyne was already up the stairs before I could speak the final word in my sentence. I was sitting on the couch still thinking about the ear piercing scream Jackson made. Over and over that awful but hilarious sound played in my head. I stood up, giggling about Jackson, and walked up to my room to put on my guard uniform. Adalyne was in there sitting on her twin bed texting someone. I wonder if it was that mysterious boyfriend she has been keeping secret from me. I sat down next to her and asked, "Who are you talking to?"

"No one you need to know about."

"Is it a guy?"

"No."

Adalyne put her phone away in her purse before I could see who she was texting. She then stood up, walked over to the closet, and started putting on her uniform. I followed right behind her. It didn't take long to put on our matching uniforms, our hair tied up in a bun through the hole in the back of our hats. If we'd swapped name tags, no one would know the difference.

"Hey, You'd think we could play a prank on Jackson."

Adalyne turned to me with a large smile.

"You want to see if we can recreate the scream he made?"

"Yes, and I have the perfect idea."

The metal suit was laid out on the floor in front of me, all of the constricting frames and support beams were exposed to the elements. I had managed to get the limbless android into the suit and had the suit collapsed to the maximum space it could provide. Wires were running from its chest into the suit's processor. Pretty soon, if the android's processor wasn't too damaged, it will be able to control the suit like it was built for it. I peered at my watch and it read 6:45. I better get the processor paired with the suit before it turns seven. The security team would be here any moment. I quickly attached my computer with a USB cord to the android's processor and the suit's processor. I opened the programming into the android, and opened another window on my computer with the suit's programming. They were different in a lot of ways, but I could still find the similarities between the android's program for operation, and the suit's program for function. I entered the program on my computer to begin binding, or pairing, the two programs together. The computer started to whir louder as the binding process began. All I had to do was wait. I looked out through the room's doorway and up through the giant skylight above the courtyard in the center of the complex. The sky was darkening quick and there was no way to avoid getting noticed while leaving the place. I'll need to leave the computer to run its program while I make an alibi for why I'm here. No, I need to leave, but first I need to get something out of Tom's workshop. Later, about ten hours should be long enough, I'll come back and check on the progress the computer has made. If it's finished, it will be up before I get there. If it's not finished when I get back, which I hope it isn't, I will meet it when it wakes up. I better come back in nine hours instead of ten. That should ensure I get back here before then.

Thomas sat down in the driver seat of the patrol car, talking into the radio, as I walked towards the entrance of the tech complex. There was nobody here except for Morgan, Adalyne, and Tom. They called in something stolen, a... body suit?... I have no Idea what they are talking about, but I will soon find out. I made my way past the giant pedestal where an iron statue of the company's first android was supposed to go and went down to the storage room. There was a giant boiler at the other side of the storage room, but I turned towards the loading ramp instead and walked into Tom's workshop. Tom was the only one in the room and he was ranting on about something.

"I knew I should've had them start yesterday!"

The room was filled with scrap metal and androids. It also had a wretched stench from the molten machines hanging on some giant hooks. There was a brand new, polished, prototype of an android sitting in the corner with wires coming from its head attached to a computer. Standing next to the newer android was the suit I believe Morgan was stuck in a couple of days ago. Was there a second one they were talking about?

"Hey Tom, what happened?"

"Well, I don't know. I opened the door to the room, and my suit was gone. There was also a fireman's axe in here as well and I have no clue where that went!"

"Do you have any operational cameras in the building?"

"No, they're all on the exterior."

I called into my radio for an investigative team to come over, but they ended up only sending three people. Thomas soon appeared next to me and he began talking to Tom.

"Do you have any Idea who would do this?"

"No, but I hope the exterior cameras picked up something."

Tom and Thomas walked over to the computer plugged into the newer android, and began to sift through the footage. I went into the storage room and spotted what looked like a person. It didn't move so I thought it was a mannequin. It had a beard and a bald head with large ears and nose. It's eyes were dark and lifeless as if it hadn't seen the light of day. I walked out and around to get a better look at this android, and almost stopped when someone spoke and poked me in the shoulder.

"Hey Jackson!"

I jumped and spun around to see that Morgan had jumped at my reaction. We both looked at each other in surprise for our reactions, but then looked at each other with warmth. Adalyne came walking in just in time to hear our conversation.

"You scared the crap out of me Morgan."

"I didn't mean to. You scared me when you jumped."

"Yea, well just don't... don't uh... Just call my name."

About a year ago, Adalyne, Morgan, and their parents came down for a giant family reunion. Morgan and I snuck off to the movie theater for a Halloween movie, The Shining. I had never seen the shining before, but I'm pretty sure Morgan had at that point. That was one of the scariest movies I'd seen in my life, besides IT. That movie was much worse. I drifted out of my thoughts as Tom walked with officer Thomas to check out the rest of the building to see if anything else was stolen. Morgan suddenly took my hand and began pulling me back towards the workshop rooms.

"Come on, I want to show you something."

Adalyne followed closely behind as I was led into a room adjacent to Tom's workshop. The lights were off and the room was dark, but there was something sitting in a chair covered by a dust sheet. The lights came on and I could see two figures sitting on chairs.

"What's this?"

The doors shut loudly behind me, followed by a quiet clicking sound where Adalyne stood with a smile on her face. She looked at Morgan and nodded her head. I have no idea what they were doing, but I bet these figures under the sheets were brand new androids.

"You'll see here in a moment."

Morgan let go of my hand and pulled up the sheet behind one of the characters. There was a short buzz followed by a low hum and the sheet towered over me by an extra foot or two. It fell off revealing a half canine half human with bright blue eyes and paper white teeth. There was hair covering its left eye and a white bow on the back of its head. It started walking towards me and extended its hand.

"Hello, what's your name?"

The design of this thing was almost perfect. It's feet, hands, and body were of a human, and the canine characteristics were the ears, fur, tail, and face.

"Am I not speaking anything, or are you deaf?"

I had forgotten that it was extending its hand for a handshake. I reluctantly reached out and shook hands with this thing.

"What's your name?"

"My name is Jackson."

The way this thing spoke was amazing. The lips were even conforming to fit the words coming from its mouth. I turned to Morgan and asked,

"How long did it take to make this thing?"

"Her name is Lexis and we didn't build her, we found her… and Jackson."

"What do you mean you found Jackson?"

Morgan and Adalyne laughed at my question.

"The 'male' android is named the same as you… Jackson."

"Really? That's not weird at all."

Morgan and Adalyne paused and looked at each other for a moment.

"Yea. I thought about renaming them, but they… know their names. I don't want to mess with that kind of programming."

Adalyne walked over to Jackson, the android, reached under the sheet behind his head and did the same thing Morgan did to Lexis. Jackson stood up as the sheet fell to the floor. He Looked at everyone in the room and then to me. We shook hands, supposedly as part of their programming, and he asked for my name just like Lexis did.

"Hey Jackson?"

The android and I both looked at Morgan.

"No, the Jackson in uniform."

The android Jackson and I looked at each other and for a moment's time, it seemed like the other Jackson didn't know why I was in uniform. He seemed to pause for a moment observing my uniform, unsure of who I was. I walked over to Morgan wondering what she wanted and she just turned to the android pair and yelled,

"Hey Lexis, Jackson. Let's show this guy what you can do."

"Shouldn't we be quiet like you asked? To keep this a secret for Tom's surprise?"

"Tom's upstairs right now and I think we can get away with you teaching us some dance moves."

Lexis and Jackson nodded their heads in agreement. They stood next to each other in synchronization appearing to be internally communicating with each other.

"What do you guys want to learn?"

The perfect idea popped into my head.

"How about the Hustle."

Everyone looked at me like I didn't know what I was talking about, but Lexis soon broke the silence.

"All right. Follow after us."

Lexis and Jackson soon began teaching us the Hustle, one move at a time.

I peered at my watch, 3:45 in the morning, realizing that I may have not given myself enough time to get inside the building. The front door was too loud and the back door had an exterior camera on it. I would need to find a way inside through an unfinished window, or something. I began driving around the building with my new car, headlights off, to find a place to get inside. The building is massive, there's no way for all of the outdoor cameras to be up this soon in construction. Plus, I'm the one that now oversees the entire camera system. I know where the cameras are looking. I kept on driving around the complex, avoiding camera views, trying to find a way inside. There were plenty of windows, but they were usually too high off of the ground for me to get in. Maybe there was a cafe off to the side of the building that didn't have the wall installed yet. Wait... I have the perfect idea.

I was walking down the edge of the second story, looking through the hole in the wall where a giant window was supposed to go. The radio lit up in static with Adalyne's voice coming in.

"Hey Morgan, guess what Ben did."

"What?"

"He got the programming done on the brand new android!"

"That's great, what did he do?"

"Well I downloaded the program from the old androids, tweaked the programming a little, and gave Ben the USB for him to work on and upload into the newer android."

Tom broke in the conversation through the radio.

"How'd you get the programming from those wretched things? We were nearly unable to get the scrap out of them."

"I worked my magic Tom, don't worry."

The radio static stopped after a short pause in the conversation. I pushed in the button on the radio in my hand and asked,

"Have any of you guys seen Josh?"

There was a moment's time of no response from the radio, but Ben came in shortly after.

"You mean the guy with the casts on the right side of his body?"

"Yea, wasn't he supposed to be working on the new android with you?"

"No. He works on it during the day."

There was a faint sound of something falling over on the far side of the complex. I hooked my radio onto my belt and began walking over to the source of the sound to figure out what it was.

I managed to get up the stairs towards the second floor and began walking over to the room where I had left him. There wasn't much left to do except talk to him once he wakes up. The watch on my left hand read 4:11 am. I'm late! What do I do if he's gone? Come on now, the first thing he would do is come looking for me. I made my way behind some drywall and through a doorway with no door. To my relief, 126-F was sitting on the floor right where I'd left him.

"Phew. I'd thought you'd be awake by now."

I knew no one would respond, but the voice in my head proved otherwise.

"Not much longer… Maybe a couple of more minutes… No, no one else knows about you… Hello? Where'd you go?"

A quiet beep came from my computer. I opened it and in big letters on the loading screen were the words, Download 100% complete. I looked over at what used to be 126-F, who still hadn't changed in any way, and asked out loud to him,

"You there?"

I sat there for what felt like an hour hopelessly waiting for a response. I decided to unplug my computer from the machine and closed it up for the night. I reached behind his head and unplugged the cord from his processor when I was violently thrown back against the wall next to the doorway, knocking the air out of me. The wretched machine in front of me stood up and began walking towards me in a large stride. For the first time in what seemed days, there was life behind those eyes. They glowed a faint greenish-yellow color, looking straight down into my soul. He reached down and picked up the axe I'd brought up from Tom's workshop. His big metal hands grasped the wooden handle of the axe, holding it up off the ground by just an inch. I thought he was going to kill me. I knew he was going to kill me. The closer he got, the more sure I became. I closed my eyes waiting for a nasty blow, but it never came. I sat there waiting for something to happen, but it never did. My body was shaking from being thrown, but I still managed to slowly open my eyes. Extended in front of me was his big metal hand, seeming to be waiting for mine. His other hand holding fast to the axe.

"I'm sorry if I hurt you."

The scratchy, robotic, wheezy voice clawed at my ears like nails on a chalkboard. I could no longer identify the voice I had heard in my head, but I knew it was him. I put my left hand into his big metal hand, and he pulled me up off of the ground like I was nothing. We stood there looking at each other for a couple of moments before a voice broke the silence.

"Hey! Show yourself!"

Chapter 7

I was walking the newer pilot suit into the room where we hid Lexis and Jackson after Tom asked me to hide it somewhere. He said that whoever broke in here could easily do it again and steal the other one. I pressed the button on the side and I was released from the suit with no problems. I walked back into Tom's workshop and reattached my radio and pistol to my belt. The radio cracked abruptly sending me a couple of feet into the air.

"Tom! Your suit never left the building! It's still here! He's running now and I am following close behind!"

"No, where are you!? Keep your distance Morgan. If you can, hit the lower spine where the metal plates separate!"

"I'm on the second floor, east side, heading towards the stairs!"

I pushed in the button on my radio and called in. "I'm heading up! I'll block off the front doors!"

Ben came in next on the radio. "I'll block the back exit!"

"Um… Tom?"

"What?"

"There are no metal plates, or at least I can't see any!"

"Then hit him anywhere on the spine!"

I ran up the stairs from the basement into the main hall of the mall. Immediately I could hear shots being fired from the second floor. In the distance behind the gunshots, I could hear the loud thumps of metal shoes running across the unfinished concrete floor. For a moment's time, I thought I saw, through the first floor east side window, a car pass with its headlights on. The thought left my mind when I heard the metal footsteps become louder.

"Adalyne! He's coming your way!"

I looked up at the second floor hoping to see the suit stomping around, but I could not spot it. I began running back and forth through the courtyard trying to get a better angle to see what was happening on the second story balcony. The footsteps became louder yet. I ran towards the sound, the footsteps becoming even louder. I followed the sound above me as fast as I could, my feet flying under me. The sound began to get quieter, skipping over the stairs and back over to the west side of the second floor. The radio came on again, "He skipped over the stairs and ran down one of the wings, I can't keep up with him!"

I ran up the stairs up to the second floor, spotting Morgan running down the hallway following the guy in Tom's suit. I began chasing the suit, watching as it rounded a corner down one of the walkways. I came around the corner and met Morgan who had suddenly stopped, almost running into her.

"Where'd he go?"

"You lost him?"

"He rounded the corner and went quiet. He might be right on top of us."

With flashlights on and guns drawn, we began looking around the area for any sign of where he could've gone. I remember how easily the suit knocked over a tree that was at least six inches thick at the base. Imagine what he could do to us. We covered each other as we moved through the west wing of the mall. Most of the walls still had the studs visible, but there was drywall up in some places. The entire exterior of the mall was finished except for the east wing's second and third floor windows. I shined my light into the opening of where a store was supposed to go. All I could see were tools, a pile of drywall, some bags of cement, and plywood that had yet to go up. The ceiling of the room was completely exposed, all of the air ducts and wires that would eventually connect to something were visible. We continued to look from room to room for the suit.

"You think it waited for us to move on into these rooms before it went the other way?"

"It could be possible. What made you think that?" asked Morgan.

She had her flashlight and gun trained on the hall across from the entryway of the room.

"We better double back and see if we missed anything."

I pushed in the button on my radio and spoke,

"Tom, Ben, you guys see anything? He disappeared on us."

There were a couple of moments before anyone came on the radio.

"No. No one has shown up in Tom's suit."

"No one at the damn front door either!"

"Sorry Tom, we almost had him."

"That suit was made to prevent such an incident. It had to be someone who works for me in the building! It had to be someone on the inside."

Morgan and I looked at each other with worried expressions. If it really was someone from the inside, who would it be? There were only a few people besides me, Morgan, and Tom who worked on these suits. It couldn't be Josh because he has a brace on, it simply wouldn't fit. And it couldn't be Ben, he was with us the entire time.

"Hey Morgan. Were there any distinct features?"

"I thought his head looked a little big, but all I could see was the outline until he took off down towards the other side of the balcony. He had removed all of the metal plating, I'm sure of it. But… Why?"

"Beats me, I don't have a single clue."

I spoke into the radio while looking at my watch. 5:15.

"Tom, did you happen to put a tracking device in the suit?"

"Hell, I did so much stuff to that suit I don't remember what all I did. I did plan on making your suit answer to a homing beacon once you call it, but I haven't even gotten started on it yet."

Morgan and I began sweeping the area again, making sure that every possible hiding spot was checked. And it didn't take long before I noticed something peculiar on the floor. It was a greasy yellow blob covered in some dark red crust.

"Morgan, what is that?"

She knelt down and picked up some of the stuff, throwing it back revoltingly to the floor.

"That stuff smells awful, almost like the wretched smell of the androids downstairs, but this smell has something dead to it."

"Where could it have come from?"

It didn't take long to realize that this is the walkway that the man in that suit came down, and I'm pretty sure that he had to have been in contact with those machines… somehow he, or she, had to still be here.

My heart skipped a beat as my six a.m. alarm clock went off. That awful buzzing sound that scares you if it crept up on you just right seemed to never fail at getting me out of bed. I immediately hit the off button on the alarm and sat up. James and Grandpa went to a put-put course while I did my daily patrol yesterday. Today though, James needs to be dropped off at school at 8:00. Grandpa told me that last Friday some group of kids were picking on him right before he flattened one of their noses. The kid can fight, but I don't want him to start the fights. I put on a fresh uniform with my gun and taser at my side. I put on my bullet proof vest, and hooked my radio with the bodycam on top of the vest. I'm all set and ready for today's events. I tuned in on my radio and immediately received the middle of a conversation.

"...tional units in and around the building."

I better get out there to see what's going on. I'll come back to pick up James later, maybe around 7:30...ish. I pushed in the button on the radio and asked,

"Go 10-9 please."

The lady from the station called into my radio.

"There's been a discharge of firearms at the tech complex called in by a worker who arrived early this morning. The first officers at the scene requested six additional units be present at the construction site. They reported that an intruder may still be present at the site."

"I'll be right there."

"10-4."

I raced out of my room and through the living room passing Grandpa on the way to the front door.

"What's the big rush?"

"There's been a shooting at the tech complex and I'm heading over there right away."

"Did anyone get hurt?"

My mind began picturing Morgan, Adalyne, and Tom wounded with a bullet hole in their bodies. I quickly pushed the thought aside.

"I really hope not."

The weather outside was cold for this time of year so I slipped on some warmer clothing. I took off in my patrol car through the freshly fallen snow on the ground, and headed over to the complex. The closer I got, the more frightened I became. The thought that something awful had happened crossed my mind over and over again, never seeming to rest. I crested the hill and spotted the massive complex covered in snow. Arriving in the parking lot, I spotted four other patrol cars along with Morgan, Adalyne, Tom, and two other guys. A wave of relief washed over me as I realized that nothing bad had happened to Morgan, she didn't even appear to be shaken. I leaped out of my car, slammed the door, and quickly walked over to her.

"Are you guys ok!?"

Adalyne came walking towards us from her car seeming to be as pissed off as Tom.

"Yes Jackson, we're fine."

"What happened?"

Morgan stood up from the bench and said,

"We ran into the guy that stole Tom's pilot suit and we believe he's still in the building."

"So… you guys were never fired at?"

"No. We fired on him."

"Did you hit him?"

"Adalyne emptied her entire clip on the guy, but we didn't find any blood."

Adalyne came into the conversation, sitting down behind Morgan with her gun.

"I know I hit him, I saw sparks fly, and he had removed all of the metal plating on the suit as well. I hit him six out of the seven times that I shot, yet… he was never injured, or we don't know that he's been injured."

Morgan, Adalyne, and Tom were all frustrated. Frustrated that they had the chance to get the suit back, but were unable to. And frustrated that this guy still has the chance to hurt them really bad if he wanted to. They also seemed to be tired because I could see the bags under their eyes, and the constant yawning going from Morgan to Adalyne, and back again.

"Why don't you guys go home. You all seem to be really tired."

Morgan looked up and said, "Yea. That's not a bad idea. Come on guys, let's allow the police to do their thing. I'm exhausted."

The trio's mood quickly changed from angry to relaxed in a heartbeat. Tom piped up and said,

"That does sound good, I can't wait to get some sleep."

"Wait, you? The coffee hog?"

"Eh… shut up."

Morgan and Adalyne giggled at Tom's humor, quickly got into their car, and drove home. They seemed to have forgotten about their frustration and put in its place, some peace. A couple of minutes later, Josh came up to me and in a tired voice, his breath condensing in the cold air, and said, "I saw someone coming back down from the south end as I was driving up to work here at about six-o-clock this morning. I couldn't tell what the vehicle was because he had his headlights off, but I'm sure he was involved."

"Thanks for the information Josh. And by the way, where did that other guy go?"

"Ben? He left in his own car right before Morgan and Adalyne left."

Josh was wearing a light bandage on his right arm, which surprised me because he had just survived a fire and explosion. He should've been more injured than he was.

"Hey, what happened to your arm?"

"Oh, I got some second degree burns. Want to see it?"

"No! No. I don't want to see it."

"Ok. Well I need to get inside, these bandages are soaked."

"All right, see you later then."

I got back into my patrol car and told the other officers that I needed to take James to school. By the time I opened the door, the time had turned 7:44. I'm right on time, or at least I thought I was. Grandpa was sitting on the living room couch watching Homicide Hunter on TV. Closing the front door behind me, I asked,

"Grandpa. Did James get up?"

He quickly turned around towards me.

"I don't know. When was he supposed to get up?"

"Ten minutes ago." I said slightly irritated.

With a small hint of frustration, I opened the door to James' room, turned the lights on, and yelled in the best non-aggressive tone I could make.

"James get up, You're late for school!"

James, still half asleep, mumbled something inaudible.

"James, want me to get an ice cube?"

"Nooooooo…"

I walked over to his bed and began shaking him a little.

"James. Come on, get out of bed."

There was no response that I could hear, so I stood up and began walking slowly to the door.

"Alright. Here comes the ice cube."

James suddenly moved like he'd been shocked by a cattle prod. Getting dressed, making his bed, sloppily, and walking out to get some breakfast. I almost had the door closed when, on his little desk, I saw the drawings of the three burned androids that were moved into Tom's workshop just a couple of days ago. These drawings were pretty good. I picked up the drawing he made and studied his artwork. He had to have drawn this from memory. There was also something different about the way he posed the androids, like they were still alive. I put the papers down and went back into the kitchen to get some breakfast myself.

"Grandpa, did you have breakfast?"

"Yep… Coffee."

"Is that all you had?"

"No, I had a banana too."

I pulled out some leftover French toast, a couple of days old, and heated them in the microwave. As the clock on the timer went down, memories about the two androids Morgan found went through my head.

"How about the Hustle?"

"Alright. Follow after us."

Lexis and Jackson did the first couple of moves of the Hustle, having us copy their moves. Eventually we got to the point where we could keep up with the duo. Almost meeting their moves with our own. Adalyne and Morgan were having an equal amount of fun. The androids were too... what's the word for it... perfect. Every deliberate move they made was on the spot every time. They never messed up and they never seemed to notice either. It was a rigid behavior, but subtle. The way they introduced themselves was weird. I've never seen any program as sophisticated as the one in those androids' heads. My thoughts were ripped from my head as the beeper went off on the microwave, telling me breakfast was ready. I sat down across the table from James, who had scarfed down his cereal in the minute I had warmed up my French toast, and asked him about his drawings.

"They're ok, I guess."

"Just ok? James, I couldn't draw those better with a picture to look at."

James finished his bowl of cereal and stuck it in the sink.

"Are you going to ask me to join an art class?"

"Only if you want to."

James stood there thinking about the option for a little bit before he shrugged it off, and went to go brush his teeth.

"You really shouldn't push him to do something. Your dad pushed him to do a lot, and when you act or appear like your dad, it reminds him of his dad. My son!"

"I'm sorry Grandpa, I just see his capabilities and think how well he could use them to benefit his life."

Grandpa began to become a little emotional.

"Well you leave that kid alone and let him make his own life decisions."

Grandpa stood up and walked over to the basement stairs, slowly walking down into the basement.

"Grandpa, where are you going?"

"I'm watching football on the damn BIG TV!"

Wow, everyone is in a grumpy mood this morning. I glanced at my watch, 7:58. James is going to be late if he doesn't hurry.

"James, you done? School's almost starting."

"Coming."

James walked out of the hallway, dressed for winter weather, backpack armed for school. We got into my patrol car and drove over to the local grade school.

"Alright James, I'll pick you up tonight and we'll go have some hot chocolate! How does that sound?"

"Good. Bye."

"Bye James."

James shut the door on my car and walked up to the school through the snow. He was greeted by a teacher at the door who let him in with a big smile. My radio crackled to life with an emergency call.

"We have an 11-78 with possible survivors at the corner of first avenue south and south twenty-fifth street. Requesting all officers in the vicinity to report to the scene."

I quickly pressed in the button on my radio and called in,

"Officer Fuelman on route."

My left arm held the new remote firmly as it vibrated in the direction of where he had hidden himself. It surprised me that Adalyne didn't see me. I was right out in the open, but I bet the giant pilot suit drew her attention away from me. I didn't know that she would open fire on the suit like that either. I'm just lucky that I was able to crawl out of the second story window before she came back, and drive around the building when I did. The remote began to vibrate a little harder than before, indicating that I was heading in the right direction. It led me down into the basement and through the boiler room. The remote began to vibrate towards a different direction, pointing to the storage room. I walked into the storage room that was stacked to the brim with boxes of supplies, tools, and entertainment equipment for when the tech center opens. I passed the storage room and entered the loading ramp area. The remote vibrated even harder this time, pointing directly at Tom's workshop. I opened the door to the room and tried to turn on the lights. To no avail, the lights failed to function. I flipped them frantically hoping that at any time they would work. Ah, screw it. I pulled out my flashlight and pointed into the room hoping that he'd be sitting in the open waiting for me. I saw the new android, on the other side of the room three wretched androids, and he was nowhere to be found. I walked further into the room looking for anything that I may have missed. The new android had some of that weird grease sitting on top of its head. Well now I know that he was definitely here and may still be here, but where. The remote suddenly vibrated even harder in an unidentifiable direction, indicating that he was right on top of me. I flashed my flashlight around looking for him, but paused at the feeling of something on my shoulder. My heart pounded on my chest feeling like it could burst out at any moment. The weight on my shoulder became heavier and began to slowly pull me around. His face, well… not his actual face, appeared in front of me showing no aggression. My fear and dramatic heartbeat disappeared as I figured out that he wasn't going to hurt me.

"Holy crap Dad, you scared the shit out of me."

He responded in his wheezy voice.

"I couldn't show myself until I knew for sure that it was you."

"Fine. Did you get hit by any of those shots last night?"

"What do you think?"

He pointed at some dents in the frame of the suit where bullets had harmlessly bounced off. Then he spoke again.

"Do you know who burned down the workshop?"

"No, I don't…"

"You don't have a single clue!?"

"No. I…I…"

"You what? You thought that some accident burned that place down? It was Tom. He was right there in the building setting a 'bomb' near the propane in the kitchen. He wanted me destroyed, thrown into some garbage dump far away from anyone."

"I know Tom wanted you gone, and I never wanted to intervene. But when you saved my life that night, I thought that the killer inside you was gone, and that my father was all that was left! I just wanted to meet you again, but I thought the only way to meet you was to listen to your voice that you put inside my head. I just wanted to talk to you again."

"And you almost lost the chance due to Tom's unthoughtful actions. He's the one who almost sent me to hell!"

"Because of your choices long ago. You murdered my friend."

"Not on purpose!"

"You killed my mother simply because she…"

"That wasn't my fault! And it wasn't my machine either."

"I… what do you mean it wasn't your machine?"

"Tom built the rotten android you see me in now, and he built the android that took your friends."

"What are you saying?"

"I'm saying that if Tom hadn't been around, your friend would still be alive and… and your mother would still be here too. I have tried to ruin his life before, and I've succeeded in some places, but failed in most others."

My father's tone became more intent, or sinister.

"And now... we have a second chance to give Tom what he deserves. He took so much of what was precious to me, it's time I do the same to him."

Memories of my friends and mother flashed in my mind. One, my friends putting together a small android cat or what I can remember of it. My mother, I couldn't remember much of. She was always distant, like she was hiding something from us. And I remember Dad telling me that she was never coming home. That was one of the saddest days of my life... until my friends... Tears began to form in my eyes, clouding my vision. I wiped them away quickly and turned to Josh Sr. with an angry tone.

"What do you have in mind?"

"Oh... You'll see."

Chapter 8

I began walking down a hallway to make sure that something was the way I wanted it to be, but I don't know where I am, or what I was doing. I just felt like I knew what to do, but I don't even know what it is. I turned into an office and pulled out a drawer with a gun in it. I grabbed the gun, and made sure it was loaded. What am I doing!? I wanted to put the gun back, but I couldn't control myself. I don't even know where I am! I heard a loud crash from down the hall, and immediately went to go check it out. I don't recognize the place, but somehow I knew where I was going. I rounded the corner into a large room, and spotted an early prototype android holding a woman up in the air by her throat. I involuntarily spoke up, and that's when I noticed that it wasn't my voice.

"Put her down Trinity!"

The android turned its head towards me and said, "But this is what you wanted."

"Not to her!"

I wanted to pull the trigger and shoot the android, but no matter how hard I thought, I just stood there pointing the gun at it.

"Trinity, you have this all wrong! She is not who you think she is."

"Oh, but that's where you're wrong Josh. She hurt you. Tom hurt you. You only wanted one thing, and I can make that a reality."

I turned my head towards two boys who I felt were family. I've never seen them before! One looked like he graduated high school, and the other looked like he was no older than ten.

"Son, take Josh and get out of here. Get as far away from here as possible. Go!"

"But dad..."

"GO!"

As the two boys ran out of the place, I turned back around and faced the android. I raised the pistol, and fired a shot into the android's shoulder.

"Trinity, don't do this!"

"But I already have."

I looked at the woman in the android's arms, and noticed that she was beginning to pass out. I raised the pistol and shot six times into the android's chest. The android sputtered and twitched as it fell onto the floor, becoming motionless as the last spark of power left its body. I ran over to the woman and dropped the gun on the floor next to me.

"Sarah? Sarah, no please... come on, wake up!"

She laid there on the ground lifeless. I could feel tears in my eyes, but they weren't 'my' tears. I still have no clue who I am. I felt the woman's chest and realized that her heart wasn't beating, and her lungs were still. I noticed something in the dark ahead of me. I looked up and saw another body. This time of a young girl no older than eleven years old. I looked past her body and saw another, and another. I saw six bodies laid out on the floor. The entire room was destroyed with tools on the floor, tool boxes and shelves tipped over.

"Why?... What did you do Trinity? What..."

"I did-d wha-at... you-u wanted Josh-sh. Y-you said... you want-ted Tom's li-ife to be r-ruined, a-and no-ow it is..."

"Shut up!"

Tom ruined everything! Trinity was just an android. Capable of only the program inside if its computer. If only Tom had just left it alone, everything would be fine and... and Sarah would still be with me and the boys. Tom, this is all your fault... this is all your fault!

I felt someone grab my arm as I awoke from the terror of sleep. Morgan was by my side, dressed in her security uniform, looking at me.

"Are you ok? You were yelling in your sleep."

Tom was standing in the doorway looking at me worriedly.

"Yea, I had a bad dream."

I stood up out of bed to get ready for the day, memories of the dream still fresh in my head.

"OH! Sorry." said Tom as he walked out of the room quickly, closing the door behind him.

"Here."

Morgan tossed me my fuzzy robe, and realizing that I was just in a small shirt, I quickly put it on faster than I have before.

"Adalyne. What'd you dream about?"

"I... I dreamt about shooting an android that choked someone to death, and then saw that the android killed six other people, including kids."

"That's… a pretty weird dream. It's almost three, so why don't you get something to eat."

"Ok, that sounds good."

I put my uniform on, balling my hair through the hole in the back of my hat. Then Morgan and I walked down into the dining room, surprised that Tom had already made omelets. The aroma of cooked food filled the space, calming my jittery body.

"This is nice. Where'd you learn to cook?"

"Since I owned a workshop for the first time, and it didn't help with my weight." Tom joked.

"You're still hanging onto that are you?"

Tom laughed at Morgan's comment until he sat down with his own plate of food.

"Yep. I'm never letting that go."

It didn't take us too long before we finished our breakfast, or mid-day meal. We didn't need to be at the tech complex until seven again, so… we decided to go sightseeing at a park at the top of the ravine's ridge. It wasn't too far of a drive from here.

I had tools scattered around me on the table as I reassembled the tendon group on the last wretched android that was hanging from the ceiling. I tweaked the tendons so more voltage could be passed through the system, giving it more power. I attached new batteries, new hoses, and reinstalled new processors that I brought in from the storage room next door. These androids could now function, but dad wanted me to add something extra. He wanted me to add something to the processors that were from inside the metal cabinet they pulled from the burned rubble. I remember that cabinet, but what happened to it? He handed me six tiny receptors, the kind you would see in something to make multiple androids function as one, but he said I didn't need to worry about the cabinet, like he'd broken into it.

"What were you doing out and around in broad daylight? You will get spotted."

"But I wasn't."

"Well don't go anywhere until I'm here ok?"

He sat there and thought about my statement for a little while then slowly responded.

"Fine."

I guess he wanted me to attach these receptors so he could control them, all five at once. I asked myself if this was really necessary, but I went on with it anyway. I continued to work on the androids as the day went by. By four, I had installed the receptors in all but two. By five, I had finished the fine tuning for function and behavior. The only thing left to do was to program the new processors I placed in their heads. I have no experience programming something from scratch, but I can try to use the program from the newer android, duplicate it, and install it to the other five. I reached into the back of the android's processor and pulled out the processor cord.

"What are you doing?"

"I'm programming the androids. Why?"

"You don't need to do that. I need their minds blank... Oh, and Tom moved the other suit. Where'd he put it?"

"I don't know. This place is so big, it would take all day to check."

Dad froze in his place, like he had locked up his servos. He turned his head to me abruptly and broken as if he'd detected something.

"You need to leave."

"Why? I'm not done yet."

"NOW!"

"Ok, sheesh. Calm down."

I picked up my coat and gloves looking back at him just to see what he was doing. He pulled himself up into the rafters, still able to cloak himself in the darkness above the lights. I walked down the loading ramp to my car through the sloppy, wet ground. The three inches of snow that fell this morning was now completely gone. Soaked into the ground like a sponge. I sat down into my car, but before I could start the engine, "Hey Josh!"

I drilled my head into the roof of my car as Adalyne knocked on my window. I rolled it down and asked, "Ow. Hey Adalyne, what are you up to?"

"Not much, just seeing what you're up to."

She was holding back a laugh after watching me nail my head.

"So, was there any reason you wanted to talk to me?" Adalyne looked down at her watch, and then unconfidently asked,

"Would you... Would you like to go get something to eat at like four or five-ish."

I looked at her with an awkward smile.

"Sure. What will be open at that time?"

"How about a Pancake House? The one close to Target."

"Alright, I'll see you there at five then."

"How about four, I need to make a grocery run."

"That sounds fine, and you mean four in the morning right?"

Adalyn was walking away when she turned her head and responded, "Yes Josh, four in the morning. Bye."

"Bye."

I rolled up the window of my car and I couldn't help contain my excitement. "YES!"

I was a little too excited, but I didn't care. I wasn't going to let my past get in our way, not one bit. I put the car in drive and drove home to get a little rest before my date tomorrow morning.

It was 4:43 in the morning when I got a phone call from Morgan, waking me from my sleep.

"Hello."

Morgan talked back to me in a distressed whisper.

"Jackson, that suit is back and it's chasing me. I need more man power over here and I need it quick!"

"Are you ok!?"

"What do you think!? I'm stuck in the damn storage room and this thing ain't going away!"

I began to get dressed and hustled out of the house, not caring to make noise that would wake up James or Grandpa.

"Hang on, I'll be right there!"

I hung up the phone and blasted through the door towards my police car.

"Not today! Not her!"

I glanced at the time on my watch, 4:32. I'll finish my sweep of the basement while Tom finishes his sweep of the third floor. Adalyne had disappeared for a grocery run, and Ben was off to Europe. It was just the two of us. I was caught off guard by the faint sound of something light falling over, like a broomstick. I walked over to the source of the sound hoping that it was the wind or a small breeze. I panned my flashlight throughout the entire boiler room starting to think that it was probably just the boiler. I began walking back towards the workshop, passing rows upon rows of shelves packed full of boxes big and small. I wonder how much money is just sitting in this place? I jumped into the air as my radio announced itself.

"H… Morg…"

I pressed the button on the radio.

"What, Hello? you're breaking up."

"What…"

"I said you're breaking up!"

There was no longer any response from Tom.

"Stupid radio!"

I looked at the radio under my flashlight, trying to figure out why it wasn't working. I turned it off and on again, pulled the batteries out to see if they had corroded, and pulled the antenna out and reattached it to see if that was the problem.

"Flipping batteries must be dead."

I heard the same sound again, this time a little closer. I turned around and noticed a bolt on the floor that I swore wasn't there before. It had the same weird grease on it, similar to the stuff the suit dropped when…

I pulled out my gun and aimed it down the rows of shelves with the flashlight pointing its direction. I pushed the button in on the radio.

"Tom, I… crap!"

I threw the radio on the ground remembering that it wasn't working properly. I began spinning around in circles, keeping anything from sneaking up on me… hopefully. I decided that my best option was to get the other suit on before he catches me. I began sneaking around the third shelf of boxes, stepping quietly enough to hear the patter of mouse feet. I slowly made my way to the door, my flashlight still in front of me. One foot at a time I came closer to my escape. This reminded me of when I was in the bunker, and I wasn't paying attention to what was hiding in the dark. I was starting to get paranoid, worried that each nook and cranny had something hiding in it. I was beginning to get this smell of something like the burned androids that we scrapped, but with something dead added to it. With each footstep I took, the stronger the smell became. Maybe I was walking in the wrong direction. I felt some air brush against my back. I immediately froze, hoping that it was just a draft. My body began to get goosebumps as I realized that I could feel something behind me. It wasn't touching me and it wasn't breathing, I could just tell that there was something there. My breath began to shutter and my heart was pounding in my chest. My thoughts were confirmed by the sight of something to my left. A face missing most of its plastic skin, its eyes black with a single, silver dot, slowly entered my field of view only a couple of inches from my face. I was frozen in my shoes, chilled to the bone. I covered my mouth to quickly hold back a scream. This thing wasn't a man. It was a machine and it was messing with me. I was shaking over fear that I could be killed, but I held myself in place. I could be picked up by this thing and never seen again. The face began to slowly recede into darkness, disappearing from view. My rapid heartbeat didn't help me be still, and my breathing was louder than before. Sweat was rolling down my forehead, dripping off my chin onto my shirt. If I bolt for it, I could make it. Don't be an Idiot! It'll catch you! If I don't do anything I'm going to die! I reared around flashing this thing in its eyes and opened fire. I didn't make two shots before I was picked up and thrown through some boxes into the other aisle, knocking the wind out of me. I got up and dove through more boxes into another aisle. The suit-thing... whatever it was, came stomping my direction, around the adjoining rows of shelves. I dove back into the shelf pulling a box over me hoping that I wasn't spotted. The stomping slowed and passed right by me. I pulled out my phone as the creature walked passed another corner. The time on my phone was 4:43. I unlocked my phone and immediately called Jackson.

"Hello."

"Jackson, that suit is back and it's chasing me. I need more man power over here and I need it quick!"

"Are you ok!?"

"What do you think!? I'm stuck in the damn storage room and this thing ain't going away."

"Hang on, I'll be right there."

The phone line went dead followed by the blank buzzing sound.

"Jackson? Jackson. Please come on."

I now realized that the stomping sound was far across the storage room. I can sneak over. There was something warm on my forehead, so I reached up and smeared blood from a cut on my head. I need to get out of here! I slowly backed out between two bigger boxes behind me and walked over to the door. I removed my shoes and threw them across the room. Immediately the thing went after the sound, and I took off with quiet feet towards the room where I hid the suit, but it was locked.

"Damn it."

I pulled out my key ring, and slowly flipped the keys to find the right one. One by one I tried them on the door, completely exposed and in the open. Wrong one... Hurry!

"Come on... Yes."

I slowly turned the key on the door knob, it clicked, and creaked open.

I made my way across the dark room down to the other side. My hand in front of me, I ran into a cushion. I felt around the object to get my bearings and I could easily identify the new suit Tom had built. I stuck my hand in the metal glove, but before I could get my other hand in, I was swept sideways across the room and slammed against the wall. I saw this mechanical face in front of me, built of the same identical materials as the other wretched androids, but covered in withered, black plastic that used to be polished and clean. He held me against the wall off of the ground with his left arm and drew back with his right. In the dark, I couldn't make out what it was but there was something in its hand. With lightning speed, his right arm swung at me. Pain shot through me as my side was cut by the blade of an axe. I could hear the impact drill the wall behind me that I was held up against. I could no longer feel my legs, and I could no longer breath properly. I had lost my ability to scream, and move. These dim yellow eyes stared into mine as I was dropped to the floor. I couldn't feel the floor with my legs and I could barely move them to hold myself up. I managed to painfully set myself against the wall and held my side. I could feel my warm blood oozing through my shirt and over my hands, running onto the floor. My eyes slowly closed as the android walked out of the room and out of sight. My mind was becoming cloudy, and I was beginning to lose consciousness. Come on... stay... awake...

I ran up through the loading ramp and over to the large door hoping it was unlocked. Thankful that it was, I slowly opened the door, letting in the night air. I shined my flashlight across the room passing the workshop, and over to the elevator. I thought I heard someone moan in the distance from what I thought was the workshop. I moved closer and swept my flashlight past the room adjoining this one. Again there was a moaning sound, but this time it came from the room where the androids were hidden, the ones Adalyne and Morgan found. I opened the door and walked into the dark room focusing my light on the untouched suit against the wall.

"Jackson."

I whipped around to a horrid sight. Morgan was sitting up against the wall with blood staining her clothes from her knees to her chest, soaking up what was lost from her body. My heart stopped, my mind froze, and my body began to shake.

"Morgan! NO!"

I ran over and knelt down next to her, partially sliding through a puddle of blood.

"Shh…"

"Morgan what happened?"

"Quiet."

"No-no-no-no. No. No. No!"

"Jackson."

Tears were beginning to form in my eyes. I didn't want to see this! I pulled my gauze and rescue strap that all police carried with them, and began tying it around her waist.

"Jackson."

"What Morgan, tell me."

"You need to… get in Tom's… suit."

She silently groaned as I began to cover her waist in gauze.

"Morgan, you're going to be ok."

I put my hand under her chin and brought her eyes to mine.

"We're going to get out of this. You're going to be fine. You're going to be just fine!"

I began to frantically wrap more gauze around her, hoping to stop the bleeding. She brought up her hand slowly, shakily, and put it on my face.

"Jackson… you know… I love you… but get… in the fricken… suit."

Each time she spoke, she choked on the blood that was in her lungs, and from the pain of her injury. I tied off the gauze, ensuring that it wouldn't come loose, stood up, my hands pure red from the blood that covered Morgan, and walked over to the suit.

"Stick your… hands… into the glo…gloves and… and your feet… into the… shoes."

I followed her instructions and the suit collapsed around me. There was this tremendous pain in the groin because there was simply no room. I breathed out a high pitched, quiet squeal that was the only thing audible in the room. Morgan choked in pain and said, "Tom built… that for… for… me and Adalyne."

I responded in the same quiet squeaky voice, holding my metal hands over my groin.

"No kidding."

I stumbled around for a couple of seconds, getting over the pain, and I created loud stomping sounds with my metal boots. I finally stood still like a newborn baby, trying to get my bearings. I had never used one of these things before, but now I know what it's like to be in a suit that moves with you. Before I had gotten into the suit, I had removed my gun holster and radio… RADIO!

"Hey this is Fuelman for station. I have an injured woman at the scene, I'm with her now, I need backup pronto, and send an ambulance. I'm at the new tech complex!"

"Officer… back…"

The radio cut in and out, unable to make anything clear.

"Hello!? can you hear me!? Damn radio."

I put the radio down and took my taser with my big metal hand. I was unable to get my fat metal hands through the trigger, so I knelt down near Morgan.

"Morgan, take this and when whoever it is comes through the door, tase him."

Morgan held the taser in the air for a couple of seconds before falling limp. My heart stopped for what felt like forever.

"Morgan?"

"I'm… still here. Let… me rest."

"Did you hear what I said?"

Before Morgan could speak another word, I was slammed into the side and thrown against the wall at the end of the room. I looked up and saw not a person, but a machine. Its face was black and molten like the other three androids, but then it spoke.

"You think I'm just going to let…"

There was a loud snap, followed by faint clicking sounds. The wretched machine fell to the floor and began to shutter wildly. I looked over at Morgan who had pulled the trigger and was holding it down with one hand.

"Ha… you thought… I… I was… dead."

I stood over this machine as it convulsed on the floor. I brought up my foot and slammed it down upon the android's head, feeling it crack and break under my foot. I brought it up again…

"NO!"

I was drifting in and out of consciousness when I saw a man standing in the doorway with a pistol in his right hand. The gun was smoking from the one shot that he'd just taken. I looked back at Jackson who slowly began to fall over with his right leg still in the air, a trickle of blood running down the center of his forehead. With a loud crash, Jackson, and the suit, fell onto the floor limp. I muttered the one word I could before I lost the strength to hold down the taser trigger any longer.

"Jackson?"

Tears, new ones, began to run down my face. I looked at the man who was shaking in his boots, stunned by his own actions. The wretched machine slowly got up and turned to look at him. I tilted my head and looked at him with my one eye that wasn't clouded with blood from the cut on my head.

"You... son... of... You..."

I finally lost complete control of my body, eyes blinding, and my body falling over. I could hear my own thoughts, but then I felt nothing. No pain, no touch, no smell. I felt like I was floating in empty space.

I ran down stairs as fast as I could yelling into the radio.

"Morgan, are you there?"

No response.

"Morgan, you there?"

Again, there was no response. I made my way down stairs and around the giant boiler, through the storage room, and finally into the loading area. I saw my workshop... the door next to it was wide open. I walked inside and almost had a heart attack. There, on the floor, was my suit with a man inside... no, Jackson inside with a bullet wound to his head. I ran over and pressed the button on the side, releasing his body from the suit. I dragged him out and removed the groin plate from the suit, and climbed in myself. I stood up and stared at the lifeless body of my great niece, Morgan. I sat her up on her back, her hair, clothes, and the left side of her face, stained with blood. Her lifeless eyes were frozen in a state of fear. It made me remember what it was like when I lost my daughter... and my wife. I knew no monster off of the street would do this to someone. Especially to my family.

"JOSH!! Get out here and face me like the killer you are!"

I reached under my work desk, and pulled out a large box. I ripped it open and grasped what I was looking for. I attached an eleven inch retractable blade, that was made specifically for this scenario, to my right arm. With the click of a button, I was able to snap the blade in, and snap it back out using nitrogen pressure. I turned around to leave, but noticed two characters sitting under some sheets. I pulled it off and to my surprise, it wasn't what I was expecting. In the chair closest to Morgan was this female canine character covered in fur. I pulled at the hair, and it had the same elasticity as human skin. These weren't made out of plastic at all. These were amazing. This character also had long hair, almost like a wig, covering its left eye and running down its back. It also had ears that I've never seen on an android before. Did Morgan and Adalyne build this? That thing is awesome. I yanked the sheet off of the other figure, and it revealed a male version of the same design.

"Huh? Why the hell did I not know about this?"

I heard a hollow thud come from the adjoining room followed by light footsteps. I walked out and shined my shoulder light into the darkness

"Josh! Stop running!"

There was this awful sound from behind me. A dozen violins playing off tune from each other, a few octaves higher than it should be, and smudged by digital static. I turned around just in time to see this burned android, with a single camera in the center of its face for an eye, jump at me with both arms outstretched. I brought up my arm to protect my face as we tumbled down across the concrete floor. It began to lay punches upon me, but I could already tell that it was beginning to slow. I continued to push it off and eventually threw it against a concrete pillar. It tried to get up, but I kept on knocking it down with severe blows to the back of its skull. It bolted underneath my legs and came up behind me, still screaming that awful scream. It clung onto my suit and started to pull on some metal plates on my back. I jumped up into the air, and landed flat on top of it using my weight as a weapon. It let me go and I whizzed around to attack, but it had disappeared. It became disturbingly silent in the room. I ran into the storage room, then into the boiler room, hoping to spot it. I heard some patter off to my left, then off to my right, circling me. I walked over to a small cement tumbler and picked it up off of the ground. I turned towards the sound, waiting for the android to strike again. I heard that awful scream to my left, I swung the tumbler around and drilled the android square in the chest, knocking it to the ground.

"Got you now!"

I slammed my fist down towards the top of its head, but it caught my hand in its fist and began to push away with force. With a loud firecracker like snap, I triggered the blade cutting clean through the back of the android's hand. I recoiled my arm and blade, then slammed it down upon the androids chest triggering the blade, killing it. It ceased movement and just lay there as a rag doll. I picked it up off of the ground and yelled,

"Is this you Josh?! You made a poor choice to fight in this thing."

"Good thing I'm not just one."

With impeccable power, my right hand received an impact beyond any that I'd ever felt before. I fell sideways onto the floor, and noticed the android tumbled past me with the blade still attached to its chest. Adrenaline was rushing through my body like never before. I put my right hand to the ground to push myself up, and that's when I felt it. The unbearable pain of my wrist receiving too much weight. I brought my hand around… and the metal glove wasn't there! My hand wasn't there anymore! It had been cut clean off, through the glove's metal frame, the metal plating, and it was bleeding profusely. I again tried to get up, but a machine had a foot on my chest holding me down.

"Do you know how I was able to find you?"

I just stared at this old machine over me, ignoring his question.

"Do you have a clue of who you're up against?"

"Well, I'm seventy seven, and I'm still able to kick your ass!"

"Your body's weak, and you're missing your right hand. Almost like me before I was put in this suit."

The machine hooked his hand through the chest plate of the suit and pulled me off of the ground, standing me to my feet.

"Now that I gave you the chance, beat me up!"

I noticed that his head wasn't connected directly to the frame of the rest of his body, exposing wires, and the all-important processor line. I stepped forward, ignoring the pain from my hand, and swung at him with my left hand. He raised his axe to swing, but that was what I planned for. I brought my hand back and caught the axe, mid swing, and ripped it from his hands. I spun around again and drilled him in the side. The frame caught the axe stopping it from damaging anything important. He reached down for the axe, but I pulled it out and scraped the axe blade on the bottom of his metal chin. I backed up and gauged what to do next, but my thoughts were becoming clouded, and unclear. I was bleeding out too fast! The wretched machine leapt for me, catching me in the legs, and lifting me off of the ground. We both fell backwards onto an unfinished floor, dust flying up everywhere. I found the old machine's shoulder and swung the axe down on top of him. I couldn't tell anymore if it was the dust clouding my vision, or my head. The axe stuck in tight, preventing me from pulling it out. It took the axe from my left hand and slammed his other hand into my right wrist. I yelled in pain as his metal hands touched my bone, exposed by the savage swing of an axe not too long ago. He pushed me down into the floor, knowingly that I would pass out at any moment.

"Your body will bleed out… you have no other choice but to give up!"

I tried to get up, but I was getting dizzy, and weak. He then spoke again in a sarcastic tone.

"Look at you, the trooper. Trying so hard to avenge your daughter's death, while keeping the real secret from the rest of your family!"

It reached down and ripped the button from my suit, crunching it in its hand.

"You're going to feel what JOSH felt, when JOSH was killed by one of your inventions. You knew it would happen, and you thought it would end him, but you were wrong."

It then occurred to me that this wasn't Josh. It was someone else. It reached behind my neck and disconnected some wires from under a damaged sheet of metal.

"You're going to die by your creation, like JOSH did by his."

It slowly backed into the dark, leaving me trapped in this suit unable to move.

"Tom."

This voice was someone familiar, and calming.

"To your right you goof."

I turned my head to the sound of her voice. I realized who it was, and a tear rolled down my face.

"Let's go home."

She reached out and touched my hand causing all of the pain to disappear. Then my mind went blank, but I could still feel her small hand in mine.

Chapter 9

I was sleeping soundly in my bed when I heard someone knocking at the front door.

"Morgan, can you get that?... Morgan?"

I turned to look at the twin bed next to me and noticed that no one was there. It was still neatly made from the day before. The knocking came again.

"I'll be right there!"

Did Tom come back? I came home at around six after my date with Josh. Tom had told me to go on a grocery run at four. "Just go home and rest when you're done shopping." Is what he said. I whipped on my robe and walked over to the front door. I opened the door and saw the B.P.D. badge on two individuals dressed in suits. Before they muttered one word, I slammed the door in their faces. I had watched too many TV shows in my lifetime to know that it's never good when you see two officers on your doorstep. I slowly opened the door again, seeing their surprised faces.

"I'm sorry, I... I overreacted. Is there anything I can do for you?"

The two detectives looked at each other with drawn faces.

"Ma-am, I am detective Daws and this is detective Harris. We have some bad news involving your sister and great uncle."

"Why? What happened? Are they ok?"

"Ma'am... I don't know how to say this, but your sister and your great uncle were found dead at the new tech complex... the one under construction."

There was this long pause before I could answer the detective.

"I'm sorry, say that again?"

"Ma'am, why don't you get dressed. I think you better come with us."

"Ok. I'll be back down in a minute."

I walked upstairs to my room, the detective's words not fitting into my head. 'Your sister and your great uncle were found dead at the tech complex.' If they're playing a prank on me, I swear someone's going to get it! But what if they aren't? I don't want to think of that! I glanced at my watch and the time was 8:45. It was early in the day and I only got a couple of hours of sleep. Maybe I'm still dreaming. I put on a pair of jeans, and a long sleeve shirt under my jacket. I walked down into the living room and saw the two detectives holding the door open, their faces blank. I followed them down to their patrol car and saw Josh in the back seat, his face blank as well. I sat down next to him and asked,

"Josh, what's going on?"

"Um… Adalyne. I'm so-so sorry, but your sister is… not coming home."

I could feel my eyes begin to water, but I did my best to hold them back.

"What do you mean she's not coming home?!"

I noticed the detective in the front look in the rearview mirror with sympathy and regret, and then he said, "Your sister, Morgan, was killed last night in the complex. Your great uncle and one of our officers were also found dead close to her, most likely killed by the same individual."

"I want to see her. I don't believe you!"

I began losing the strength to hold back my tears as the car turned the corner towards the hospital. I couldn't believe a word of what I was told. There's no way any of this is true! The patrol car stopped and the two officers let Josh and I out of the back seat. I didn't want to go in there, but I wanted to see Morgan. I refused to believe that she was dead.

"Adalyne, please follow us."

The two detectives led me through the building, passed a couple of corridors, past the coroner's office, and down into the basement. We then walked past a few more corridors, but soon the detectives opened a door on the right. I froze in my shoes. There, on three tables, were three figures covered completely in blue sheets. One had long hair running off of the edge of the table, the same color as mine. Josh held out his hand for me to take, but I just stood there, knowing that it wasn't a prank, and stared at three lifeless bodies on the tables.

"Adalyne, please come look."

"I…"

Tears began to form in my eyes. Josh took my hand and led me over to the table that had the woman on it. The doctor pulled the sheet off of her face, and as soon as I saw those lifeless eyes, I buried my face in Josh's shoulder so I couldn't see. I let myself go, my body completely breaking down, and tears soaking into Josh's coat. Through my sobbing, I managed to yell,

"Cover her up! Cover her up."

I overheard the coroner in the room talk to the two detectives.

"The young lady died from multiple complications due to her injury, including her spine that was completely severed. I also think that if you had found her alive, she wouldn't have made it long enough to reach the hospital. The officer has one clean bullet wound to the head and the older man here lost almost all of his blood due to his severed hand. I have no Idea where they found him, but they said they destroyed the 'suit' getting him out of it. I was able to identify the possible murder weapon for the two. It was most likely an axe or a sword. I also placed the time of death for all three of them at around five-o-clock this morning."

Josh had his arms around me, and I had mine around him. I couldn't believe that my sister was dead, I saw her not too long ago! Memories of her began to flood my mind and with each passing memory, my mind broke and twisted. My thoughts then brought me to who the officer was. I broke free of Josh's hold and walked over to the table at the end. I pulled the sheet off of his face, confirming to me that it was in fact Jackson. I reached over to the table in the middle and pulled the sheet off of the other face, who was indeed Tom. My crying turned into screaming as I realized that everyone I was here for was now dead. I was all alone! I collapsed to my shaking knees, my throat screaming as loud as it could go. I could feel Josh's hand on my back as my stomach began to turn over. I got up and ran over to the nearest garbage can and hurled up everything I had in my gut. I knew that Jackson and Morgan would've most likely gotten married in the future, having a family and living a life. But all of that future was now impossible. I would have no nieces or nephews. If I had any children, they would have no aunt or uncle or cousin to play with. What I dreaded most was the thought and memory of everything my sister and I had done when we were kids. Playing together, running together, and messing around with any high school crush by switching places with each other. Our secret handshake that we've had for years replayed in my head. But the chance to make new memories with her was over. I left the garbage can and began to stumble out into the hallway. Josh put his hands under my arms before I could fall over, but I shoved him away. I ran over to the stairs and up onto the first floor, sprinting as fast as I could. Josh tried to keep up, but the brace on his right ankle slowed him down.

"Adalyne!"

I slipped and fell as I tried to stop in my tracks, landing on the cold tile floor. I looked up and saw my parents, who were also distressed for they must have heard the grave news too. I got up quickly and ran over to them, throwing myself at them. My father caught me in his arms, my mother holding me in hers as well. I cried into their shoulders not caring to hurt them if I held them too hard. I still had the fresh memory of my sister's dead eyes, almost like she was frozen in fear before she died. I did not want to go back down there and look at her again. I feared that I could no longer control myself while looking at her.

"Adalyne, we came as soon as heard about Morgan."

"When... When did you hear about it?"

"Very early this morning. We arrived at a hotel late last night to surprise you with a visit, but..."

My father began to slowly raise his head towards the stairs. I turned to look back at Josh and the two detectives who were standing at the head of the stairs. My father then spoke to me.

"Adalyne, why don't you go home and rest."

"No. I can't sleep, not after what I saw. Not after..."

I was too upset to finish my statement, my mind unable to form a sentence and hold that image in my head. I started to collect myself and I loosened the grip on my parents, their faces as distraught as mine. Josh came over with a box of tissues, and held them out for me and my parents. I took a handful and cleared my eyes of tears, then I took a few more. I noticed that Josh's right arm was wrapped in bandages to cover the still tender skin. His elbow was exposed, but other than that, his arm was completely covered, even most of his hand. An officer came up to us and spoke in a calm voice. "I need to tell you this."

The officer reached into his pocket and pulled out a small black case, one that would hold a ring. He then spoke the words that nearly killed my parents.

"This was found in Jackson's patrol car, and the entire police department was told by officer Thomas..."

My mind only found one answer, "Jackson was going to propose to Morgan."

The officer nodded his head slowly and handed the ring to me. It was obvious that he didn't want to be the one to tell us, but he managed to bring himself to it. My parents, on the other hand, began to cry again. I knew they were thinking about the grandchildren that they would never have, and the son-in-law that they will never meet. The two detectives led them down into the coroner's office, and Josh and I were left alone in the lobby, standing next to each other wondering... what now?

"Excuse me, Ma-am!"

I turned around to the sight of a woman with short blond hair, and a nose ring. She was carrying a journal and a backpack with who knows what inside.

"Are you Adalyne?"

"Yea."

Josh stepped between the woman and me.

"Now is not the right time to talk to anyone. Go find someone else."

"It's my job to report on important town events, especially when it's about J.T. Cybernetics. It's what I do."

I could feel the pain from my heart begin to boil up into anger. This reporter was never my favorite, nor Morgan's favorite… I'm even surprised that she has the nerve to come here! Josh and the reporter continued to argue as I sat there getting more and more agitated.

"Go away, you can't talk to her!"

"Well, why doesn't she just tell me."

I could feel my hands run cold as the two continued arguing. I walked around Josh and slowly towards the reporter and responded,

"I don't want to talk to you!"

"Alright fine. But I'm still going to get what I came here for."

I watched as the reporter walked around us and towards the coroner's office. I began to follow after her, but Josh reached up and put his hand on my shoulder.

"It's not worth following her. She always gets herself in trouble."

I realized what Josh meant as the reporter came back up the stairs with an officer right behind her. She was escorted out of the building by the officer, and I watched as she drove away. I was going to beat her up if Josh hadn't stopped me, and I'm glad he did. I know that my sister would never come back no matter what I did. My parents slowly came up the stairs with the same distraught faces they had when I met them, and they were no closer to calming down as I was. I walked over to my parents and again hugged them, calming myself down.

My mother spoke up to me and said, "Who's this Adalyne?"

"Mom, this is Josh. He's a good friend."

My mother glanced at him for only a second before she continued to sob into Dad's coat. I began to think of the injury that caused Morgan's death. I overheard the coroner, but I needed to see it for myself. I stood back a little ways and began to compose myself. I could keep myself from crying any longer, but I still shook in place. There was an officer standing next to the basement stairs, so I walked over to him and asked in a very shaky voice,

"Can I see Morgan's injury?"

"You can't go back down there."

"I need to see Morgan's injury."

"Ma'am, there's not much I can do right now. I'm sorry, but you can't see her injury."

I again lost my composure to keep myself from breaking down. I walked over to my parents and hung onto them once more. I could hear the patients of the hospital walk past us going to their appointments, and the doctors going about their usual day.

"Adalyne, you should go home and rest." said Josh.

My father spoke up too and released me from his arms.

"Yes, we all need to rest. Adalyne, come with us to the Hotel."

"No, I… I want to go back to Tom's. I want to rest there."

"You can't be there by yourself…"

"I'll take her." said Josh.

My father seemed to be against the option for a moment, but soon seemed to understand that I wanted to be alone.

"Alright, but you call us if you need us ok?"

I nodded my head yes. My father began to walk my mother out of the hospital, but before I could leave, an officer came up to me and asked, "I'm sorry that you can't see Morgan again, but there's an investigator that has agreed to show you a few pictures. He's waiting for you right over there."

The officer pointed at a man standing in the distance with a suitcase in hand. I nodded my head and Josh and I began walking over towards the investigator. We sat down next to each other in a small office while the investigator sat down by the desk in front of us with a notebook. I was holding onto Josh's hand while he asked me his first question.

"When was the last time you saw Morgan?"

"I… I saw her right before I went to go see Josh for breakfast at five, after my shift. After that I went to the grocery store at six and then I got home and fell asleep at about seven."

"And… what was the last thing she said to you?"

"She said…"

I again almost lost the ability to keep myself from breaking down, and the investigator noticed.

"Take your time. I overheard you talking to the officer out there and… you… you wanted to see the injuries?"

I nodded my head yes and he seemed to be hesitant to take out the images, but he did so anyway. I tightened my grip on Josh's hand as the investigator set the first image of Morgan's injury onto the desk in front of me. There was a gash that started on her left side just below her breast, and it ran over to the opposite side of her back. There was another image that he placed on top of the other and it was the same injury from a different angle. My grip on Josh's hand tightened as I could feel my stomach twist as if I would throw up.

"Are you going to throw up again?" asked Josh.

I shook my head no as I restored control of my body. The investigator spoke up once more and asked,

"Your shift begins at seven the previous night, right? And you don't sleep until six the following morning?"

"Yes."

"Ok. Go home and rest, and when you're ready… I'll come back and ask you some more questions."

"Ok."

Josh pulled me up to stand, and we walked out to the officer that took us to Tom's home in his patrol car. I opened the door to the home and for the first time since I was here, I couldn't hear any noise from anyone. It was too quiet.

"Go rest Adalyne."

I looked at Josh for a little bit before I pulled my hand from his and walked up into the bedroom that I was supposed to be sharing with my sister. I laid down and looked at my sister's empty bed and wondered what to do next. I pulled out the ring to look at… and it was really beautiful.

I stood in the living room as Adalyne walked up the stairs to her bedroom. I knew she wanted to be alone, but I wanted to do something for her. I looked at my watch and it read 11:45. When my mother died, I didn't eat for a few days. That was a mistake that I didn't want to repeat. I knew that if Adalyne didn't eat, she'll definitely be tired, hungry, and she won't think straight. After searching the freezer for something easy to cook, I found a rib steak and began defrosting it in the microwave, but then I heard a small sound from upstairs. I walked towards the stairs and I could hear Adalyne crying. I slowly made my way up towards the bedroom and when I stood next to the door, Adalyne just let herself go. I wanted to knock on the door, but I knew Adalyne wanted to be by herself. Never the less, I brought up my hand and knocked on the door a couple of times. There was a moment or two, but the crying slowly calmed down.

"Yes?" Adalyne responded.

"Do you mind if I come in?"

There was another moment of silence before she said yes. I opened the door to see Adalyne curled up in her bed with a pile of tissues sitting on the nightstand. She was still sobbing when I sat down next to her on the opposite bed. She sat up and looked down at her hands that were holding tissues. I reached out and put my hands on top of her hands and she seemed to relax for a moment. Then I told her,

"When… When I lost my mother back in 98, I completely lost it. I didn't want to do anything or go anywhere. I was completely shut down. That same day, I lost some of my friends… My father was more distant from me than he ever was, and then a few days later… he was dead… and I don't know why. My brother disappeared into the world, and I haven't seen him since. I remember the time when my brother and I were building this rabbit, and all the sudden, there was chaos and… that was the last time I ever saw my family.

Adalyne abruptly hit me with a heavy hug and said, "Thank you for making me feel like I'm not the only one who's lost half my life."

I held her tight as she continued to sob. We sat there for a while until I heard the microwave downstairs beep.

"Adalyne, you didn't have any breakfast or lunch, and I know that eating is the last thing you want to do, but please eat something. Starving yourself won't help."

"I…"

Adalyne was interrupted by her phone in her purse that buzzed loudly.

"Can you get that Josh?"

I reached over and pulled out her phone. It had an unknown number to it, so I asked Adalyne if I could answer it and she said yes.

"Hello?"

"Ummm… Is this Adalyne's phone?"

"Yea."

"I'm Jackson's Grandfather."

"Oh, ok. Umm…… I'm sorry, about Jackson."

"Don't apologize." He said in a worn voice. "James wanted to know if he could see Adalyne. I guess James just wants to leave the house because he doesn't want to see me… well… let's just say I can be scary when I'm upset."

"Isn't there another family member he could stay with?"

"Not here in town, no."

"Yes that's fine." said Adalyne, thinking a distraction would be a good idea.

"Ok. I'll drop James off when you're ready. Bye."

The phone line went dead and I put her phone back into her purse. Adalyne seemed to be calming down quite a bit, but she was still shaking and teary. We held each other until Adalyne released me from her hug while taking in deep breaths.

"Fine, I guess I could eat something."

"I need to go back to my apartment so I can get some of my stuff situated, but I promise I'll be right back. It'll take me a few hours but call me, ok? I'm also making you something to eat. Please eat some of it."

Adalyne nodded her head yes. I stood up to continue my cooking down in the kitchen, and when I looked back, I saw Adalyne slowly pulling the covers of the bed over her head. She laid down quietly, so I turned off the lights, and shut the door as she began to rest.

I blasted my eyes open to the sight of a room that I kind of remember, or at least what I could see of it. The room was almost completely dark, so I reached around and felt the side where the nasty cut was, but didn't find any. In fact, I felt well rested. Maybe I nodded off in the middle of my shift. What kind of dream did I have? My hair was in the way of my left eye, so I repeatedly pushed it aside. I felt weird and numb. Like every limb on my body was dead, but I still had the feeling in them. I pushed myself from the chair, and out of the dark room again shoving my clump of hair off to the side of my head. I stumbled out into the parking lot looking for my car. Where is my car? I left it right here! The sky was only lit by the crescent moon coming over the mountains in the east, allowing the stars to shine bright in the sky. I tried to say something to myself, but I couldn't make any sound, not one squeak. There are no taxis in this city, and there are not many bus routes that come up this way. I patted myself down looking for my phone to call Adalyne, and that's when I noticed that I was kind of exposed. What kind of clothes am I wearing? I was wearing a top, and pants, but there was nothing over my belly. I looked down at my hands, but all I could see was the outline of them. Frustrated, I decided to walk home. I heard something behind me rustle against the ground, causing me to spin around to find it. The sound occurred behind me again. Was something behind me? Maybe I'm still dreaming. Without a second thought, I began my long walk home, somewhat excited to get a good long rest.

Chapter 10

James was sitting at the dining table observing the steak on his plate. Josh had made a salad that he scarfed down, but he hadn't touched the meat, like all nine-year-olds do.

"James, are you going to stare at it, or are you going to try Josh's cooking?"

"I'll try it… eventually."

I smiled at him. Is this like what a child of mine would be like? Or is he still thinking about his brother Jackson? Will I ever have a family? The questions reminded me of Morgan and Jackson and what their family would've turned out like. I managed to eat a small piece of steak, but it was all that I could handle. James finally took a piece of meat with his fork and put it in his mouth. He sat there and chewed on the piece until he swallowed.

"Do you have any steak sauce?"

"Yea."

I stood up and went to the fridge, pulled out some A1 sauce, and set it on the table in front of him. He took the bottle and nearly drowned his steak with the sauce.

"Wow, Josh's cooking isn't that bad is it?"

"No. I just don't like meat."

James ate one piece of steak at a time, covering each bite with too much sauce. Later, he seemed tired, bags clearly visible under his eyes, so he found himself a fine spot on the couch to lay down. It was getting late, almost 10:30, so I sat next to him and turned the TV to a cheesy Halloween movie, one James could watch. I turned the lights off and began to fall asleep myself when I heard the front door shutter, and the door knob turn. I got up and walked to the door, but before I could look through the window, the door came open. I noticed that the outside door knob was held by a black hand. The figure then walked inside and looked at me.

"Lexis?"

I got no response from her, and I immediately yelled at James.

"James, get to the back bedroom and hide, now!"

James, seeing the tall figure, took off following my instructions without question. Lexis watched him run off and tilted her head to the side just a little. She seemed to be confused, or disoriented, and why hasn't she said anything yet! She had also pulled her hair back in disarray. I began backing away cautiously towards the stairs.

"Lexis, what are you doing here?"

She opened her mouth in surprise and appeared to say something, but her voice was absent. She also appeared to be a little offended by my question. Lexis reached out with one hand, trying to take mine, but I slipped away and ran upstairs towards the bedroom. As soon as I made it into the room, I reached under my bed and pulled out the case to the gun that Tom gave us. I pulled out the gun and loaded the magazine. Behind me was a mirror leaning up against the wall, and in its reflection, I could see Lexis stare into the bedroom. Her ears were pinned back and her face was riddled with confusion. I took a flashlight and held it in the opposite hand of my gun. Would this gun kill it? Let's find out! I stood up from behind the bed and flashed the light at Lexis, but something stopped me from pulling the trigger. I wanted to shoot, but Lexis wasn't looking at me anymore. She was staring into the mirror with wide eyes. My flashlight illuminated her white clothing like a bright star, brightening the room just enough to see. She brought up her hand and waved it in front of her face, her eyes still focused on the mirror. She took a step back, looked at me, then dashed into the bathroom across the hall and turned on the lights. I slowly walked behind her and saw her face in the mirror. Her mouth was wide open as she stared at her reflection. Lexis took her hands and put them on her snout, running them up her face and over her head. She then pulled at her ears like she didn't know they were there, and ran her hands through her hair frantically, almost seeming like she was trying to pull it out. She then looked down at the rest of her body. Lexis held up her arm, tugged at her fur with her other hand, and then began pulling at the fur on her neck, belly, and other arm. She ran her hands down her back to the head of her tail, rearing around sideways to the mirror to get a look at it. Her mouth was still wide open exposing her uncovered metal tongue, and bright white teeth. She seemed to stumble a little bit, let go of her tail, and held herself up with her left arm on the counter. Lexis reached into her mouth, cautiously feeling each tooth, and moved her tongue around seeming to test it. Her eyes spotted me in the mirror and she spun around quickly. I backed off into the hallway not knowing what to expect, my gun still in my hand. I heard a solid thump and the clatter of a toilet lid, so I slowly peered around the corner of the doorway and spotted Lexis. She sat herself on the floor in between the corner of the room and the toilet in an uncomfortable position. She had her knees pulled up to her face with her arms wrapped around them. Her head was tucked under her arms and her tail was shoved out to the side. She was breathing unsteadily and seemed to be scared. Was this a malfunction? Or is this something else? I took cautious steps towards her, not knowing what was going on, reached out to touch her arm, and for a moment's time the skin of the android felt warm. It had never felt warm before. As soon as my hand broke contact with her arm, she freaked. Her arms shot out sideways, denting the wall and her feet pushed out from under her. I fell backwards into the shower causing the shower curtain to fall on me. I pulled up the curtains just in time to see Lexis run out of the bathroom and down the hallway towards the stairs.

I stood up and dashed after her, but by the time I got to the stairway, the front door was wide open allowing the night air to rush in. James was also nowhere to be seen. I really hope he's still hiding. I ran down and shut the front door.

"James?!"

"Yea."

Oh thank God he's still here.

"You can come out."

James walked out of the back bedroom and stared at me with wide eyes. I knew I couldn't leave him here, Lexis could come back. And if Lexis is behaving like this, then I bet Jackson, the android, is behaving in the same way. I picked up my phone from the coffee table in the living room and called Josh. I heard someone pick up the phone and before he could answer I yelled,

"Josh?! Josh, you won't believe what just happened!"

"What? Adalyne, calm down. What's going on?"

"A while ago, Morgan and I found these androids down in an underground bunker. Tom didn't know about them so it was going to be a surprise, but…"

"You found what?"

"It came to my house Josh! It found me!"

Josh seemed to stutter for a few seconds but soon responded.

"Adalyne, hang tight. I'll be right there!"

With the quiet sound of a dead line, I ended the call. James was looking at me curiously. I knew that those androids can carry twice their weight and that they can easily kill a person. Just the design of the frame raises some questions. I wonder... was it them that killed Tom, Jackson, and Morgan? They have the power to do so, but what about the guy in the suit? He could easily do the same damage. I remember when Morgan and I chased him on the second floor. He could've killed us then, but he didn't. I waited for Josh's car to pull up into the driveway for what seemed like an eternity.

"Adalyne?"

"Yes James."

"What's going on?"

"Um... Josh and I are going to go chase that thing, ok. I can't leave you here because it may come back."

"Can I chase him with you?"

"You will stay in the car with Josh."

I could see the headlights of a car shine through the front windows of the house. I ran outside to Josh's new car, and buckled James into the back seat. I then go into the passenger side, sat down, and buckled up.

"Adalyne, where did it go?"

"I believe she may have gone back to the tech complex. But if not, she's roaming around town somewhere."

Josh put the car in drive and we sped off towards the complex. I had my pistol in my hand, still fully loaded. Josh reached under his seat and pulled out his eleven mm glock, dwarfing mine.

"Where'd you get that from?"

"My Dad got it at an auction."

James piped up from the back seat.

"Cool!"

Maybe bringing James wasn't such a good idea.

I ran up along the ridge back towards the complex. If I could cry, I would have tears, but I'm not sure what I am. The crescent moon was still just over the mountains, shining enough light for me to see in front of me. My feet were carrying me at a speed I never knew I could run at, and every so often, I'd trip on a log or a rock and land on the ground. It didn't hurt, but I could feel where any sharp object had cut 'my' skin. I finally reached the front door of the massive place, and pushed it open not caring to damage it. I heard something in my head, but it was coming from someone else. I followed the sound in my head, wondering if it was leading the way instead of me. I stopped in front of the basement stairs as the android, Jackson, was at the bottom of the stairs in complete darkness. I could hear him talking, not out loud, but in my head like we were wirelessly connected.

'What the?'

I saw him look up at me and freeze.

'Lexis. What are you doing powered on?'

I tried to figure out how to talk, but all of this is new to me! I still have no idea if I'm dreaming! I tried to say the words 'I'm not Lexis', but no sound came out.

'What do you mean you're not Lexis?'

What? I didn't even say anything.

'You just did!'

Wait, can he hear my thoughts? I waited for a response, but none came. I thought about something to say,

'I'm not Lexis, I'm Morgan.'

'No!... I watched her bleed out on the floor!'

Ok, I think I'm getting the Idea of this.

'Wait, who are you?'

'I'm Jackson.'

'The canine android?'

'No!'

Jackson seemed to become frustrated as he walked up the stairs towards me. If I've become this... thing, then I think Jackson... as in the Jackson I loved before he was shot had become this android! I covered my mouth... snout as I realized what happened.

'Jackson, the police officer?'

'Oh my God! YES!' Jackson said in frustration.

I broke down in happiness and sorrow. I wanted to show him, prove to him that I was Morgan trapped in this body. I wanted to hug him, but he still thinks I'm Lexis. Instead, I took his hand and dragged him across the building into the nearest bathroom, but he fought me the entire time. I don't think he knows his current appearance yet. I dragged him into the unmarked bathroom that thankfully had a working light, and turned it on. I yanked him over in front of the mirror, but he had his eyes trained on me.

'What the hell Lexis! What are you doing!'

'Jackson, look in the mirror.'

Jackson, slowly turned his head to the mirror. He stared into the mirror curiously, slowly walking forward. He touched the end of his snout to the mirror, getting as close as he could. He pulled on his ears, his fur, and his tail in almost the same way I did when I stared into that awful mirror back at Tom's.

'What… this is a dream. This has to be a dream!'

'I don't think it is.'

Jackson punched the mirror, crashing it to the floor. He backed up and fell backwards into the opposite wall, and sat there staring into empty space. I let him sit there until I thought I heard him begin to shutter his breathing. I now believed that this wasn't a dream, but… how do I prove that I'm Morgan? I knelt down a few yards from him and looked at him. He was still staring straight ahead, his breathing unsteady. I thought of the perfect thing to say to him.

'Jackson… when I was on the floor with that slash in my side, you came in and started wrapping me in gauze.'

'What about it? And it was Morgan!'

'Listen to me!... I told you to get in the fricken suit and when you did, the suit Tom designed specifically for me and Adalyne, pinched you in the groin!"

Jackson broke his stare and looked right at me, but I continued.

'Before that, I called you instead of the police and told you that I was being chased by the man in Tom's stolen suit. You told me you would be right there, but… you weren't there in time.'

Jackson slowly stood up and looked at me with his ears pinned up. Is that an involuntary thing, or does that happen on command?

'Morgan?'

I jumped over and hung onto him, hugging him tight enough so he couldn't move.

'I thought you were dead! I saw you get shot in the head by that man.'

'How are we not dead? Or what I mean… I thought we'd move on, but…'

'I don't know and I don't care! I thought you were gone.'

Jackson reached around with his arms and held me close. I didn't know if I was truly dead, and this was all in my head. But the fact that I saw Adalyne acting the way she was, this really couldn't be a dream. Jackson spoke to me again.

'So… What do we do now?'

I sat there and thought about it for a little bit. No idea came to my mind but one.

Josh parked his car right in front of the tech complex, its big glass windows reflecting the night sky. The stars were very pronounced tonight despite the city in the ravine.

"Josh, I want you to stay and look after James."

"What? I'm coming in."

James was hyped up and ready for something he knew nothing about.

"Neither of you are coming in!"

I stepped out of the car and headed into the tech complex. My body was shaking for the fear of what I may find, but I pushed myself to end everything in there that wasn't human. I had Josh's glock, and my nine mm pistol with me. Slowly, I opened the door to the place, shining my flashlight into the large and empty entrance. My shoes were not making it any easier to keep quiet, and I needed to find a place to hide if these things came looking for me. There were plenty of rooms that didn't have any drywall up, and there were plenty of cement bags stacked across the place. My flashlight dashed back and forth, looking down every possible place these things could be hiding in. I needed to get up to the second floor and look over the courtyard, so I ran up the stairs onto the second story balcony, and stared across the great football field sized opening. In the distance on the ground floor, I could make out the soft glow of a light. I ran across the second floor until I was above the illuminated area, and turned off my flashlight. The stairs next to me were lit just enough that I could see my footing. I slowly, step by step, made my way down the stairs and onto the first floor. Down the hall was a room brightly illuminated. With my back pressed against the wall, I slowly inched my way towards the room. I noticed that there was a shadow on the floor coming from inside the room. The shadow began to grow and I ran back down the hall and around the corner. Lexis and Jackson were next to each other as they walked out of the room, their mouths moving like they were talking, but no sound came out. I looked down at my pistol and clicked off the safety. I glanced back up and saw the duo looking directly at me. I pulled my head away from their view, hoping that I wasn't spotted. I held my breath and pulled my pistol up next to my face. Right now is where this ends! I slowly peered back around the corner and met Lexis' bright blue eyes only inches from mine. I launched myself backwards from her, screaming, and shot into her face. She covered her head with both of her arms as I emptied the clip onto her. Lexis stumbled backwards and took off running down the hallway, veering left into the maze of the building. I took off running after her, uselessly trying to catch up to the speedy android.

Adalyne was far behind me as I realized that I needed to disappear. My body is completely black, and I hope I could use that to my advantage. I turned the corner and ran into a stack of wood planks. I leaped over and hunched down behind the wood as Adalyne ran by. I felt around the top I was wearing and noticed a lip on the back of it running with my spine. I tucked my fingers under the lip and pulled on it. I'm going to hate this.

I stopped dead in my tracks as the sound of velcro being torn flowed through the air. Behind me there was a stack of wood planks that Lexis had to be hiding behind. I walked up to the wood and hopped on top of it. There, on the floor, was Lexis' top, bow, and bell bottoms.

"What... is it doing!?"

I remembered turning the lights off in the bunker when we found these androids in the first place. When I shined my flashlight on her in the bunker, the only thing visible was her clothes, teeth, eyes, bow, and earrings. The rest of her body was perfectly blended in with the darkness, even with the flashlight directly on her. I guess that's kind of smart if she's trying to hide from me. As I pulled her top from the ground, I heard a couple of small metal objects hit the floor. Two earrings, with a small chunk of fur attached to them, were on the floor covered in what seemed to be their skin's adhesive. Wow, this android is going to great lengths to get away from me? The thought left my mind as I heard a crash from the courtyard. I stepped down from the stack of wood and took off running towards the sound, my pistol gripped firmly in my hands.

I ran up the stairs as I neared the end of the courtyard. This opening is like the size of a football field. I heard gunshots not too long ago, so I hope that Adalyne is ok. I hope that she killed whatever she had found. I heard some light footsteps above me on the third floor balcony.

"Adalyne!"

The footsteps stopped and seemed to walk over to the hand railing on the side. I walked over and looked up hoping to see Adalyne, but instead a black figure jerked his head down and looked at me with bright blue eyes. This wasn't Adalyne. I've never seen anything like this before. It took off running towards the second-third floor stairs. I thought to myself, it looked like a dog. I began running in the opposite direction as I looked to see the pitch black body of an android appear on the stairs. I hobbled along with the brace on my leg, the loud footsteps of the android closing in behind me. Each step I took was two for the android. I turned into a room that had a hallway leading out of the back and sadly no place to hide. I felt two hands on my shoulders, hairy ones, push me down onto the floor with immense power. I had no choice but to give in. He took the back of my neck and swung me around to his face, holding me back up off of the ground. He had a snarl in his teeth, and he was choking me. He slammed me back onto the tile floor and raised his right hand into the air with a fist. I closed my eyes waiting for the impact, but instead I felt his grip on my throat release as Adalyne's voice sounded from the distance. I coughed out the fluid in my throat, happy that I could breathe again.

"Josh! I told you to stay with James!"

I sat up and looked at Adalyne who was standing over me.

"Sorry... I heard some gunshots and I thought you needed some help."

"Well you almost got yourself killed!"

"I thought I could help."

"Please get back to the car!"

"What was that thing?"

"It's... I can't explain right now."

Adalyne handed me her nine mm pistol and took off running down the hallway after the black dog-like android. I really hope she kills that thing.

I walked down a dark stairway and into the basement. I swear I saw Josh coming down this way.

"Josh? Adalyne?"

There was no response. If I'm found by either of them, I'm going to get in so much trouble. I walked past a room with a giant tub in the middle of it, and then came into a room with a bunch of shelves. As I walked through the room, my foot kicked something on the ground. I picked it up and it felt like a shoe. It was too big for me, and it felt like it was for someone athletic because the soles were so big. I continued walking through the dark and came across two massive garage doors. They were metal and cold. They must be the doors where they unloaded the burned androids a few days ago.

"Well, look at what came down here." Said an awful, ear scratching voice.

"Hello?"

"This is about the last thing I expected to find wandering down here."

"Who are you?"

"Well let's just say, um… Do you know the Circuit Cafe?"

"Yea! I went there for my birthday!"

"Oh, well that's nice. Do you know of the old J.T. Cybernetics workshop?"

"I have heard of the Circuit Cafe."

"No. Do you remember the original workshop?"

"Circuit Cafe?"

"No! before that!"

"I don't know what you're talking about."

I sat there completely confused, but the strange voice continued.

"Of course you don't. You're just a child. Long before you were born, I was working with a friend named Tom. Him and I were set on creating these machines that could do everything a human could do, including speech and individual thought. Soon after our fist few failures, and a couple of processor lines, we finally created one. It even named itself Trinity. Soon after though, my wife Sarah, and my two sons went there to see our work, but then… everything fell apart. Trinity was behaving out of its programmable range. It killed Sarah, and I knew whose fault it was. But before I could confront him, I was attacked and hung by six prototypes in the workshop. They didn't have any existing program in them, and at the moment of death I knew that it had to be Tom's fault!"

"…What?..."

"Never mind. I don't even know why I'm telling a child this."

The man stepped out of the shadows, showing this torn metal face with patches of charred black plastic. The rest of his body was built with metal frames, connectors, and exposed hydraulics. I began backing up from this horrific monstrosity, but it kept the distance between us the same. In a moment's time, a black figure darted out from the darkness, picked me up off the ground, and ran with an unhuman velocity. I didn't hear the burned monster chase after me, and I figured that was because the person carrying me was running too fast for it to keep up. I was being held tight in two fuzzy arms as I flew up the stairs. I couldn't see who it was, but I could tell that its body was completely covered in fur. Before I knew it, two glass doors came open and I was placed on the ground next to Josh's car. I looked back at this dog like character and I could see a clear outline, including a tear in each ear. It took off back inside before I could say something, leaving me by the car. Well… at least I'm back here so I can't get in trouble.

"James get in the car!"

I turned to Josh who came limping around the corner of the building far to the west.

"Fine."

Chapter 11

I ran past the first and second story balcony as the canine android leapt over the edge of the stairway, and awkwardly landed on the main floor. He then took off back down into the basement. I ran down the stairs as fast as I could trying to keep up with him, but it soon became obvious that he was much faster than I was. I leapt down into the basement and into darkness, my flashlight the only source of light in the building. If this android decides to hide the same way as Lexis, I could easily over look him with the flashlight. Thankfully though, this one hadn't made that choice yet. His bell bottoms were still illuminating brightly when my flashlight shone on him. I turned the corner where he had disappeared and I could no longer see where he'd gone. I wandered into the storage room and hung a left against the wall. As I shined my flashlight down one of the walkways, I spotted what looked like a blue shoe. It was Morgan's shoe, the one she wore the night when she... Shut up! Now's not the time to break down! I walked down past the other row of shelving and came upon the other shoe. Why are they scattered apart from each other? I ignored the question and kept on going through the rows of shelving. Eventually I came to the entryway of the loading ramp. I believe this is where he passed through, but there are two hallways splitting off in two different directions, including the one where Morgan had unintentionally scared Jackson. I walked into the room where we hid Lexis and Jackson the android, and for the first time, I saw the giant blood stain on the floor that no one had cleaned up yet. I felt like I was going to throw up again. I fought back the feeling and left the room. Maybe Jackson hid in the workshop. I slowly opened the door to the room and shined my light over the space. I saw two of the three wretched androids hanging from the ceiling, but I wasn't sure where the third one went. The two metal bars that it used to hang on were bent and broken. I walked down the room and slowly observed them hanging on their steel arms. Something caught my eye as I passed the half destroyed waitress. There was a pair of white eyes staring at me from behind the android, judging me. I pointed the flashlight at the ground beneath it and saw the feet of Tom's stolen suit. I backed up a few feet as a metal hand reached around, pushing the waitress off of the steel hooks, and dropping her onto the floor with a loud crash. In front of me, was this horrid sight of a machine filled with life of evil. I could tell by the way it stared at me, it had no good intentions. The suit's protective shielding was completely removed exposing what was wearing the suit. An android with no limbs, connected from the back of his head to the suit's main processor, stared at me giving me goosebumps. It tilted its head sideways and said in an ear scratching voice, "Hello little girl."

I raised the glock pistol and shot it in the face multiple times, not seeming to have any effect. I took off running back towards the stairs by the storage room. I heard the doors behind me slam open, followed by the sound of a dozen violins playing off key, torn in a digital tone. I didn't look back though I heard the sounds of heavy footsteps behind me. I didn't know how close it was but I could tell it was getting closer. Each second I thought, now is when I die, now is when he gets me. My feet carried me up the stairs and into the courtyard, quicker than before. I kept going and going, the footsteps behind me becoming closer, close enough that I could feel their impact on the floor. At any second, I felt that I could be knocked onto the ground and killed with one massive swoop of its fists. I rounded the corner out of the courtyard and began running to the front doors of the complex. I got closer and closer to the pedestal where the iron statue would go, and I was so close. My feet were swept out from under me and I was whipped under the pedestal. A black hand covered my mouth while the other arm held me tight. I screamed into the furry hand and tried to kick my way free. But instead I was dragged around to the opposite side of the pedestal, and spotted the wretched suit standing a little distance away from me. I now realized who had a hold on me as a snout came into view above my head. Lexis was holding me, keeping me from screaming and moving. I tried to free myself, but every time I moved, she tightened her grip. It felt like she would crush me, holding me so tight that I felt my joints pop. The suit looked back and forth for where I disappeared, unaware of my proximity to it. He began walking towards us when Lexis backed around the pedestal and out of view. I breathed against her hand with my nose, choking on the fur that I inhaled. In the distance I heard quick footsteps as I made out the light shape of bellbottom pants and bright blue eyes.

Jackson came fast from the distance and leapt into the air sending both him and the suit crashing down onto the floor, sliding the axe off into the darkness. The two tumbled for a little ways until Jackson managed to get a choke hold on the suit. The wretched thing managed to twist its head and arms backwards to push itself and Jackson off of the ground. It turned its legs back in a full one-eighty, now facing itself at Jackson. The suit managed to pry Jackson off, and threw him backwards into a wall. Jackson caught a flying punch and kicked the head of the android causing the metal connectors to snap and pop. Jackson stood up and threw a few punches himself, but they were harmlessly blocked off. Lexis stood up with me in her arms, still covering my mouth and brought me into a closed space. She put me down releasing her hand from my face and turned her head to look at me. I didn't yell or scream because it seemed that Lexis did not want to hurt me. In fact, I think she's been protecting me the entire time. She had her hands up in a gesture to stay there and slowly backed away from me. Her body was perfectly blended in with the darkness, except for a faint outline. Behind her I could see Jackson land through a stack of boards with the creature over him, holding a broken wooden plank like a knife. Lexis flew over and drilled the creature in the side. She landed on all fours as the creature rolled across the floor, tumbling from the impact. But as quick as it was knocked down, it got back up. Jackson stood up from the pile of now broken studs and walked over into the dark, seeming to be searching for something. The suit swung at Lexis, but was easily outmaneuvered. Lexis took a hold on the android's neck and began pulling on it. Again a popping sound came from too much pressure on its neck. Lexis fell into a choke hold as she tried to get away, but the machine had both of its massive metal hands around her neck, holding her in the air. It brought her closer to its face and said, "You, and your friend will never make it out because you simply don't understand what you have gotten yourselves into."

Lexis brought up her hands in fists and slammed them down onto the machine's elbows. She brought her head down as it collided with the android's, causing it to let her go. The creature's head seemed to be a little loose as it stumbled from the impact.

"Come on stupid suit, work!"

An object came sliding past me and bumped Lexis in the heel. She picked up a double sided axe stained red from only one thing, blood. Lexis held the axe with her right hand as she slowly advanced towards the wretched android. Her body was seemingly glistening in the little light from the adhesive in her skin, cuts loudly pronounced by an exposed metal frame. She, again, ducked under a swing from the android, and swung the axe.

A loud metal shear echoed across the room as a large chunk of metal fell off of the suit, clanging as it hit the floor. Lexis backed off as the machine began swinging wildly with its hands. She swung the axe directly into the foot of the android causing it to fall belly first onto the floor. She hopped onto its back as it tried to get up, and swung the axe sideways into its neck. She took hold of its skull frame that stuck out from its head and pulled on it. The android managed to stand up, and it began whirling in circles to throw Lexis off of its back. She pulled as hard as she could on the axe, and with a loud snap, her body flew backwards towards me, sliding right into my feet. The machine slowly stopped and I could see the bottom jaw of the android still attached to the suit. The top half of the head was in Lexis' hand, and a broken axe was in the other. With a loud thud, the wretched android fell onto the floor, finally giving up Tom's suit. Lexis looked at me with a sense of relief. I knew she was trying to help me, but I didn't like the thought of an android being able to reason. It scared me that something made of metal and numbers was capable of so much more. I never liked these things in the first place and I don't like them now. As Lexis reached out her hand to lift me up, I backed away and took off for the door. Looking back, I saw her standing there with her ears flat, almost seeming sad. I burst through the front doors of the entrance and sprinted for the car.

"Josh! Start the car!"

I jumped into the passenger seat of the car not caring to figure out what just happened.

"Go-go-go-go!"

Josh took off, the tires screaming on the parking lot pavement creating a comfortable distance between us and the building. In the rearview mirror I saw two dark figures, one with bellbottoms, staring at us as we entered the highway towards town. I wonder what would happen since we left these things alone? They would probably be wandering the town, looking for someone to dance with.

'How come you didn't speak to her?'

'I don't know how! I can't figure out how to speak out loud. We are talking in each other's heads.'

Jackson seemed to be puzzled by my statement. I looked down at the fur on my body which was covered in a sparkly adhesive from my skin, glistening brightly in the starlight like glitter.

'Um… Morgan?'

'What.'

'What did you do to your clothes?'

I realized that I was standing in the open with nothing but fur to cover me.

'I took them off to hide in the dark, and it worked! I caught Adalyne and hid her from that wretched thing.'

'Well…'

'Well what!? Don't look!'

We walked back into the complex looking for the stack of studs where I left my clothes. I knew I was an android that had the characteristics of a human, but it was weird to be in a body that wasn't human. I glanced at a cut on my arm that was shining in the little light there was, and managed to conjure up the courage to stick my hand inside. It didn't hurt like I thought it would, but I stuck my hand through my arm and poked it out the other side. It was disturbing to see what I really was, a metal machine with this fake body over it. A cloth item hit me in the head as Jackson poked his head up from behind the stack of wall studs. As quickly as I took them off to hide, I had my clothes on the way they were before. I held the lip on the back of my top as I tried to find the velcro, each time accidentally sticking my arm to it instead.

'Hey Jackson, can you get this?'

I pulled my hair up as Jackson pulled the two ends together.

'Morgan, you have two perfectly cut holes on your shoulder blades.'

'I have what?'

Jackson took my right hand and put it on the hole on my left shoulder blade. It was the size of my hand and It felt like something was connected to this thing, then was ripped off. Jackson felt his back for such a hole with both hands.

'Do I have it too?'

Jackson turned his back to me, but all I saw was fur. No holes, and no exposed metal.

'No, You have just a regular back.'

'Weird, it's like they were put there on purpose, but it gets covered up by your top.'

I thought about what they were for, but I couldn't think of any reason. My thoughts turned to my tail that was somehow uninjured from the fight. I twisted my body to get a better look at it, then I tried to move it.

'What are you doing?'

'I'm trying to figure out how to move my tail.'

Jackson started laughing a little.

'What?'

'It looks like you're doing a weird dance.'

I finally got it to twitch just once, almost like waking up a dead limb. Trying to move a separate limb was more difficult than I would imagine.

'Hey Morgan, look at this.'

I turned to Jackson who was repeatedly bringing his ears to a point, then back down against his head.

'How are you doing that?'

'I don't know... I move them as if it was a um... a... I don't know. I also figured out how to make a shushing sound. I don't know how, but I can still breathe.'

'Oh wait! We could whisper to people.'

I again tried to move my tail and finally, I pulled it to the left without turning the rest of my body. My hopes went up as I was able to make a full circle with my tail.

'Yes. I got it!'

Again and again I contorted my tail into different angles, testing where I could and couldn't go with it. I heard some electronic whirring and when I looked back at Jackson, he had managed to get the entire skin off of his android body and onto the floor. He stood there, only in his skeletal frame, and looked at the entirety of his metal body.

'Wow I look...'

'Ugly.'

'Hey.'

Jackson began turning around and I stood there observing all of the inner parts of his metal body. The metal frame was indeed a very close replica of the human skeleton. Hydraulics were in places where the metal covers were missing, and the plastic plates that covered his body appeared to be made for holding the shape of his skin. I walked over and picked up his skin from the floor. I felt happy. Happy that the monster that killed me and Jackson was dead. I bet Adalyne must have been heartbroken when she found out. Imagine what she'll do when she discovers that it's truly me, just not in my regular appearance.

'Great, now how do I get that skin back on?'

Jackson began reaching for the skin, but I pulled it away from him."

'Morgan, come on. Give me the skin... my skin.'

I took off running down towards the main hall with Jackson close behind."

'Morgan!'

I dropped the skin onto the floor, and he picked it up quickly. I watched as he put it on as a coat, his arms and legs sliding into the skin. There was the quiet sound of servos as the skin became part of his body again.

'Come here you!'

Jackson leapt for me but I managed to slip away from him. I squealed as he tried to grab my arm, running down the grand hall. I could hear him laugh from behind me as the distance between us closed. I laughed almost the entire time.

'Jackson, quit chasing me!'

I felt a hand take a hold on my shoulder pushing down a little too much, causing me to fall forwards and slide to a stop. I rolled over and saw Jackson's smile. He was probably enjoying our time just as much as I was, until his smile faded away. He rolled off onto the floor next to me, and sighed.

'What's wrong?'

'Oh… since we're… dead, what are we supposed to do? We can't eat, we can't sleep.'

'Only because we haven't tried.'

'Well I still feel alive, like I didn't die. I still want to have a family, but we both know that's impossible. I still want to go out and see the world. I fear though, that when other people see us, all they will see is a very sophisticated robot, like we're still someone's belongings.'

I now knew what Jackson meant. I felt like a person, but I clearly wasn't. I still had the desire to raise a family… he's right. We should be dead, but we're not? How could we still be on this planet even after experiencing death? Are we supposed to do something? Maybe we were supposed to save my sister from that thing, but that's over now. She's safe and sound with… my eyes widened as I realized what we'd forgotten. Before I could mutter one word to Jackson, someone in the distance spoke.

"Hello?"

Jackson and I stood up and looked at a woman sneaking in through the front doors.

'Jackson, who is that?'

'I bet it's that reporter.'

I wonder if she would freak if she saw us? I began walking towards her in the open.

'Morgan! Stay back! She'll run from us!'

'No! She might not be scared of us.'

I turned back around to the woman who was looking in our direction with a flashlight shining on both of us. I waved my hand at her to come over, but she just stared. I took a couple of steps towards her, and just like Jackson said she would, she took off running in the opposite direction.

'Well you've done it now.'

'Oh shut up. She can't be here, so you go that way and we'll catch her in the middle.'

Are we going to try to scare her?'

'Without hurting her, so she leaves.'

'All right.'

We both took off running, Jackson to cut in front of her, and me to stay behind her. I caught up to her quickly, but I kept my distance at a few yards. She shined her flashlight behind her expecting me not to be there, but when she saw me, she let out the loudest scream I've ever heard, and took off running faster. I didn't know it when it happened, but my ears had flattened themselves to my head when I recoiled to her scream. She made an unexpected turn down into the skinny basement stairway, slipping, and stumbling down onto her face. She slowly slid down the stairs, belly down, and came to rest at the bottom. She rolled over and clasped her face with both of her hands to stop the blood that was running from her nose, through her fingers, and onto the floor. As I got close to her, I noticed that she had her eyes closed gasping in pain. I hated the way she talked about J.T. Cybernetics, she was always so negative. I pushed the thought aside as she tried to stand up, but quickly fell over again. I caught her in my arms before she could hit the floor and I elevated her head. She still had her eyes closed and her nose clasped in her hands when Jackson crested the top of the stairs.

'What happened?'

'She tripped, fell on her face, and slid down the stairs.'

'Ouch, that's going to leave a mark.'

She finally opened her eyes and stared directly at me. She took one hand and pushed against my face, rocking her body to try to get away still dazed from her fall. She started whimpering too, scared to death of my appearance. Her breathing didn't slow and I could feel her heart rate through her back begin to skyrocket. I thought about what would make her calm without speaking to her. The only thing I could do is speak with motion.

'Jackson, take her hand.'

'What? I thought we were scaring her off...'

'Just do it!'

Jackson reached out and lightly took her hand in his. She tried to push it away, slowly becoming stronger after her fall, and began to fidget even more. I looked at her again with a worried face. Will anyone not be scared of us? Even after we saved Adalyne's life, she still ran away in fear. As I stared into the reporters eyes, I could feel her heartbeat begin to slow down and she didn't seem to fight us so much. She pulled her hand free from Jackson and held her nose with both hands, but this time she said in a shaky voice,

"Holy crap this hurts!"

She tilted her head back and pinched the ridge of her nose, her face streaked with blood.

'Jackson, go find a towel or napkins, something to get the blood off her face.'

Jackson walked off towards the storage room looking for anything of use. The reporter opened her mouth, breathed in quickly, and breathed back out slowly. For the first time since I remember being this android, someone asked me a legitimate question.

"What are you?... Why..."

I wanted to say something, but I simply couldn't figure it out! Her heart beat slowed to its normal rate, and her breathing became more stable. She moved to stand up and I assisted her, holding her arms as she began to put weight on her shaky feet. She stood there for a couple of seconds before she began to fall over, but she whipped her arm around and held onto my shoulder. My mind raced along as I realized that she was becoming more and more used to me, beginning to believe that I was no threat. She was finally able to stand, capable of catching her own falls. I let go of her hand and she stood there pinching the ridge of her nose. I noticed that the nose ring she once had was now gone, ripped from her face during the fall. Jackson finally appeared with a rag in his hand, partly dirty from the construction in the complex. He looked at her for a couple of seconds, and then gasped.

'Oh her nose ring!'

'Yea... it's gone.

I took the rag and held it out for her to take. A couple of seconds passed before she took the rag and wiped down her face while still being careful around her nose. She didn't run, and she didn't appear to be that frightened anymore. She removed the rag from her face, reached into her purse, and began dabbing her nose with some tissues from her purse. It would've been nice to know that she had tissues. Once the blood was clear, I could see a tear on the left side of her nose where the nose ring used to be. I'm really glad that when I tore out my earrings, I couldn't feel the pain of my tearing skin.

'This is why, Jackson, no one should have nose rings.'

'So they don't fall and get them ripped out while being chased by a robot?'

'...Sure.'

The reporter found a box and sat on it, partly crunching the box. She held a wad of tissues on her nose as she stared at both of us. We stared right back at her and I noticed that she was sitting on something wet. Wait, actually... oh. I guess I would wet myself to if I had a nose ring ripped out along with a concussion.

'Um... Jackson? You wouldn't have happened to spot a pair of pants laying around would you?'

'Pff. No. It's a construction site. Why do you ask?'

'No reason.'

The reporter began rubbing her ears while looking at us. Though we were moving our mouths, only me and Jackson could hear our voices. She soon asked, "How come I can't hear you?"

We just stood there not knowing what to do.

"Can you talk?"

We both shook our heads no.

"Are you part of this place?"

We shook our heads no in response. I looked at her purse and saw the notebook inside. Yes! All reporters carry notebooks. I gestured to her if I could come over, but she didn't seem to understand. I slowly walked over to her, not knowing if she would take off again, and sat down on the ground next to her. She looked at me like she was expecting me to do something violent, but I just pointed to the notebook in her purse.

"Oh... Yes you can write."

I took the notebook that had a pen clipped to it and began writing. I handed it back to her and she read aloud,

"'I'm Morgan.' Like you have the same name as the one that died?"

I took the notebook, wrote down some more words, and handed it back to her.

"'No, I'm the one that was killed.' What do you mean?"

Jackson had made his way over to the other side of the reporter and sat down on the floor.

"Prove to me that you're telling the truth."

I took the notebook and wrote the words, 'I was cut into the side by an axe and Jackson was shot in the head.' She read it and suddenly became scared again.

"Wait, what if you killed them!?"

I put my hand on top of hers, holding her there calmingly as Jackson took the notebook and wrote something down. He handed it to the reporter and she said,

"Wait, You're saying that you're the one who arrested me when I blew in the building's front windows!"

Jackson nodded his head yes, and the reporter began to rock back and forth thinking about her current situation. She dabbed her nose with her tissues and said to Jackson.

"If you really are Jackson, and you are actually Morgan."

She looked at me and continued.

"How did you end up like this?"

I didn't know how to respond, or what to write. I was clueless on how I became the thing I am. I looked up at Jackson who appeared to be sad. He had his ears pinned back and his eyes closed.

'You alright Jackson?'

'Morgan… I need to tell you something.'

'Ok… what is it?'

Jackson and I walked around the corner of some shelving, I turned around and he put his hands on my shoulders.

'Before we died, I… I…'

'Come on, you can tell me.'

'I … was going to ask you to marry me.'

I stood there, frozen in my feet. All of my responses had been thrown out by his sentence. I was kind of expecting anything but that one sentence.

'Morgan?'

I broke eye contact with him, not knowing what to say, my mouth hanging open.

'I … I don't know…'

Jackson looked at me square in the eyes and asked,

'If we were still alive, what would you have said?'

I stood there frozen in my thoughts.

'I …'

I couldn't help but stutter, trying to tell him yes, but all that came out was,

'I um, uh … I …'

I pulled from Jackson's arms and walked off into the darkness of the room. Thoughts of what would've happened if I were still alive played through my head. I was so close to having a family?! I fell onto my knees, crying if I could, thinking about everything I would miss out on. A wedding, having kids, watching those kids grow up to have their kids.

'Morgan, I'm so sorry. I should've kept my mouth shut.'

Jackson was kneeling next to me with a hand on my back.

'No it's just… I would've said yes, but now it feels impossible. What are two possessed androids supposed to do in life? Perform?'

Jackson didn't say a word. He was caught on the thought of being here, stuck in this situation for God knows how long.

'I want to leave so bad, but I don't know how. And if I did, you'd be stuck here by yourself for as long as this body lasts, and I don't want that. I want to be together even if we don't appear as we once did.'

I realized that we can still do so much, and we still have a family. My sister Adalyne, and our massive family back home was what I still had. Our conversation was ripped away as a screeching metal sound came from the loading ramp room.

'Jackson, we need to leave.'

Jackson nodded his head as I walked over to the reporter. She asked, "What was that sound?"

I ignored her question and took her hand, gesturing to her to leave with us.

"Wait. What's going on!?"

There was a shriek of a dozen violins playing off tune from each other, faded with a digital voice. I picked up the reporter as Jackson ran by.

'Not friends! Let's go!' yelled Jackson.

I carried the reporter up the stairs and out towards the front door, setting her down right at the entrance. I saw her car outside and pointed at it.

"You want me to leave?"

I nodded my head quickly and began pushing her towards the door. She finally took the message as a loud crash sounded from the distance.

'Morgan!'

'I know Jackson!'

Jackson held the door open for the woman, seemingly slow compared to us, and we ran out into the parking lot. I looked back and saw four pairs of eyes staring through the entrance's front windows. I continued to run further from the place not looking back. The reporter was in her car already near the highway, and Jackson was at the parking lot edge watching the eyes in the windows.

'Come on! I don't know if they'll follow us!'

I caught up to him and we took off towards town. We both had the same plan and the same destination to go to. We needed to find Adalyne.

Chapter 12

Josh closed the door of the rear passenger seat and led James up to his Grandfather. They stood and talked for a little bit before James and his Grandfather walked into Jackson's house. Josh sat down in the driver's seat, tired from staying up so late.

"What time is it?"

I looked at the car's clock and said, "It's 12:54."

"No wonder it feels so late."

I laughed at his comment and he laughed with me. I yawned and said, "Why don't we go to your place. They found me at my home, and they will come back looking for me."

"Well what if they know where I live? It's not like there are plenty of places to hide."

"I think it'll be ok."

Josh drove out of the residential zone and onto the highway through town down towards the RV rental center. We made a U turn back down on the freeway and drove a ways until we turned down an exit and onto Mullowney lane. Eventually we made it to the Grand Slam apartments and parked next to the tall oak tree at the end of the apartment building. I awkwardly walked to the front door as Josh unlocked it with a pair of keys. My body was tired, sweaty, and hot from so much running. I never knew I could run like that. But when you're facing death, I guess you'd do anything. We walked inside, happy to be in a somewhat comfortable home. Josh flopped face down onto the couch, and I sat down in the chair across from the coffee table. We didn't turn on the TV, and we didn't do anything else. My throat was dry and sore, scratching at me like I swallowed a bug.

"Do you have anything to drink?"

Josh refrained from lifting his head from the pillow his face was stuffed in, and spoke in a muffled voice.

"Yea, there's cups in the cupboard left of the sink, or there's Cola or Pepsi in the fridge."

I filled a large glass of water, drank it quickly, and filled it again. I sat down on the chair and put my glass of water on the coffee table. I wondered why Lexis was protecting me. Was it part of the programming? Or… was someone controlling her by remote? I left that thought as I took another mouthful of water. Josh sat up on the couch and stared at his TV with bags under his eyes. I could smell the sweat from my body, covering me in a fog of dread.

"Josh, do you mind if I take a quick shower?"

"Yes, that's fine."

I finished my glass of water and walked into the bathroom. There wasn't much stuff in here, only simple hygiene products. A shower was probably the best idea I could think of. It would be relaxing.

I sat there toggling the TV remote between stations trying to find something interesting to watch. The news? On the news, there was a video of main street being flooded with protestors. They had pictures of Morgan, Jackson, and Tom on signs strewn across the crowd. Nope. I flipped between more stations. Football, Castle, Forged in Fire, Alone, Twilight, Star Trek, a weird cartoon. There was simply nothing worth watching at the moment… ah here we go. I finally found a channel playing a rodeo, and it was even from the local arena. I leaned back on my couch enjoying the rodeo when I heard a neighbor's dog go nuts.

I let the warm water massage my back as I peered out of a small window in the shower. I was beginning to fall asleep, tired from all of the running I had done. My arm was bruised from doing something I don't remember, probably when I was in the tech complex. One of my toenails was chipped, bleeding only a little. And there was only a small cut on my leg, but other than that, I was relatively unharmed. I began to go through more memories of me and my sister from the past twenty or more years. I remember when I was about thirteen, Morgan had brought her boyfriend home to play some games. She left him in the basement as we put on exact matching clothing upstairs to play a prank on him. There was a laundry chute in the back closet that I used to climb my way down into the basement, and Morgan distracted him while I landed in a pile of laundry. She told him she'd be right back, and went upstairs. I got out of the pile of laundry and snuck up behind him and yelled, I'm back! He jumped so high, he must have hit his head on the rafters. And then he couldn't figure out how I got down here. Morgan came back down and he realized we were twins. We laughed until our ribs hurt. I haven't laughed like that in a long time. I pulled myself away from my thoughts as I found a clump of some sort in my hair. I pulled on it, tried to comb it out, and I tried holding it in front of my face to see what it was. Its texture in my hand was somewhat rubbery, but it still held its shape. I pulled on the individual clump, feeling progress as it made its way, slowly, down my hair. It got to the point where I could see what it was. A chunk of glue was frozen in my hair from one of the androids. I finally pulled it free, taking a couple of hairs with it. I reached around the curtain and set it on the counter next to the sink. I felt the floor shake a little, but I thought it was just me. Then the floor shook again, much harder than before. Is Josh moving something around? The floor shook a third time as I turned off the shower, shaking the mirror above the sink. I heard Josh yell something as I stepped out of the shower. Is he in trouble? I took a towel, wrapped it around me, and slowly opened the door to the hallway. I saw, at the end of the hall, a window broken in with shattered glass on the floor where something had forced its way in. I heard heavy footsteps as a black figure holding Josh by the throat, dragged him over into the living room only a couple of yards away. Lexis had a large kitchen knife in her other hand, holding it very threateningly. She threw Josh onto the couch sideways and raised the knife into the air. I knew that if I didn't do something, Josh would surely be killed by her. I ran out of the bathroom and over towards the couch. I lost my sister, my great uncle, and I'm not going to lose my friend! As Lexis began to bring her arm down upon Josh, I threw myself on top of him and held my hand out towards Lexis, my eyes shut tight. I stayed there for a couple of seconds before I opened my eyes to the sight of a giant steak knife in my face. Lexis had her eyes wide open as she stared into my eyes, seemingly confused by my actions. She took a few steps away from us and looked back and forth at me and Josh. Each glance seemed to make her more and more agitated, until she dropped the knife. She threw her hands down onto the coffee table, breaking the glass out of frustration. Lexis was pacing back and forth, running her hands through her hair and over her ears. She seemed to calm herself down a little and looked back at us. She slowly reached over to us, but I kicked her hand away with my bare foot. Lexis reached over to the chair and took a blanket that was on its head rest, and as I stood up off of Josh, she tried to throw the blanket on top of me.

"You stay away...!"

"Adalyne!"

I turned to Josh who was still sitting on the couch.

"She's here to protect you from me. There was only some miscommunication."

Lexis looked at him with a confused face, one ear pinned up to a point.

"What do you mean Josh? How do you know she's here to protect me? She almost killed you!"

Josh stood up from the couch and slowly walked over to Lexis.

"She is just a trapped soul in one of my father's wretched inventions."

My mind could not comprehend what he was saying, twisting to fit his words. Josh continued talking to me.

"Over the years of my life I had seen this happen only twice. She's scared, frightened of what she's become."

"Who Josh!? And how do you know!?"

"Your sister Morgan! That's who it is! And I know because I have seen this before. Not to her, but to people that I have known."

Is it true? The reason that Lexis has been protecting me this whole time was because she's... my sister? Lexis leaned toward Josh, seeming to understand his reasoning. They both looked at me and then Lexis held out her hand for me to take. I resisted the urge to do so until Josh reached for my hand.

"Adalyne, trust me. She isn't going to hurt you."

Josh took my right hand and put it into Lexis'. I didn't know what to expect from her, and I didn't want to find out. Lexis put her other hand on top of mine and then formed my hand into a fist as she began the first few steps of me and Morgan's secret handshake. I eventually caught on and we went through the handshake over and over again until we made no mistakes. She stopped, held my hand in both of hers, and stared into my eyes.

"Morgan?"

This had to be her. There's no way an android could remember my secret handshake from almost fifteen years ago. A tear formed on my wet face as I began to truly realize that this really was my sister.

"Morgan!?"

Lex... Morgan leaned in and wrapped her arms around me happily. She seemed to be crying, but there was no sound of her sobs. Only her unsteady breath was heard as she held onto me. The longer we held onto each other, the more I believed that since Lexis was Morgan, Jackson had to be… well Jackson. Then the thought occurred to me that she hadn't spoken one word to me yet.

"How come you haven't said anything yet?"

Morgan leaned back, folded her ears against her head, and broke her gaze upon me. Maybe she doesn't know what to say. Josh stood there scratching his head, puzzled by the same question. Before I could say anything else, Morgan took my hand and led me back into the bathroom. She picked my clothes up off of the floor and handed them to me, shutting the bathroom door behind her. I quickly put my dirty clothes back on and stepped back out to the duo standing in the living room. I saw Morgan disappear into the bedroom looking for something as I walked over to Josh who had his arms crossed, looking at his smashed coffee table.

"Darn that thing was expensive."

I was drying my hair in a towel as I stared at the shattered glass on the floor.

"Don't get too worried. I bet Tom has a spare coffee table I could give you."

"Thanks Adalyne."

I turned around and saw that the cabinets above the kitchen counter were knocked onto the floor from the struggle.

"And I think I could pay off the damage to that."

"Thanks, but that won't be necessary. My security deposit will cover it."

I heard the front door open as the sight of Jackson came into view, threatening to harm Josh. Morgan finally returned from Josh's bedroom with a pen and a stack of printing paper. Before Jackson could do anything, Morgan had already said something to him that was inaudible to us. Her mouth moved to fit words, but her voice was absent from the conversation. Josh leaned close to my ear and said,

"I have no idea why they can't speak. When I was around other androids like this, I couldn't get them to shut up."

"What happened to them?"

Josh seemed to ponder on the question for a moment, but soon responded.

"It's almost as if their souls have been… what's the word?... Digitized into the machines."

I felt Josh get ripped away from me as Jackson had a hand on both of his shoulders. Was Jackson keeping Josh and I separated? I reached out and took Josh back from Jackson, and Jackson let him go with a puzzled face. Morgan put her hand in front of Jackson, keeping him away from Josh.

He pointed at us and looked at Morgan seeming to be asking a question. Morgan answered him with a simple nod of her head. Jackson threw his arms into the air in frustration and let them fall back down to his sides. Josh and I sat on the couch, and watched Morgan write something down on a piece of paper. Josh took it and read it aloud.

"I'm so happy you didn't run. I haven't figured out how to speak yet, but I will."

Morgan handed me a piece of paper and it said. 'I'm sorry if I scared you before, I was protecting you.'

"Morgan, for a couple of seconds I thought about that also, but I was too scared of what was going on. Everything moved so fast after..."

I held myself from saying those awful words. Morgan seemed to catch on as I wiped away a tear on my face. Morgan then quickly wrote down some more words and handed me the paper.

'You saw my dead body didn't you?' Seeing those words brought me back to the moment when I saw pictures of her injury. That sinister gash running across her spine and around her side, exposing her inner organs. I burst down into tears and said,

"Not just yours. I saw Jackson's and Tom's, and I felt like I was the only one that was here anymore! I felt completely alone."

Morgan seemed to be sad. Sad that I had to go through what I did, and sad that she couldn't be her usual self anymore. She walked over, knelt down to my eye level, looked at me with those bright blue eyes, and held my hands in hers. She leaned in and gave me another hug hoping to calm me down. I wonder what it's like to be an android? I still don't like how these things were so humanly accurate in the first place. The ability to breath, to move like a human, to speak like a human. Even the fact that you can style these androids with different clothing scared me. It scared me by how close they are to being humans, yet appearing completely different. Morgan reached over, took a piece of paper, and wrote down a few more words. 'It's weird being this body, but I've figured out a few things.' Morgan backed right into the front of the TV. She flattened her ears and brought them to a point repeatedly, sometimes only moving one ear. She then moved her tail around without moving the rest of her body. I'm really curious on what it's like to be in her shoes; to have a tail? That would be something to get used to. Morgan then took her left hand and stuck it under her right arm's skin. It made me cringe to watch the other side of her arm get pushed out by her fingers. It reminded me of Dr. Pimple Popper. I never knew why Morgan liked to watch that show, it would always make me gag. My thoughts were interrupted by the neighbor's dog going berserk.

We all looked at the open window and then back at each other. Was it a neighbor? I went to the door and almost opened it when Morgan put her hand on the doorknob first. She pushed me back as she opened the door by a crack. As she peered out into the darkness, she brought up her hand and waved for us to back up. She slowly closed the door and turned the lock. Morgan leaned up against the door, turned out the lights in the room, and as soon as the lights went out, a pair of dim white eyes stared in through the broken window, searching... observing. It began to poke its head into the room and turned towards Morgan. She brought her shadowy tail up in front of the creature in an attempt to hide herself from its gaze. The creature continued to stare into the room, the parking lot lights shining through the gaps in its body. I could make out the shape of a half molten face that looked like one of the burned androids I scrapped back at the tech complex, but... what is it doing here? It slowly pulled its head back out of the window, walked out into the parking lot, and disappeared into the darkness. My heart was hitting the ribs of my chest like a hammer, audible to me and Josh. Morgan seemed to relax a little and left the front door, still concentrating on the shattered window. Jackson, who had both of us crammed in the kitchen, walked over to Morgan and stared out into the dark abyss.

"Josh, you can let me go now."

"Sorry."

Josh released his arms from around me and walked out of the kitchen.

He seemed to be embarrassed by his own actions, perhaps scared of that wretched thing as much as I was. He walked over to the bedroom window on the opposite side of the apartment to keep an eye out for the android. Morgan and Jackson were looking out the front door windows, and I decided to watch out of the kitchen window. There wasn't much to see, but a couple of times there were headlights that shined on something that may have been important. Some people walked by, unaware of the lurking danger. I continued to stare into the dark, hoping that whatever stared in through the window was gone. I looked back at Morgan and said,

"I think it's gone."

Morgan slowly shook her head at me, telling me in plain English that this wasn't over. I dropped down from the window and saw the lever action twelve gauge shotgun over the couch. I bet that thing would do some damage to androids. I stood up and looked back out of the kitchen window... and... I wanted to say something but my throat choked. I stared out through the window and into the white eyes of a monster. The street lights were just bright enough to shimmer off of the screws in its mouth that once held its rubber teeth. I tapped the counter rapidly with my right hand to get everyone's attention. I began to move sideways, its eyes following me, and out of the kitchen. I jumped in place as a hand touched my shoulder, but calmed myself when I realized that it was Jackson's. He pulled me back further from the window as the eyes backed up and out of view. I looked at Morgan who had a deadlock-stare on the window, making sure that if it did come back, she'd be prepared for it. This awful sound of off key violins shook the room as an android came blasting through the front door, knocking it flat to the ground. He jumped on top of Jackson and bit down on his arm. Morgan tackled the burned android and slammed it into the wall. I slid behind the fight and took the shotgun from the case above the couch.

"Josh where's the ammo!?"

As Morgan held the android against the wall, Jackson took a leg from the broken coffee table and slammed it down on his head, resulting in no effect. The machine launched Morgan across the room, pinning me to the couch as Jackson took the full force of the machine's attack. Morgan stood up, whipped around to see if I was hurt, then turned her attention back to the fight. Josh came right up to me and started to load the shotgun.

"Adalyne listen,"

My mind was torn by the sight of the android's broken mouth taking a hold on Jackson's tail.

"You have five shots before you run out. It's all I have!... Adalyne!"

"Yes Josh, I got it!"

I responded to him though I didn't hear what he said. I took the shotgun and loaded the rounds as Morgan was thrown into the kitchen, and Jackson into the bedroom. The android crookedly turned his head to me as I aimed at his left eye. With a loud boom from the shotgun, the left side of its face shattered and broke from the rest of his body. He looked back at me, his left eye gone, and was smashed in the head by the fist of my sister's hand. It stumbled a little before Jackson tackled him with full speed, launching him through the doorway and into the oak tree outside. I reloaded a round with the lever of the gun, throwing the expended shell onto the floor. Before I could fire another shot, the android threw Jackson backwards and took off running. I walked over to Josh's car, and almost had a hold on the door handle when Morgan put her hand on it first, keeping me from opening it. Morgan looked at me and I could tell that she wanted me to stay.

"Morgan, I'm coming to help you, you saw what this gun will do to it."

Morgan shook her head no, and took off running after the android, Jackson following close behind. Josh was standing in the doorway of his home, his face riddled with fear.

"Let me guess… you're going to go kill that thing and you want me to stay here."

"Yep, you have a brace on your leg, you'd be an open target."

Josh walked over to me and closed the door as I sat down in the driver seat of his car. I rolled down the window and said,

"Josh I promise I'll be right back."

"Please don't get hurt. It's been so long since I've had anyone to care about."

My heart felt… oh what's the word for it? I motioned for Josh to lean in closer as I put my hand on the back of his neck. He seemed to be caught off guard by my choice to kiss him, but he let it happen. Josh then broke off and said, "Now you promised to come back."

I put the car in reverse and backed away from the apartment.

"I will Josh!"

I took off towards the tech complex with the shotgun in the passenger seat, and Josh standing in the rear view mirror. This may have been a mistake to return to the complex. Who knows what will happen when I get inside. I sped down the freeway, across the river. Made a U turn at the RV rental center, and crossed the river again into town. I could see the giant building from the bottom of town, the giant glass windows on the side reflecting the moon and stars. Trees were planted around it, partially blocking it from view. What did Josh tell me in the apartment? Something about the gun? And how did Morgan and Jackson make it through town without anyone noticing, especially since they were chasing that android? I don't know but I'm going to find out what is going on in that place! I turned the corner around the edge of the ravine and drove up towards the complex. As I drove down the road off of the highway, I could see the front doors of the entrance wide open, and the parking lot completely barren. I parked the car a little ways from the place so I could prepare myself on the walk over. My body shook at the unknown mysterious creatures that may or may not kill me. With the shotgun in my hands, safety off and trigger ready, I entered the building. I had a flashlight by my side that I found in the glove box of the car and shined it into the darkness of the grand hall. Each step I took assured me that I was making a huge mistake coming back, echoing through the vastness of the great dark. I walked up the entry way stairs and stared at the pedestal in the middle of the Grand entrance. I turned and walked sideways to the left, but was stopped in my tracks by a hand that came out of the darkness and pushed against my body.

Chapter 13

A hand pressed against my body, keeping me from moving any further. I looked up to see Morgan standing right in front of me gazing deep into the dark.

"Morgan, what is it?"

Morgan took my right hand and pulled me over to the side of a wall. She was looking for a place to hide me. She pulled me back behind what looked like a check-out booth. Morgan seemed to try to say something and I finally heard, in a whisper,

"What are you doing here?"

"You… you said something."

"Shhh!... Damn it Adalyne, I told you to stay with Josh."

"I want to help you…"

"No-no-no-no, you can't fight these things by yourself, you'll die!"

"Morgan, I'm helping you…"

"Shh, quiet."

"I'm going to stay…"

Morgan put her hand over my mouth and as I tried to pull it off, light footsteps sounded from the distance towards our direction. I shut my mouth as a figure appeared at the top of the stairs from deep in the building. It ran down to the pedestal looking for something. I realized it was Jackson from the bright blue eyes glowing in the dark. Morgan stood up and hopped over the counter to meet him, talking to him in her head. I poked my head over the counter and looked into the dark. I peered down the halls back and forth a couple of times, and I thought I saw dim beady eyes staring around the corners in the distance. As soon as I looked directly at them, they would dart behind where they were hiding.

"Morgan."

Jackson and Morgan continued to talk to each other, unaware of the creeping danger. I hopped out and walked over behind Morgan. I never realized how tall she was until I tried to poke her in the shoulder. In the bunker I thought she was maybe six feet tall, now she was almost seven feet. When I poked her in the shoulder, my hand was level with my eyes. Morgan still talked to Jackson, waving a hand at me to wait. I poked her harder on the shoulder as something dashed across the darkness.

"Morgan-Morgan-Morgan!"

She whipped around partly irritated.

"There's something over there."

I backed up from the sudden sound of a loud footstep in the distance. Morgan lowered her mouth down to my ears and whispered,

"You shouldn't have come here."

She stepped in front of me, putting me in between the two of them. I glanced around and saw a pair of eyes staring into mine. I looked in the other direction and saw two more eyes… then they disappeared. My heart began to throb in my throat and my hands went cold.

"Morgan… Wasn't there more than just the androids we scrapped?"

Jackson froze in his place, reached over and tapped Morgan on the back of her neck. She looked in the same direction as Jackson and stared at something in the dark. I leaned over from behind Jackson to get a view of what they were looking… at. I could see a dark animal figure with a row of shiny teeth. It stood there, twitching, looking through Jackson and straight at me. It had dim yellow eyes that resembled something of a cat. Its mane was loosely moving sideways as its head twitched back and forth, and its mouth snapped at the uncontrollable urge to jump after me. It growled the sound of a lion stalking its prey, and at that moment, it crept out of the shadows. I moved to look from the other side of Jackson and as soon as I looked at the wretched thing, it ripped its head sideways with my motion. I heard something in the other direction, so I pushed down Morgan's tail to get a good look. I could see, past the pedestal, two figures standing side by side. One was burned and molten from the fire while the other one looked human. It was that bald humanandroid the company built for the showcase. I held the shotgun firmly in my hands as heavy metallic footsteps sounded on the stairs as the half destroyed waitress android came into view. Her legs were backwards as she crookedly walked from the courtyard to us. Each step caused loose plastic plates to shake. On her face, the left side was exposed with wires and hoses hanging uselessly, but she was still able to function. Most of the plastic plates were molten, formed together from the heat of the workshop's fire. I spun around in circles looking at each android. They all twitched and seemed to be staring straight at me, ignoring Morgan and Jackson. The only way to survive these things is… well… There was the sound of awful violins and digital scratching that roared through the air, shaking the atmosphere around us. I heard the sound of metal impacts on the floor as these things charged forward. Jackson went after the lion as Morgan took off towards the other two figures in the dark. I was left in the open as I slowly turned back towards the stairs. The waitress walked down the stairs towards me, well aware of the shotgun in my hands. I could hear the sounds of fighting in the darkness, unable to see what was going on. Jackson reappeared from the shadows and slammed a wood post into the waitress. She fell back as the wood shattered into pieces accompanied by a crackling sound. The lion, who ran towards Jackson, stopped and seemed to change its mind. Its twitchy head slowly turned towards me and locked its gaze upon me. As machines fought in the smell of burning servos, the lion took quick steps towards me. I raised my gun and fired at his head, but it ducked sideways from the shot and landed around corner of a doorway. I reloaded my weapon and aimed to fire again, but before I could, the lion took off into the dark scrambling on all fours. I heard a sound of metal screaming in my ears, followed by a loud bang. I looked over and saw Jackson's foot on the waitress's broken neck hanging over the edge of the pedestal. Jackson hopped off and ran to help Morgan with the other two wretched creatures. I could see the lion in the distance continue to watch and observe the action occurring before us. I knew that he was avoiding me because of the shotgun. Morgan was on top of one machine flying her fist down upon it while the humanandroid stood up in the distance from being knocked down. I could hear the sounds of fighting all around me, and the smell… that awful smell of burning rubber accompanied by something dead consumed me in a dense fog. I ran over to the pedestal and ducked down beneath it, the waitress's limp head hanging in front of me. I poked it with the gun and it twitched. It then began to twist and turn, slowly pulling itself back onto its body. The head flipped up above the edge of the pedestal and with a small creak, it snapped back onto its body. I looked past to see a wretched android fly through the air and land near the front door. As Morgan freed herself from the clutches of the humanandroid, I stood up and began making my way up towards the courtyard to regroup and plan what to do next. There were stacks of cement mix bags just high enough to hide behind. I leaped over and peered across the top of the stack to watch Morgan fight the waitress. She swung her feet to take out the waitress's legs but since they were backwards, they would bend out of the way. The waitress then came up and delivered a heavy fist into Morgan's face. Jackson was holding the lion's jaw only inches from his arm, while the humanandroid took off towards Morgan again. Now's the perfect time! I got up and ran towards the lion to help, bringing up my gun to shoot. The two rolled and tumbled, keeping me from getting a clear shot. They moved towards me, and I almost had a good chance when the lion turned its body in such a way that it pulled Jackson in the way. He finally wrestled himself free and kicked the lion off into the nearby wall. Jackson then turned to me and pointed to the front door.

"No! I'm not leaving."

Jackson held my shoulders seeming to beg for me to leave.

"Jackson, I'm not leaving you two to fight these things by yourselves."

I could see Morgan in the distance fending off the humanandroid as the waitress slowly stood up from being knocked down moments before, and the half destroyed android with the wires for a hand stand up from the entrance where it was thrown before.

"You could get destroyed!"

Jackson shook his head, but before he could do anything else, the lion took his bare claws and sank it into Jackson's shoulder, pulling him back into the fight. I looked back at Morgan who was now swarmed with three wretched androids as they began to lay blows on her like hail on an umbrella. She took the humanandroid by the throat and threw him into the half destroyed android, knocking them both to the ground. The waitress gave a pretty hard hit, but was answered by Morgan with a severe blow, by her foot, to the stomach. The impact was enough to send the waitress into the air, landing her upside down on the pedestal. I was too close to the action so I took off running. I looked back once and I could see the half destroyed waitress slowly get up from the pedestal. I looked forwards and saw what appeared to be an unfinished room at the end of the hall. I heard some heavy footsteps behind me, so I craned my neck to look back. Behind me, on all fours, was the waitress crawling after me like a crocodile rushing after a meal. I could see Jackson and Morgan preoccupied by the other androids, blind of my situation. I sprinted faster towards the room that may not have had a sufficient hiding place. I looked back again and saw the distance between us close by more than half. My heart was beating fast and my feet couldn't move any faster. The waitress android was closing in faster by the second, and it was clear that she would reach me before I would get to the room. Behind me, the quick thumping of her feet and her legs twisted backwards made her appear as a creature of the paranormal. I turned around and fired a shot at her head. She stumbled to avoid the shot and I was able to increase the distance… for a second. She got back up and continued her endless pursuit to catch me. I saw her white eyes track me like the laser pointer on a gun. I managed to pick up the pace a little more as I approached the room, but I could feel the thumping of her footsteps behind me getting closer and closer. I heard the snap of metal springs that could only be her mouth biting at my heels. My body felt a great impact launching me forwards, arms closing tight around me. I closed my eyes and screamed as I feared the worst. I tumbled in the air expecting the impact of the floor at any second, and the fists of the wretched thing to end my life. I landed, but I felt the body of something else break my fall. I opened my eyes and saw the waitress in the air above me mid-flight, her jaw wide open and the screws that once held her plastic teeth shining in the dark room. A pair of legs came up around me and stopped her approach towards my head, shoving her off towards the side. The arms that were wrapped around me came loose, and laid me down on the floor of the room as I realized that Jackson had tackled me before the android could. Jackson turned to the waitress with his arm pulled back with a fist. She pushed Jackson away and backed up to gauge what to do next. Jackson glanced at the box next to him, still keeping an eye on the android. She leapt forwards on her two reversed legs and tackled him to the ground. Right before, Jackson's hand disappeared into the box and pulled out a large pipe wrench. He swung that wrench around, throwing sparks as the tool made contact with the android's face. Jackson shoved the handle into her eye, ripped it out and laid a savage punch to the other eye. The waitress fell to the floor and kicked Jackson's feet out from under him. As Jackson fell face first into her, she opened her broken mouth and snapped it shut on Jackson's snout. She held onto Jackson as they wrestled on the floor. The pipe wrench slid away as the two tumbled around. Jackson took his hands and pried the nail teeth off of his snout before being launched into the ceiling of the room by the waitress's two backward legs, but Jackson used the rafters to angle himself back upright. He landed on top of her and took the wrench from the ground. He held her down on the floor as he hammered her with it, each impact shooting pieces of plastic out in all directions. She finally fell limp as something important was destroyed, but Jackson sat there and continued to pound in the face of the waitress, like he was driving a nail into the hardest wood there ever was. I laid there on the ground shaking uncontrollably, my lungs quivering unnaturally. As Jackson finally gave up hitting her with the pipe wrench, he turned to me and exposed his half ripped up face. I jumped at the sight of his exposed metal frame that I never wanted to see, and imagined what my face would look like if Jackson wouldn't have been here to save my life. I curled up on the floor and let all of my anxiety free, causing my eyes to run like a river. The android's deathly appearance was still fresh in my mind. My body was shaking and my heart was pounding uncontrollably. Jackson's face left its mark in my mind, ensuring that I will never forget my near death experience. I felt a hand slide under my knees and another under my shoulders as I was pulled up into Jackson's body in a comforting hug. I was still alive! I sat there in his arms and wrapped mine around his torn neck. I could feel his bottom jaw press against my back as we held onto each other. I didn't want to let him go. I was still shaking from the trauma that total fear causes. I heard something static erupt in my ear, and then a voice came through. Jackson's clear familiar voice that was his own before he died, spoke to me calmingly.

"There is no need to sob Adalyne. You're ok."

"I know, I'm just happy to be alive!"

"Wait… You heard me?!"

I didn't answer his question and instead continued to cry into his fur.

"I… I figured out how to speak? YES! Oh my God there is so much I wanted to say like, why could this thing pull its head back on, and how do these things function after they were scrapped…"

"Jackson, please."

"Oh, sorry."

My eyes ran dry of tears and my body was becoming too exhausted to shutter.

"Take in a big breath Adalyne. Calm down. Nothing is going to get you as long as we are here to protect you."

I began to feel frustrated towards whoever was behind these heads. Controlling them to do despicable acts upon people they may have never known. I opened my eyes and peered down upon the wretched android that lay on the floor with no recognizable face, flattened by Jackson's rage. I could feel my adrenaline pushing my body to move, wanting to expend energy, so I let go of Jackson.

"Ok, I can stand."

Jackson cautiously put me down onto my feet. I looked at his body that was torn in places exposing the steel skeleton underneath. His left hand didn't have any cover on it anymore and his snout where the waitress had bitten was missing its skin too. The pants he wore were ripped at the knees and shredded at the ankles. He still had the majority of his skin, but it made him look like a zombie.

"You all right Adalyne?"

"Yes I'm fine."

I checked my arms and legs to make sure I wasn't bleeding from anywhere, then I realized my finger was cut severely on the knuckle. A burning pain came up from the screams of fear and adrenaline that had swallowed my body when I knew I was going to die. In my search for injuries, I hadn't noticed the shotgun in Jackson's hands. He handed it to me slightly covered in the adhesive from his torn skin. I asked, "Are you ok? You're torn to shreds."

Jackson looked at his hands for a couple of moments before he answered.

"I can't feel pain. I can feel, if you understand that, but I can't get the pain, the one thing that makes me human among so much more."

I could see him contemplate the thought of being stuck for as long as his body lasts. I wonder if he's seen his body, the one at the morgue. I could see that his tail had the very end ripped off exposing steel joints that resembled something of a spine wrapped in tendons of wires.

"How are you and Morgan going to get out of this?"

"I don't know. Something in me wants to stay-don't get me wrong, I miss my own body. I know Morgan misses hers, especially after I told her about the ring I bought."

My heart erupted in a cold pain. Nothing would eat away at my sister more than the thought of losing the chance at anything... especially her life. We heard a crash sound from the distance, and rushed out to the pedestal, and over to the courtyard. Jackson and I stood there in amazement as Morgan fended off the three remaining androids. The lion jumped into the air, but Morgan swung her foot up into its face using his momentum to worsen the impact. The burned android came from behind and the humanandroid from the side. She ran towards the burned android and jumped into the air hoping to take hold of its head, but it used the wires hanging out of his left wrist as a whip, and threw Morgan off balance as she landed. The trio jumped on top of her and held her face down to the ground.

"Well, let's see how much speed I have."

Jackson took off running, accelerating at an unhuman velocity. The spaciousness of the main hall was big enough to allow Jackson a few seconds of running before he collided with the humanandroid. Jackson drove him right into the cement floor throwing more sparks into the air. Morgan brought up her feet and drilled the other android in the head as the lions claws were twisted backwards to keep its hold on Morgan as she stood up. The burned android whipped its wires into her arm tearing a gash into her skin. The second time the android swung, Morgan took and held fast to the wires and put her other hand under his armpit. She swung him around into the lion and the two went tumbling onto the floor. Jackson, on the other side of the room, took a couple of bricks and threw them at the humanandroid. He then grasped a shovel and swung it at the android repeatedly. I looked over at Morgan who was chasing the burned android down a hallway and when I looked back at Jackson, he took off after the humanandroid. The lion scrambled his way up an unfinished escalator, so I ran to the second floor up a separate flight of stairs hoping to catch it off guard. The lion came running my direction when I aimed the shot gun at it, ready to fire if it came close enough. The lion stopped in his tracks and stared at me. He waited for me to advance but I knew that I needed to hold my ground. He took off down one of the many hallways, disappearing from view. If I was going to catch that android, I needed to get the jump on it. The last time I remember, most of the third story floors were still rafters near the middle of the structure. Perhaps I could climb up there to get a good angle to hit it.

There were stairs up to the third floor so I carefully made my way up. I walked around the semi-finished third floor and to my dismay all of the flooring was completely laid down. The workers, since my last patrol up here, had put down what must have been hundreds of square feet of flooring. Maybe there was a balcony I could find, or a garbage shoot? If I do find something like that, how am I going to lure the lion into the trap. I continued walking around on the third floor looking for such a place to set up my trap. I came across a window peering into the massive soon-to-be testing area, and looking down at it from the third floor made the room look bigger than it really was. I continued on from the view of the giant room, and through a door into what looked like what was going to be a retail strip. There were openings for display windows, shelving was already up, and there was tile laid across the entirety of the hall. Eventually I came across a square hole in the floor where workers were doing something between the two floors. The second floor, in the pitch dark, seemed just close enough for a stable landing. If I decided to jump on top of the creature to get to point blank, I had bags of concrete mix to soften my landing. Anger continued to build in my mind. Whoever killed my sister was going to get it, and they were going to get the total frustration and anger I had built up. But… Morgan and Jackson are still here. They are still… alive. I wonder what kind of thoughts must be going through their heads. WAIT! Jackson was going to propose to Morgan! Where did I put the ring? I remember putting it down on a night stand in my bedroom. I had to have left it in the bedroom back at Tom's somewhere. I continued to think about it until I heard a scratchy violin scream off in the distance. I immediately ran for some cover. There was a stack of wood, tools, a corner, somewhere I could hide! I could hear the thumping of a creature running around in the dark, the impacts of its feet shook the floor hard enough, that it had to be on my floor, they were simply too close. I crawled under a sawhorse and pulled some wood up to hide behind, placing the shotgun on the floor. The footsteps became louder until I could hear them in this room. I glanced out through a gap in the wood and saw nothing. I could hear the servos of a wretched machine standing so close, but there was nothing in the room. I slowly scooted the wood aside and took up the shotgun. There was nothing in the room that I could see. I crawled over to the hole and slowly, a figure came into view. It was that lion. It was twitching and moving in a way that would make your skin crawl. He was standing there ripping his head side to side to peer down hallways that mirrored mine. If I was to shoot him now, it wouldn't do enough damage. I want to get right behind his neck. There was a ladder set up against the hole in the floor for the workers to climb up or down. I made my way over to the ladder and continued to observe the lion. I bumped something with my foot and I heard the sound of a hammer hit the floor. I cringed and watched the lion with an eagle's eye. He didn't react to the sound and instead continued to observe the second floor hallway. In curiosity, I tapped the end of the barrel against the ladder making a metal bang, yet it didn't react. I tapped it harder and again it didn't react. The lion must be deaf. It turned around and began walking down towards the testing arena. Now's the chance to sneak up on him. I quickly made my way down the ladder and walked up behind him. His exposed claws were scraping the floor as he walked crookedly, but it was very obvious that it could still outrun me. It waddled along like a regular lion would, unaware that it was about to get killed. I walked up closer behind it and moved my shotgun right up to the back of its neck. I was aimed and ready to fire, my finger on the trigger. My breath was steady and my hands were firm. Now's the right time. I began to pull the trigger with my finger and with high hopes, pressed it all the way down.

Chapter 14

The gun in my hands made a loud click as I held it there. I forgot to reload! I backed off a little ways and pulled the lever back on the shotgun to reload it, taking my eyes from the lion. Everything in my body froze as I looked up. It was no longer anywhere to be seen. Its footsteps could no longer be felt against the floor, and his beady eyes were nowhere around. I aimed the shotgun into the darkness around me, hoping to find it before he found me. The image of the lion's claws tearing through Jackson's fur played through my mind. What would happen to me if he caught me? I would probably suffer the same fate as Jackson and Morgan when their bodies were found. I continued to search around for the lion, looking for those beady eyes should be like finding a red dot in a green patch.

"Come on, where are you?!"

I was still in the hallway, wide open to be attacked. I looked to my left and saw a room with shelves set up. I ran into the room and leaned up against the end of a shelf. I leaned the shotgun up against my forehead as I stood there going through my options. My breathing was shuttering and my hands were shaking. If I don't know where the lion is… a breath quietly sounded behind me. He's right next to me! I made a risky choice to scoot off to the left of the shelf not knowing if that breathing was on the right side, or to the left. I scooted down the side of the shelf and slowly stood up on my feet. There, through the gaps in the shelving were beady white eyes staring at me. They followed my movement as I shuffled side to side… until they disappeared.

"Come on, where'd you go?!"

The lion tore through the wood shelving with its paws and began to crawl towards me trying to squeeze through the hole it had just made. I took the butt of the gun and hit it in the arm over and over until I believed that

I was damaging the gun instead of the lion. I took off running across the hallway looking back to see it struggling to get out of the hole. I looked forwards again and saw studs in the walls where workers hadn't put up any drywall yet. As I entered the room on the opposite side of the hall, I looked back to see the horrid sight of the lion running after me with its jaws wide open. I continued to run towards the studs in the wall wondering if this thing could fit in between them. I heard his roar right behind my head as I squeezed in between the studs. There was a loud thud, followed by the sound of splintering wood. I looked back and saw the lion breaking through the studs one at a time. The room I was in had studs everywhere, and the rooms all the way down as far as I could see had studs up as well. I began running through the walls with the lion not that far behind. The first few studs I could fit through easily, but then I came into a room that was covered in drywall except from where I entered. I then spotted a doorway that had crates of cement bags in the way, leaving a gap about half a foot wide. The sounds of the lion's claws tearing away at the wood studs echoed in the space. I could see its eyes glaring at me through the stud forest, not resting until he had me. I began pushing my way through the gap with the shotgun still at hand. Inch by inch I made it further through the gap. I could hear the lion getting closer as the sound of snapping wood shook the atmosphere. I pushed myself further and further into the gap feeling the open space on the other side. The lion's eyes met mine as it began freeing himself from the wood studs. I hurried myself to get through the gap. My face entered the space on the other side and I was able to pull my body free just in time to see the lion's paw reach for me. The room was completely dark except for a faint light shining through the gaps in the walls, allowing just enough light to see the outline of my hands. It suddenly stopped reaching through the wall and took off in a blind direction. I walked through the darkness with the gun in my hand until I saw the light shining through a doorway. I ran for it. The thought of getting out of the dark overwhelmed me, controlled me. I ran back into the hallway and heard another awful roar. I felt something knock me over onto the ground as the lion came sliding by. He jumped at me as I brought up my shotgun. His mouth was aiming for my head and its teeth shined in the light. The end of my shotgun stabbed him in the back of the throat as he landed on top of me. There was a sting of pain in my left calf muscle and my shoulder as I took the weight of the wretched thing. Again and again the lion's jaw snapped down on the barrel of the gun keeping it just far enough from my hand on the trigger. I felt my back sliding across the floor until my head hit the wall on the other side of the hallway. I screamed in pain as the shotgun began to slide off of my shoulder bringing it that much closer to my face. I pulled on the trigger with everything I had. There was a bright light and a loud bang. The lion stopped, twitched a couple more times, then fell limp onto the floor. I pushed its paw off of me as I tried to stand up and run away from this thing. I yelled out as loud as I could as a sharp, burning pain cried out from my left leg, pulling me back onto the ground, dropping my shotgun. I slowly rolled over, careful not to hurt anything else, and felt my leg in the dark. I could see my leg, on it something shiny, and as I reached the shiny object with my hand, I discovered what it was. The lion's six inch claws had been pulled clean through my calf, holding me to his body. The claws had pushed all the way through my leg down to its joints. The rest of the claws were embedded in my leg or sticking out the other side. I could feel a warm substance on the sharp weapons that stuck to my hands and ran down my leg. If I pulled the claws out, I was going to bleed out. If I stay here, who knows what will find me. In my haste to get away, I hadn't realized where the shotgun had gone after I fell. It had to be laying around here somewhere. I held onto the lion's paw as I crawled over his body. Again I felt a sharp pain in my leg telling me I had pulled too far. I looked around for the gun and finally, in the little light there was, I believed to have spotted the shotgun. I pulled myself towards the gun and almost reached it when my leg was pulled on. I held back a scream as I pushed my body back towards the lion to relieve myself from the torture of its pain. If I couldn't reach that shotgun, I could not defend myself from anything else that comes along. I reached over to its shoulder and began pulling on it. My right foot slid on the smooth tile from the heaviness of the android's. My body was shaking and I could feel the jeans on my leg become soaked with warm blood. My mind told me that I needed to rest, so I laid on my back and stared into the empty dark ceiling. My mind began to give up, but I fought back to stay awake. If I fall asleep, I may never wake up. I heard a thumping in the distance coming my direction. My mind gave up and my eyes closed. The last thing my ears heard before I slept was the deathly scream of a woman.

I ran down the hall towards the source of a scream I heard not too long ago. And as I rounded the corner, I let one out of my own. Running over to Adalyne's still body, I picked her up into my arms. I tried to stand but noticed that one of the lion's paws was pulled through her leg. I put her back down onto the cold tile and began pulling on its arm. I pulled and pulled, trying to free my sister from the clutches of this wretched android. I looked behind me at the shotgun on the floor, took it, and opened the magazine. Only one shell had not been fired. I loaded the round into the chamber and aimed it at the lion's wrist. With a loud bang the paw came loose from the rest of his body. I picked up the lion's body and threw it with everything I had down the hall and away from my sister. I ripped the jeans off of Adalyne's left leg and tied it above her injury in hopes to stop the bleeding, leaving the claws in her leg as well. I scooped her up into my lap and held her face close to mine.

"Adalyne? Adalyne please, I just learned how to talk! Please!"

I sat there and stared at her face waiting for her to open her eyes. I put my hand on her chest and felt a quiet, mild heart beat, and I relaxed as I realized that she wasn't dead, but unconscious. I stood up with my sister in my arms, and began walking to the front entrance. I knew that if Adalyne didn't get to the hospital soon, she would die.

My body felt hot as I continued to chase after the humanandroid. These things really don't know the words give up, or quit. I rounded a corner and came across a four way intersection, the android nowhere to be seen. I had no idea where he could have gone, unless he was still near. I turned around to find any signs of the thing. To my left, darkness. To my right, darkness. Everywhere I looked there was darkness. I glared at the emptiness of the junction I was in, completely exposed. I froze to the sound of something walking in the dark. Then the sound occurred again behind me. The third time, two separate sounds came from opposite sides of me. I followed the sounds with each ear in a circle looking for those beady white eyes. I spun around tracking their position, making sure that if they charged at me, I would be prepared for it. They suddenly stopped and shone their eyes. They were on opposite sides of me standing silently, watching me with unknown intent. I heard someone speak from the hall behind me, causing me to turn around.

"It's been quite a while since I could do what I wanted. Years of sitting and waiting has really paid off."

Deep down the hallway were brighter, taller eyes staring into mine. It took its first step towards me and shook the floor, heavier than the other androids' steps. The eyes were also taller than the other two, and over my height by a foot.

"I have been planning for such a long time, but I didn't imagine it to be like this. You have been stuck for just one day, but I have been stuck for decades. Your mind will begin to break as you sit and watch your body fall apart over time, knowing that you can't fix it, and you'll be completely alone."

The nine foot figure stopped just inside of the shadows, staying out of view.

"Are you blind!? I have Morgan and Adalyne and James! You literally have no one." I responded.

"Wrong… I will have everyone!"

At that moment, the two androids came running over like football players ready to tackle. I stepped towards the burned android and ran into him first. I took a hold on his partly broken arm, and pulled him into the other's path. The burned android reached up, held my snout, and yanked it downwards with his right hand. The humanandroid came up with his fist into my nose causing the coolant line to become exposed. I slipped out of the android's hold and ripped off his arm that was already missing its hand. I threw the arm at the humanandroid as his came charging in and tripped him as he swung his wiry fist at my face, causing him to land on the floor. I reached down, holding him against the floor, and grasped his right eye. The burned android jumped on my back as I ripped out the humanandroid's right eye. I flipped around as I wrestled the now one-armed android and shoved the eye into its other eye, shattering them both. Before I could stand, an impact that would crush a human sent me flying down one of the hallways. I slid to a stop and peered at the mysterious character. It was a new android, about nine feet tall, looking straight at me. It had a bottom jaw with no teeth and a domed head behind two protruding eyes of white. His limbs had servos that were bigger than the other androids, and the frame appeared to be sturdier. The trio stood close to each other and began making synchronizing steps towards me. The two androids walked crookedly, twitching in every step, as the giant android however walked in a smooth stride. I was no match for the three of them, especially when I was knocked away in one graceful swoop of his hand. I need to find Morgan before he does. I took off running without knowing where I was headed. In the pitch dark, I couldn't see small objects, but I could see the walls around me. I felt something hot touch my chest. I reached up and held my nose, realizing that there was a small coolant leak. I ran down the dark halls holding my nose hoping that I could get to Morgan in time.

I felt my body shake from someone walking around. My mind became more self-aware and I realized that I was being carried in someone's arms. I moved to reposition myself causing whoever was carrying me to stop.

"Oh my God… Adalyne!?"

I opened my eyes to see Morgan's bright blue eyes staring back at me. I smiled in relief as I thought I would never see her again.

"Yes. I'm still alive."

My mind became more aware, and that's when it hit me. There was an awful pain in my left leg tearing away at my mind. I cringed and squeaked as I held in the urge to yell.

"What is it Adalyne?"

Morgan knelt down onto the ground, seeming to relieve the pressure on my leg for a couple of seconds.

"My leg hurts."

"I know… don't look at it."

I reached out and held onto Morgan's neck to pull myself up, bringing to view the nasty injury I had sustained.

"You left the claws in!?"

"I can't pull them, you'll bleed out."

She had torn the bottom half of my left pant leg and used it as a tourniquet to cut the blood flow, but it made the rest of my leg cold and numb. The memory of the lion came back into view, and I remembered its giant mouth snapping down on the shotgun as I fired through the back of his throat. I also faintly remember that as I tried to leave, its claws pulled on my leg causing me to fall over and drop the shotgun.

"Morgan where's the shotgun?"

"It's back where I found you."

"No! Morgan that thing…"

"That thing is out of ammo. I used the last shot to break the lion's wrist."

I laid back to rest in Morgan's arms, tired of staring at the metal piercing through the middle of my calf. I could see a window shining with moonlight, and outside were the stumps of small trees telling me that we were on the first floor. Morgan stood up and continued her way to wherever she was taking me.

"Where are we going?"

"I'm taking you to the hospital."

"Did you destroy them all?"

"N…No."

"Well then let me help."

"For Christ's sake, you almost died Adalyne! I'm taking you to the hospital whether you like it or not."

"What will happen if the doctors see you?"

"I guess I'll find out when I get there."

I could tell that Morgan was frustrated with me, angry that I came here, yet happy that I was alive. She continued on down the hallway not saying another word, filling the air around us with an awkward silence. I was helplessly sitting in her arms while she walked across the complex, but I couldn't help but wonder where Jackson was. We approached a door that opened into the courtyard. Morgan stood there and glared into the area, careful to catch any danger. She pushed the door open with her tail and closed it silently behind her.

"I don't think this is a good idea."

"It's the quickest way to your car. I need to get you to the hospital."

Morgan began to cross the expansive darkness, clueless if we would encounter something or someone. Morgan paused and twisted her ears back and forth.

"Morgan, what is it?"

"You need to find another way out."

Morgan looked around and stopped at the staircase at the corner of the balcony.

"You need to get up and over the fight so you can get out of here."

My heart began to beat a little faster.

"What do you mean? Is something happening?"

Morgan reached the stairs and laid me down onto the first few steps.

"You need to get across the second story to the other stairs near the entrance of the courtyard. I'm going to delay him long enough to let you escape."

"No Morgan, I want to help."

Morgan flattened her canine ears against her head and yelled in an angry tone.

"Help how Adalyne?! Get up the damn stairs, there's nothing you can do!"

She was leaning over me and for a moment, I thought she was going to hurt me. But she realized that she's much more intimidating than she used to be, and backed off.

"I'm sorry, I… I just want you to live. You have no idea…"

Morgan began to quietly sob without the tears.

"You have no idea what it's like to be in my shoes. Do you have any clue on what I'll miss out on?"

I shook my head no, but I knew what she meant.

"I will never live a true life with Jackson because… because people are difficult. They would never fully accept two androids that happen to be possessed by two dead people. I will never have a family, or children. I will never see my child take their first steps, I will never hear their first words."

Morgan sat down next to me, calmed herself down a little, and continued her explanation.

"I will never have a wedding with Jackson because no one wants to see what we are now. We will never be able to leave the confines of this prison just to stay safe from those who want to exploit us. I still feel like my own spirit, but… I'm not in my own body. The desire to move on with my life still exists in me. How do you explain that?"

I felt awful for Morgan. My heart hurt and I felt like I would throw up again. I remembered the ring Jackson had bought for Morgan before they died, and I remember when the officer handed it to me after I saw their bodies. Nothing will let me forget the awful sight of that gash running across her body, making me sick.

"I don't know what it's like to be in your situation…"

"And I hope you never find out."

We smiled at each other for a little bit before being interrupted by a faint crash in the distance.

"Morgan, don't go."

"You need to get up those stairs."

Morgan stood up, but before she could leave, I took a hold of her torn hand.

"Please come back."

She knelt back down to me and said,

"I promise."

She took off towards the sound as I began my way up the stairs. I hopped on my right leg up each step. One at a time, I slowly and methodically creeped upwards. The sounds of fighting slowly arose from the distance as Morgan and Jackson backed out of the shadows followed by two androids. I was barely up ten steps before one of the eyes peered in my direction. I ducked down flat against the stairwell hoping to hide from it. But it soon became obvious that it didn't work.

"Adalyne GO!"

I stood back up on my one foot, using the handrail, and continued my ascent. I could hear the patter of their footsteps, the clashing of galvanized steel, and then I heard something different. Footsteps, heavier than what I heard before. I looked into the darkness and spotted a pair of bright white eyes staring into my own. I ignored it and continued up into the darkness hoping that there was an escape route I could easily take. As I made my way up the tenth step, I watched Jackson launch himself onto the taller android in the dark. He stuck his arm under the android's frame and threw it off balance causing both of them to fall onto the floor. The android flung its arms in the ways of a contortionist reaching for Jackson. Morgan, on the other side of the giant room, held one android in a leg lock as the other swung rapidly at her face. I looked back at Jackson who had been pulled off of the newer android's back and fought it without restraint. The android kept trying to grab Jackson on the back, but each time Jackson successfully laid a blast of a steel fist into the machine's head. I watched closely as Jackson began to pry on something inside of the android's neck. It fell to the ground and put Jackson into a leglock, holding him there as it reached around and buried its hand under his skin on his back. Suddenly... his hand pulled up, and Jackson froze. The android pulled his body off and dropped him to the floor. Jackson held his position as if he was made of one piece of metal, frozen by the very design that made them safe. The nine foot tall machine stood up and looked straight at me. It was tall enough that even though I was up at least fifteen steps, he could've easily jumped and touched me. I frantically rushed up the stairs as the android came my direction. I watched Morgan look up at me in terror, unable to assist me. The humanandroid and the one-armed android were holding her down on the ground as the newer android approached the bottom stairway.

"Adalyne, RUN!!"

I broke the stare with my sister and moved as fast as I could with one leg. The newer android, slowly walking up the stairs behind me, spoke to me in a scratchy voice.

"You pathetic little human. You all think you're indestructible when all you really are is a fragile glass ball. One drop and you shatter."

I took another step and almost fell backwards when two beady eyes stared at me through the reflection of the stairs.

"You get away from me!"

The android ran with a bolt of speed up the stairs and caught me, knocking me onto my face.

"You think you can get away even when, deep down, you know you're going to die."

The wretched machine took a hold on the claw in my leg and began dragging me back down the stairs. I could hear Morgan in the distance fighting to get up, but failed. I cried out in pain as each drop in the stairwell pulled on my limp left leg. Each time I thought, this time it will rip out, this time it will tear through my leg, but it never did. Morgan continued to struggle herself free only seeming to get a little ways, but then fell repeatedly back into their grasp. I was whipped around to face my sister as she lay there on the floor, both of us helpless, both of us seeing the end of our lives.

"Look Morgan, at how lucky you are. How you can't feel pain. I gave you this gift, but still you fight me."

She turned her head over and looked at what I believed to be Jackson, frozen on the floor from the hydraulic lock in his design.

"I was killed by you! You took my life from me!"

"I gave you life in this form. All you have to do is accept it. However, your sister…"

He took a hold with one hand on my wrist, and held my arm above the elbow with his other hand.

"If I kill her now, she will be truly gone."

I began to realize what his evil mind had thought up. I began to push away at his arm, hopelessly trying to free myself.

"Then, I will have taken everything from you."

I felt the pressure build on my left arm. He was going to break it, but slowly. Sharp pains began to erupt through my arm, followed by faint snapping sounds. The pain was so tremendous, I wished that I would faint. I lost the feeling at the tips of my fingers as the pressure continued to build. I lost the ability to scream and all of the muscles in my body became tense. There was a loud crack along with bolting pain shooting from my elbow. The feeling of something hot stabbing me over and over again paralyzed me. I was thrown down onto the ground and I laid there cringing at the pain. It hurt too much to move, so I laid there and stared at the pitch dark ceiling. I gasped over and over again, unable to take in full breaths. I began to feel light headed, and looked at Morgan who lay there on the floor trapped by two wretched androids. But then I spotted something standing behind the androids holding what looked like a remote.

"Hey jackass!"

With the click of a button, a high pitched whistle blasted through the air causing the two androids holding onto Morgan to twist and convulse at the sound, but the newer android didn't seem to be affected by it. Morgan reared up and slammed herself into the duo that were holding her down. The giant android walked over and with one swing of his hands, sent Morgan flying into the dark, destroying both of the other androids in an instant. I now realized who it was that had the remote, Josh. He held the remote into the air hoping to stop the android.

"Dad?"

But with another big swing with its arms, the android sent Josh flying back into the dark followed by a loud bang as he landed on something metal. The wretched android turned around and looked straight at me. My eyes were watering from the pain that had enveloped my entire body, keeping me from moving. In the distance, I could see Morgan stand up and run over towards the android, but something was different about her eyes. Instead of her usual bright blue eyes, they were completely dark. They were so dark that they stood out in the darkness as two separate black holes, pulling in any light that was around them. She yelled out in anger, causing her voice to change into a monstrous tone. She tackled the android and slid across the concrete floor. As the android held her from his body, Morgan began shredding at his arm with her mouth. Whatever fighting style she had was gone, replaced by this horrific machine shredding its opponent. My mind again began to fade away into darkness as the sounds of snapping steel echoed throughout the room. I could see Morgan rip pieces from the android's body and I could see that her anger had taken over her emotions, like a wild animal protecting its young. She continued to tear away at the machine as if it were cardboard, completely ignoring everything else. I began to feel a severe lightheadedness as my mind continued to blank in and out of reality. Through the choking and the spit that shunned my speech, I finally made a sound.

"M... Mor..."

Morgan stopped and looked back towards me, her blue eyes returning to her body. She took a hold on the android's head and placed her feet on its shoulders. With each snap, the head moved further from its shoulders. My ears suddenly went numb as the android's head snapped off of its shoulders, sending the rest of its body limp. Morgan immediately turned around and ran to Jackson. She reached into his back and released the hydraulic lock on his body allowing Jackson to become free from his locked up position. I reached out towards her with my right hand as I could not figure out where my left hand was. She spoke to me, but the sound came through like we were talking through a wall.

"Adalyne, It's ok. I'm going to get you out of here!"

I wanted to respond, but the gagging and the choking from the pain in my elbow was too great, I was going into shock. Jackson ran over to where Josh disappeared hoping that he was ok. Morgan picked me up and held me as I began to feel the weightlessness and numbness take over my body. I could feel my hand holding onto Morgan's hand become numb, and the feeling to rest overtook my body.

"Don't close those eyes Adalyne. Don't you close those eyes!"

Chapter 15

My body tensed up as I laid on the floor next to a stack of support beams. My entire body cried out in pain, keeping me from thinking straight. I couldn't believe that my father could still take people's lives, or mine. But why? I don't even think that was my father. I managed to roll over and see that Morgan had already beat the hell out of the newer android, and freed Jackson from his locked up position. He came running over as fast as he could and knelt down next to me.

"Hold on Josh... oh my God. Um..."

He slowly picked me up off of the ground and began carrying me through the halls of this place. Soon I was outside and carefully placed inside the backseat of a car. It was still dark outside, but I could tell that the sun was coming up. I leaned my head up and gasped in pain as I saw a massive piece of metal sticking up through my stomach.

"Oh, crap!"

"Josh, I'm going to lean you up against the seat. Ready-1...2...3..."

I yelled out in tremendous pain as I was adjusted up in the back seat. I looked over in the seat next to me and I could see Morgan sit down with Adalyne in her arms. I saw her bloodied leg, and then her arm... or what was left of it. I felt like I was going to throw up, but every time my stomach twisted it pinched the metal in my gut. Adalyne's arm from the elbow down was missing. I could see flaps of skin dangling over her exposed elbow joint, and blood was excessively pouring out of severed veins. Morgan reached forwards as Jackson handed her a charging cord. She tied it on Adalyne's arm as a torniquet, and began wiping some adhesive from her skin onto the injury to stop the bleeding. The car suddenly lurched forwards as Jackson began driving towards the hospital. He took out a phone from Adalyne's purse sitting in the front passenger seat, and handed it to Morgan. I could see that Morgan's attempts to stop the bleeding were almost working, but blood was still running out onto Morgan and the car seat. I reached down and began pulling my shirt off. I painfully slid it off the metal fragment as Morgan spoke into the phone desperately.

"Tell the hospital to get people out at the emergency entrance!"

As Morgan talked on the phone, I reached over with my shirt and began holding it around the end of Adalyne's arm.

"Don't give me that crap! I have two people that are severely hurt and we're heading to the hospital right now, so tell them!"

Jackson began driving the car through traffic at a very high speed under the dark night sky, and soon I heard the sounds of a police siren behind us.

"Jackson, they aren't going to know what to do with you and Morgan once we get there?"

"Not right now!"

Jackson continued to weave in and out of traffic, but soon seemed to contemplate what I said. He slowed down and asked, "Are you able to drive?"

"What do you think?! I have a piece of metal in my belly!"

Jackson sped up once more, ignoring the police car behind us. I looked back at Adalyne and noticed that her injury was still bleeding, but not as bad as it was. Morgan put the phone down as she finished her conversation and held her bloody hand on Adalyne's chest.

"Jackson, her heart rate is dropping!"

I could feel my heart rate drop as well, and I began to black out. I looked down at my injury once more and saw that I wasn't just bleeding blood. I could tell that there was another fluid oozing from my wound. It had to be my stomach or bladder, and either of them could spell death for me. I looked back over at Adalyne and saw Morgan looking at me, she had to have noticed the fluid too.

"Josh, I'm so sorry…"

"Morgan, I've been in bad situations before, but I think my body has finally taken enough."

The car finally came to a stop and out of my window I could see the giant red EMERGENCY sign. The doors of the car came flying open and a group of doctors came running out of the hospital, but stopped short at the sight of Jackson and Morgan. Morgan stepped out with Adalyne still in her arms as Jackson carried me out.

"Get you stretchers! What the hell are you waiting for?!"

The doctors, seeing me and Adalyne, snapped at it. I was laid on a stretcher and watched as I was pulled away from Jackson and Morgan.

Adalyne was laid on a separate stretcher and taken down a different hallway from me. I could tell by the way I was shifting in and out of consciousness that I wasn't going to make it. As soon as I was wheeled passed an office counter, I managed to take a piece of paper from it, a pen from one of the doctors pockets, and began writing sloppily. I had to tell Adalyne... I had to tell her as much as I could. I came to a stop in a room and I could hear the doctors around me hustle.

"Put him under quick."

A doctor began putting a gas mask over my nose and mouth, but I slapped it away and kept on writing.

"Let me finish!"

"Take it away from him!"

I managed to write another sentence before it was pulled away from me, and the doctors held me down as they put the gas mask over my mouth.

"NO! Let me finish! Let me finish. Find Adalyne! She has blond hair-she came in with me, blue eyes, and she lost her arm... she needs to know! She needs to know."

One of the doctors in the room picked up my note and looked at it. He looked at me and nodded his head as I blacked out for the last time.

I stood there watching Josh and Adalyne as they were wheeled away on stretchers. Morgan and I were going to follow them in, but a police officer stepped in front of us with a gun pointing at our heads.

"Get... get down on the ground!"

It was my friend Thomas! He was caught off guard by my appearance, and he should be. Morgan began backing away slowly towards the trees behind the hospital, and I followed.

"Stop! I will shoot!"

We both ignored him as he kept the distance between us constant.

"This is your last warning!"

I decided to stop him, so I dropped my half torn up skin onto the ground with a simple thought.

"What the hell."

Thomas was again caught off guard by the sight of my metal design, and I grabbed my skin as he let us disappear into the woods. I had my torn up skin in my hands, following Morgan to wherever she was leading me. She soon stopped and began walking back towards the hospital, a little quiver in her breathing becoming audible.

"Morgan, we can't go back."

"Why not?! I need to see my sister!"

I grabbed her arm and held her in place.

"Let me go!"

"Morgan, she's going to be ok!"

"No! I need to…"

"Morgan, You can't!"

She stopped fighting and looked at me while holding back her sadness.

"We can't go back. You saw what they'll do to us. Even if they were ok with us… it wouldn't be right for Adalyne."

Morgan slowly lost the ability to stop her sadness, and began crying with no tears. We held onto each other until the sun began to peak over the hills in the east. We could easily be spotted in the open like this, and if we are found, what will happen to us?

"Morgan, we need to find somewhere to hide."

"Ok." said Morgan with a wavy voice.

She soon calmed herself down a little and said,

"I know where we can go."

I felt, well I don't know what I felt. I hurt, but I don't remember the reason why. I began to become more aware, and moved my right hand over what felt like a bed sheet. It had a soft texture to it. I began to feel a heavy pain in my left leg, along with a mild headache. Someone in the room spoke up as I swayed my hand back and forth across the bed I was laying in.

"She's awake. Honey, Adalyne's awake!"

I opened my eyes to the sight of dad standing at my feet. He had his arms angrily crossed and appeared have tired red eyes as if he were crying. My mom came running in and looked at me.

"Oh Adalyne! I'm so glad you're ok."

My mother came over to my left side and gently hugged me without moving me.

"What were you thinking?" Said dad with red, watery eyes "We thought you got yourself killed!"

I forced myself to speak up.

"I'm happy to see you too dad."

"I'm sorry… I'm… I'm so glad you're alive."

I became more aware of my body, feeling the injury in my leg and…

something else. I couldn't feel my left hand. I began to pull out my arm, and when the covers fell off... I...

"Mom?"

"Adalyne, I'm sorry."

My heart sank at the sight of my missing arm from the elbow down. My mother knelt down to my eye level and said,

"The doctors did their best to save what they could, and when I heard that my daughter was in critical condition at the hospital, I thought that we'd lost you."

My mother was beginning to cry, my father walking over to soothe her. I sat there staring at my useless limb, covered in bandages all the way up to my shoulder. I reached out with my right hand towards my parents, and we held hands together for a long time. I tried to remember what happened to my arm, but all I could remember was Morgan sitting next to me on a staircase, talking to me. Then another question popped into my head.

"Mom, how long have I been out?"

"You... you've been out for three days Adalyne."

Three days?! I wanted to move, but the pain in my arm, and the soreness of my muscles held me in place. Dad seemed to notice and said, "Stay still Adalyne. You aren't leaving this bed anytime soon."

All I could focus on was my arm in front of me. How did I lose it? All of my memories after sitting on the staircase were gone. A couple of days went by, and each day a nurse came in and changed the bandages on my leg and arm. My leg had stitches running down a few inches, and my left arm was just covered in stitches running every which way. I was told to stay still as much as I could, but it nagged at me every second of every minute. A few more days passed before I was allowed to stand, my parents by my side. Slowly and painfully, I made my way back and forth across the room. I would sit down on my bed each hour and imagine that I still had my left hand. I was wheeled out of the room a day later and into the cafeteria where I could choose to eat anything that was on their menu. I ordered a variety of food, not caring what it was, and ate it all by the time I began my therapy a half hour later. The next day, the bandages over my leg came off and I saw the nasty scar that was swollen and itchy. I began putting my weight on my legs and the muscles in my body cried at me to stop, but I didn't. I walked across the room again and again until I could ignore the pain. I looked over to a window peering into the hallway and saw a doctor stop and look at me. The doctor suddenly walked into the room with a stressed frown on his face. He had a card in his hand as he slowly walked over to me.

"Is your name Adalyne?"

"Yes."

"Oh, ok." The doctor was a little sad as he spoke. "I… I don't know how to say this. The man that came in with you, Josh, wanted you to have this note. I completely forgot and didn't remember until today."

"Is he ok?"

The doctor just sighed a sad sigh, and at that moment I knew that Josh was gone. I felt my heart rip apart. After losing my sister, my great uncle, and now my best friend, I didn't have the will to stay awake. I felt drowsy again, but I held myself in place as I began to cry.

"Adalyne, I'm sorry."

I couldn't believe that after so much tragedy, I would be hit with more horror. I wanted to see Josh's body, but I pulled the thought out of my head. I knew that if I saw his eyes, I could never be with anyone else. Three more days slowly passed, and on the last night I spent in the hospital, I remembered that my sister had to be waiting for me. She had to be out there somewhere, wondering if I was ok. That morning, a nurse removed the bandages from my stubby arm, and I could see every scar and every callous, making it appear like lizard skin. I put on a long sleeve shirt, careful not to pull on any stitches, and slowly stood up to go home. My father was going to drive his car home, and Mom was going to drive me home in Morgan's car when it was packed. Once I got in though, I couldn't help but break down once more. Morgan had a selfie of us at one of our massive family reunions tucked away in the glove box. I held onto this picture as I tried to sleep on the way home. For hours I counted every mile marker, every passing car, and every single second. I could not rest even after sitting in a hospital recovering from an injury I don't remember sustaining. I arrived at my parent's home near sunset, and the mountains in the distance seemed to glow on their own. The environment was too different, and it didn't even feel like home anymore. The funeral took place a couple of days after I got home. All I could do was sit there while my family gave their speeches. I was handed Morgan's ashes soon after the ceremony, again causing me to break down into tears. Morgan hadn't decided whether she wanted to be cremated or buried. The next day, my parents and I drove up to the highest point in the mountain range, and released Morgan's ashes over a blue sky with copper colored clouds smeared with a pink and red hue. I stared at the cloud of ashes that slowly dispersed across the mountain range, but something came to me in a rush. It occurred to me that she was still alive! Another week or so after the funeral, my mother finally let me drive. I told her that I was going home, but I decided to drive the eight long hours back to find Morgan and Jackson. It was a Sunday and I knew that nobody would be working at the tech complex. When I got there, I drove up to the front doors and slowly walked inside.

"Morgan! Jackson!"

There was no response besides the echo of my voice. I walked around the upper levels and found the hole where I tried to destroy that lion. Memories of that lion snapping its teeth down on the shotgun reverberated through my head. I could never forget that. Another memory of that waitress android chasing after me on all fours gave me goosebumps. I also remember Jackson saving my life, but his face... his metal skeletal face was what I remember most. I imagined what my face would look like if he wasn't there in time, and it made me gag. I continued walking throughout the complex and saw a strand of police tape hanging from a hook on a wall. I wonder what any detective's conclusion would be on that. They don't know that human spirits could take over androids, and they don't believe that an android could save my life, or take someone else's life. The only person that they could talk to is me. I'm the only survivor from the night shifts here. I told myself that I wasn't the only survivor, but each time I see my sister in pictures before she 'died', I can't help but weep. I continued to walk through the building yelling out their names, but still no response from them. I saw the entrance into the basement and froze. How could I be in this place? I didn't want to be here, but I pushed on. I entered Tom's workshop and spotted a pile of android parts on a table. Its body was almost unrecognizable with bent and broken frame supports, sheared joints, and snapped beams.

"Oh my God, what happened to you?"

I could faintly remember my sister tearing away at a body of metal similar to this. Maybe this was the wretched android that... I remember! I took a hammer out of the nearby toolbox and began to slam it down upon the machine's already destroyed head with my right arm. I suddenly stopped and dropped the hammer. These inventions of humanoid designs should never have existed in the first place. I ran out the back doors next to the loading ramp, through the parking lot, and out into the trees. I wanted, needed to get as far away from that place as I could. I started to cry as I ran through the trees almost tripping on every bump in the ground. I broke free of the forest and stopped over a cliff edge. I was breathing heavily and crying when I heard someone to my right yell in excitement.

"Adalyne!"

I looked over and saw these bright blue eyes staring back at me. Morgan and Jackson were sitting together on the cliff edge looking at me. I found them! Through my tears, I began to laugh. Morgan stood up and began running towards me, and soon I was running as fast as I could towards her. The moment we met each other, I was lifted off of the ground in a hug as I hung on with my only remaining arm.

"I'm so happy to see you Adalyne. It's been too long."

"I'm happy to see you too."

We were both crying and laughing at the same time, holding onto each other as tight as we could.

"I thought you were gone. Every Sunday I came here and waited for you to come back, but after the first two weeks, I thought that you never would."

"I… I was at your funeral Morgan. I saw our family… and I spread your ashes over the Rocky Mountains…"

We continued to hug each other for a while until I noticed that Morgan's skin wasn't cut or damaged. I didn't even realize it at first but she was also wearing different, regular clothing. Morgan was wearing a very large pair of women's jeans that still seemed to be too small for her, and also wore a green long sleeve shirt. I then noticed that she ripped a hole in the back of her pants for her tail. She put me back down onto the ground and I looked at her undamaged face.

"What happened to you? I thought you were all tore up from the fight."

"Jackson and I stayed at the bunker for a few days and found our 'replacement skins'. Then we raided some stores for clothing among a couple of other things. It took us forever to find clothing our size, but we did eventually find some."

"And we were about to leave this place in search of you." said Jackson.

He stood next to Morgan and looked at me with his blue eyes. Jackson was also wearing jeans that were slightly too small, and a red T-shirt. They both wore shoes, large ones at least twice my size, and no socks.

"It's good to see you Jackson."

"It's good to see you too Adalyne."

We stood there and talked to each other for a little bit before I remembered that I brought the ring with me.

"Oh! Here, I brought something for you and Morgan."

With my right arm, I reached into my purse and pulled out the ring Jackson bought for her. I handed it to him and he looked at it with more warmth than sorrow.

"Is that the ring?!" Morgan yelled in excitement.

"Yes, now let me put it on your hand."

Jackson began sliding the ring onto Morgan's left hand, but her fur and the size of her ring finger were in the way. It hurt me to think that they couldn't live normal lives no matter what they did to prove they were actually people.

"It doesn't fit."

Jackson tried to fit the ring on her pinky instead, but the ring was simply too small for her hand. I spoke up and said,

"It's ok. I'll get it adjusted."

They both looked at me and smiled. Perhaps they could try to live a regular life at home, but will anyone else accept them?

"I want you guys to come home."

They looked at me with surprised expressions, their smiles slowly fading away.

"I don't know Adalyne. What will mom say? She won't know that it's me."

"It's ok if mom doesn't know. I want you to come home for your own sake… and mine."

Jackson and Morgan began talking to each other without sound, their mouths moving to fit words. They continued to talk while I found a rock to sit on, but when I looked at my phone to tell what time it was, I realized that it was much later than I wanted it to be. My place has more than enough acres to hide two androids. There were trees and a river, and I was at least ten miles away from my nearest neighbor. Morgan stopped talking to think for a moment or two before Jackson spoke up.

"I think we should go home."

Morgan looked at him in surprise.

"Jackson, I…"

"I know this is hard, but we can only go forwards. We are together forever no matter what happens."

Morgan seemed to drop whatever she had in her mind and smiled at Jackson. They began talking to each other in their heads again, and I could tell that they were still considering if they wanted to go home… if they could go home. I turned my attention to my stubby arm, and felt the scars and stitch marks with my right hand. It was a little tender around my elbow, but… I could still hold my hand over the rounded end. I closed my eyes and began to imagine my hands together. Folding cards, playing a piano, sewing… things that I'll miss doing.

"You ok Adalyne?"

I opened my eyes to Morgan and Jackson standing in front of me.

"Yea."

I looked towards the sunset over the mountains in the west, and saw another amazing arrangement of color similar to the sunset when Morgan was stuck in Tom's security pilot suit. I reached into my purse, and took out Josh's note. I had refrained from opening it because of fear that I would never be able to be with anyone else. I opened the note and inside it said,

Adalyne. The day I met you, I had these unexplained feelings for you. I wanted to tell you so much, I needed to. I should not have killed Jackson and let your sister die. I was wrong. I love you and I'm sorry I couldn't save you... I'm sorry for everything.................

I could feel my lungs quiver and my eyes began to tear up. The man I loved was the man that killed Jackson, and let my sister die?! I did my best to refrain myself from crying. I don't know how often my life would be hit with so much sadness, death and death again. I felt a hand on my shoulder as I stood there looking over the sunset in the west.

"Adalyne?"

"How could I be so blind? Josh was with me the entire time, and he didn't tell me until this note. And... now he's gone."

Morgan and Jackson looked at each other. Perhaps they were considering what to say, what to do. I soon spoke up again.

"You knew didn't you?"

"Yes. We knew. We were trying to protect you from him..."

"Why didn't you tell me?"

"By the time we figured out how to speak, we realized that you and Josh loved each other."

I couldn't respond because what she said was true. I held onto Morgan's furry hand and gazed at the sunset with her. There were copper colored clouds with pink and red hues smudged across the dark blue sky. Jackson looked like he wanted to say something, but soon... the three of us just stared out over the ravine, happy that we were still together.

"Hello?"

"Yea, uh... Jerry Zerchophski right?"

"Yes that's me."

"It's me, Ben. A while ago I came over seas to represent J.T. Cybernetics..."

"Yes, I know who you are. I got the security footage by the way and I was curious about this black canine-like character wandering out of the loading ramp. Did your team build that?"

"No. The twins found it shortly before... before these events happened, and I..."

"Sorry Ben, I need to go take care of some buisness. I'll talk to you later ok?"

"Oh... Ok. Bye."

I put my phone away into my pocket as I stared at the destroyed android piled onto the counter. An employee came up behind me and asked, "What do you want us to do with all of these parts?"

"Let's take the processor. It should still work."

Made in the USA
Middletown, DE
12 April 2022

64020341R00108